YOU DON'T HAVE TO DIE TO GO TO HELL!

When he first saw Vietnam from the air, Mack Bolan had a flash impression of a beautiful land. He touched down on its earth to find that the beauty was indeed there.

But a beast lurked in its heart....

Mack Bolan is a star. The Executioner is a beacon of hope for people with a sense of American justice.
—*Las Vegas Review Journal*

DON PENDLETON's

MACK BOLAN

DIRTY WAR

A GOLD EAGLE BOOK FROM
WORLDWIDE

TORONTO · NEW YORK · LONDON · PARIS
AMSTERDAM · STOCKHOLM · HAMBURG
ATHENS · MILAN · TOKYO · SYDNEY

First edition October 1985

ISBN 0-373-61404-7

Special thanks and acknowledgment to
Stephen Mertz for his contributions to this work.

Printed in Canada

He knew that the essence of war is violence, and that moderation in war is imbecility.

—Lord Macaulay on
Lord Nugent's *Memorials of Hampden*

Grim experience has taught me that there *is* no moderation in war.

—Mack Bolan

To the 58,022 names
etched in the black granite of
Washington, D.C.'s
Vietnam War Memorial.

Prologue
Southern California ——————————————

Death stalked the night and its name was Mack Bolan.

The big man in combat black crouched below the outcrop of rock.

A sharp coastal breeze gave bite to the rainy mist that reduced naked-eye visibility to zero beneath a low cloud cover. The hiss of rain and the crashing surf against the base of nearby cliffs were the only sounds in the moonless night.

The Executioner made a final touch-check of his weapons and gear before moving out.

Big Thunder, the stainless-steel .44 AutoMag, rode in fast-draw leather, strapped low to his right hip.

A silenced Beretta 93-R nestled snugly beneath his left arm, near a combat knife sheathed midchest for quick cross-draw.

The head weapon for tonight's hard action was a short, compact, deadly Ingram-10 submachine gun, equipped with a MAC suppressor.

The nightstalker's combat blacksuit had been designed to his specifications: skintight, nothing to get snagged or impede movement.

He toted extra ammo in canvas pouches on military webbing.

He rapidly final-checked the wire garrote, penetration gear and lightweight assortment of grenades and packets of plastique that encircled his waist.

Ready.

Now or never.

Black-gloved fingers lowered the last piece of equipment over his cosmetically blackened face.

As the night-vision goggles slid into place over his eyes, the surrounding murky gloom of wet night was transformed into shimmering, surreal "daylight" for the man in black. At the same time the night-vision devise blotted out the whites of his eyes, rendering Bolan an invisible, shadowy oneness with the pitch-dark coastal terrain.

In his hands the SMG traversed the rocky landscape before him, tracking the surrounding veil of night for any sign of danger.

Satisfied, he moved out.

His target was a walled estate perched on a promontory high above a small inlet several miles from Balboa along California's irregular coastline. The specter who was the Executioner advanced across the night-shrouded killzone, zigzagging from tree to tree toward the base of the ten-foot-high stone wall surrounding the country estate.

Bolan had been doing this sort of thing for a long time.

It seemed like forever sometimes, ever since his combat tours of duty in Vietnam ended, and along successive miles through Hell on earth.

Then, as now, Bolan perceived his life as but one sustained heartbeat in a continuum wherein the survival and self-destructive instincts of his species wrangled for dominance. And Bolan had an idea that the world could be much more peaceful if and when that species' dark impulses could be subdued.

Sometimes one heartbeat made all the difference.

Bolan gained the base of the wall.

The misting rain rolling in off the ocean increased in intensity, pinpricking the exposed flesh of his darkened face.

He crouched at the bottom of the high stone barricade and he reached for the looped climbing rope with the multipronged metal hook at the end.

With his left hand he unhitched the rope. His right fist gripped the Ingram, his trigger finger curled in place.

Bolan knew that another man of his combat experience could become jaded by the hellgrounds, and then would come the carelessness born of familiarity, followed by death.

But in this warrior's case, the familiarity served only to hone the survival instincts to a razor sharpness with the knowledge that every mission was different from any that had gone before.

Death could materialize on the next heartbeat, especially on a hit like tonight. But Bolan was going beyond the impossible here, all senses alert to the overwhelming odds he would be walled in with once he penetrated the perimeter of this Mafia hardsite.

He stepped away from the wall to give the rope a loose-armed toss.

The hooked clamp arced leisurely to grab with a barely audible *snick* atop the wall ten feet above his head.

He tugged the rope sharply a couple of times to test it, then began climbing as fast as he could, a soundless, spectral shadow walking up a night-shrouded wall, invisible...unless any prowling guards in the vicinity and inside carried night-vision devices, too.

The Executioner made the top of the wall and stretched out flat. He quickly tugged up the rope after him, coiling it to reclasp onto his belt.

He remained sprawled a few additional seconds, scanning the layout inside the walled perimeter.

The grounds of this estate—this Mafia compound—appeared to slumber in the early-morning quiet. Through his NVD goggles, Bolan saw the main house, a sprawling, three-level millionaire-class dwelling, perched one thousand yards away across a shrubbery-covered incline.

A one-story, ranch-style guest house marked the halfway point between the main residence and Bolan's position on the wall.

The guest house, which Bolan knew to be packed with off-duty security personnel—in this case one dozen street goons drafted from the L.A. and San Diego Mafia families—also appeared dark, restful, peaceful.

Bolan knew from hard intel, channeled to him from Hal Brognola, head Fed and long-time Bolan ally, that this snoozing, rain-washed setting belied the magnitude of what was taking place here.

Bolan completed his final recon from atop the wall before penetrating deeper into the belly of this monster to deliver what one official had long ago dubbed The Bolan Effect: a raging hellfire of destruction from a one-man blitzer.

There would also be one dozen wide-awake hoods within these estate walls, roving the main house and grounds with enough firepower to hold off an attacking regiment, if it came to that.

It would not come to that, of course.

Not tonight or any other night.

Which is why a government-trained "combat specialist" in nightfighting black had marked this particular "country estate" for a Bolan blitz.

This acreage might have looked innocent enough from the outside. But in fact it was no less than a walled fortress, operating beyond touch of the law, local or federal.

The Executioner had long ago understood that operations such as these were part of the wholesale rape of a nation from within, an attempt to debase a great society.

And like a cancer, this evil was gnawing away at the fiber of America, encouraging and pandering to the worst of its weaknesses.

The Mafia, *cosa di tutti cosi*, the "thing of all things"—an "invisible government," in the words of one worried law-enforcement official—neutralized cops and had officials in its pocket.

This so-called invisible government was composed of criminals grown fat and powerful from exploitation of the weak, from blackmail, murder and torture. It spun a web of tainted power reaching into the White House of two recent administrations, a spreading stain of sin unchecked by an intimidated U.S. government.

Law courts appeared hamstrung, or unwilling to jail or deport the scum who sold heroin to school-children and enslaved women and, increasingly, young girls for prostitution.

Untaxable billions were skimmed from every legitimate industry in the country via threats of acid splashed into the face, or the murder of a loved one. And these incidents occurred for more often than people cared to believe. "You don't think our trucks should haul your goods because we charge double the going rate? How'd ya like your daughter to be gangraped some night on the way home from school? How'd ya like your kneecaps shattered with a base-ball bat? You wouldn't? Fine, here's the contract...."

Nothing had changed since the bootlegging days of Al Capone and Dutch Schultz, Bolan knew from grim firsthand experience, from too many campaigns, such as this one tonight.

There had been advances and setbacks; tough posturing, with some laws outdistanced, before they were passed, by the tightening organization of national and international Mafia families into one central power; one mobster kingdom controlling everything, infiltrating by coercion the pinnacles of legitimate power.

The preceding dozen years of Bolan's life had been spent paying back an uncollectable blood debt Bolan owed these walking scumbags; vermin who would corrupt and destroy everything this trained warrior considered worth fighting for.

The Executioner had declared a one-man war against the Mafia and others some years ago, channeling combat skills developed in Vietnam to take on enemies closer to home.

Bolan's "crazy" war had made him perhaps, as one media scribe dubbed him, The Most Wanted Man in the World.

This "vigilante" was not only on the hit list of the Mafia and every terrorist group extant, but also wanted by every law-enforcement, national-security and espionage organization around the globe.

Apart from his unsanctioned activities in sensitive areas, this one man, during his twelve-year, lone-wolf campaigns, had executed no less than two thousand cannibals without due process of law, except perhaps for the due process of those laws these "cannibals" themselves operated under.

Bolan was not a violent man by nature, surprising as that might seem to the casual observer.

"He is perhaps the most misunderstood man of our time," one sympathetic network news commentator had stated. "A real living, breathing hero and the last of his breed."

Bolan had submerged his life into his mission, a peaceful man in a violent world; he had been pushed to the limit, the line beyond which no man of honor can be pushed and still keep his ideals intact.

Bolan's reverence for life was the very reason for his war.

Animal Man, the dark force of the world, had to be stopped.

Bolan meant to do everything he could do to stop them, even if it meant sacrificing his life in the attempt.

He had found no shortage of work on a troubled planet that seemed to be moving inexorably toward the precipice of world anarchy and terrorism. Day by day, hour by hour, Mack Bolan watched the doomsday clock ticking away while the savages grabbed and destroyed everything in sight, while decent people tried to understand why reason and sanity did not rule the day.

He hoped they would understand before it was too late. There were indications that some were listening.

Some things had changed, sure. Bolan had changed. But one constant remained: the savages ran loose through America and the world, avariciously devouring, growing fatter, using society's laws and civilized aversion to violence as a weapon.

The Executioner had brought the Bolan Effect all the way to this secluded promontory on the Southern California coast to do something about that.

Right now.

He spotted a couple of two-man patrols at different points along the periphery of the rain-splashed estate. One of the pairs of Mafia soldiers was beneath and behind his position, close enough for him to hear the low mumble of their conversation as they came toward him.

And thanks to the magnification capability of the NVD goggles, he could make out the other two barely discernible figures across the property, patrolling the base of the opposite wall.

Inland on a clear day the undulating San Joaquin Hills would be shimmering in the desert heat, but now the darkness and the rain made the men across the way, and those approaching Bolan, march their beat with heads bent, the outlines of shotguns showing beneath their dark rain slickers.

Bolan did not mind the rain at all. He welcomed it. He used it, taking advantage of its effect on the patrolling sentries. The rain bettered his odds, which needed all the help they could get.

He might not have to kill going in after all, which meant he would not have to leave a trail of bodies that could be discovered and blow this operation before he had a chance to execute the main hit, the vital objective of this night's assault.

Two sentries could be seen standing inside the bullet-proof window of a brick gate house just inside the double iron gates in the center of the eastern wall, across the compound from Bolan.

That meant six guards unaccounted for, if his intel on enemy strength was on the money. They were either inside the main house or undetected by Bolan somewhere about the grounds surrounding the main building and the ranch-style barracks.

The two sentries strolled by ten feet below Bolan's perch, neither man scanning the perimeter, their heads remaining bowed against the elements, their weapons aimed at the ground. Neither sentry gazed anywhere near the infiltrator lying prone atop the wall as they passed by beneath.

"My left nut for a dry place to grab a smoke," one of the sentries grumbled as they strolled on in the direction of the brick gate house.

"Chuck and Scar will let us grab some dry when we reach the guardhouse," the second sentry said as they continued on their rounds. "Unless Bobby Trick's got the same idea. This whole bunch is jumpy with Bolan fever."

"Guess I can't blame 'em at that," offered sentry number one as they proceeded out of Bolan's ear-shot. "They don't call that bastard in black The Man from Blood for nothing."

"Yeah, yeah. Just wish we'd lucked out and pulled house duty. Later for this wet crap."

"Our turn comes again tomorrow night."

The men's voices faded.

"Wish this damn Bolan thing would blow over...."

And they were gone.

Bolan landed with catlike grace in the deepest shadows at the inside base of the wall, watching the two sentries distance themselves several dozen feet away toward the guardhouse by the iron gates.

Bolan froze for another second, not making a noise, glancing around him with combat-iced eyes and ready weapon.

No backup patrol followed the two sentries.

The guards reached the gate house. They went inside out of the hissing, cold rain.

The Executioner angled away from the wall and made his way toward the guest-house barracks used by the off-duty Mafia hoods assigned to guard this fortress by the sea.

He had noted that the sentries did not wear night-vision devices, which did not mean a damn thing, really; they could have been toting NVDs in their rain slickers. Other roving sentries might be equipped to spot an intruder in the darkness.

Bolan advanced from cover to cover with extreme caution. He moved quickly from shrubbery to tree on an undetected approach to the slumbering ranch-style barracks. The building marked the midway point between the wall and the main house where the unaware mission objective awaited.

That would change during the next five minutes, if the numbers fell right and this hit unreeled as Bolan intended it to.

In the opening days of the Executioner's war against the Mob, Bolan had staged an audacious attack on this same walled estate above the cliffs of Balboa.

At that time, a Mafia savage named Julian "Deej" Di George, Mob capo of all of Southern California, had lived on this estate.

Until the Bolan Effect ended all of that and Deej along with it.

A dozen-plus years later another boss had risen to power and taken over the scattered pieces remaining of the Di George organization after Bolan's first strike, all those years, all that blood ago.

Kenny Ensalvo was referred to as the Kid these days, but only behind his back. He had not lost the cruel, brazen flare of ambition and amorality that had made his rise in power, to fill the leadership vacuum left after Bolan's execution of Di George, meteoric without precedent.

Kenny the Kid had simply bought off or killed anyone who stood in his way, except for pockets of resistance from some of the racial minority gangs who, in fact, were becoming the criminal majority in some parts of Southern California.

The black and Hispanic street gangs continued to quarrel among themselves, but for the most part the streets belonged, or would belong, to the Ensalvo family.

Especially after tonight, if things went the Kid's way.

Kenny the Kid was holding a top-level meeting inside the main house of this walled fortress, if Brognola's intel to Bolan was correct.

Hal Brognola was one of several highly placed contacts in the law-enforcement community who sympathized with Bolan's activities to the extent of actually offering assistance. This he did primarily by channeling intelligence to Bolan about the underworld, such as the report that had brought the warrior back to this deathground near Balboa.

Ensalvo had summoned the leaders of the various underworld factions from the Los Angeles area to his mansion for this early-morning conference. This top-level sit-down of syndicate chieftains was convened to pave over any remaining pockets of dissent, hopefully to emerge with a smooth-running crime machine that would be unbreakable by the most well-intentioned, dedicated efforts either government or local law-enforcement agencies could ever hope to muster.

To Bolan's way of thinking, this particular Mafia hardsite was long overdue for the Executioner's attentions, as was a savage street hood named Kenny the Kid.

Bolan gained the east wall of the sentry barracks. He paused again, taking care to survey the shrub-spotted grounds surrounding the guest house.

When he felt certain no one had as yet detected his presence, he slid the Ingram against his waist. He utilized both hands to unwrap a glob of plastic explosive.

Crouching beneath one of several evenly spaced windows from which drawn draperies blocked any light, he carefully wedged the powerful explosive along the foundation of the house.

He reached for the timer fuse, set it for five minutes and forced the fuse and blast cap into the deadly putty.

The hiss of needling mist abruptly stopped, the sounds of rain fading to the *drip-drip* of moisture from trees and shrubs.

Bolan inched along the wall of the house to a corner of the structure. He wanted to make an appraisal of the distance separating the ranch-style building from the main residence where the meeting called by Kenny Ensalvo was supposed to take place. No, scratch "supposed," definitely taking place, Bolan's recon now confirmed by the heavy concentration of manpower guarding these grounds.

He left cover of the guest house and continued his approach to the main building, advancing on it from the southeast.

This was the killzone, he knew. This was where their security would be tightest.

He moved hurriedly, the Ingram again held ready, poised to kill.

Death stalked the night and its name was Mack Bolan.

And ghosts stalked alongside the Executioner.

The last time Bolan had attacked this hardsite, those twelve-plus years ago, when he had decimated the Di George stranglehold on the citizens of Southern California, Bolan had not been alone, as he was now; as he preferred to go, after the bitter lesson learned that night on this killground.

At that time, in those first days of his one-man dirty war against the Mob, Bolan had reluctantly accepted the assistance of several Army buddies from his Vietnam war days, a disparate unit of ruthless, disillusioned men. Most of them were hard at war with their own inner values in those first confused, troubled days after Nam.

They had seemed to need Bolan and his cause as much as he thought he could use the help they offered, but that had all ended on the first campaign of Bolan and his Death Squad.

Nearly all of the Executioner's hell team had lost their lives in the assault on this and other Di George hardsites on that day twelve years ago.

Bolan could not shake the eerie sensation that those fallen good men, those large-living brothers-in-arms, were with him now.

The ominous quiet after the rain only seemed to intensify their spectral presence.

Bill Hoffower. Demolitions expert.

Tom Loudelk. Infiltrator and scout.

Angelo Fontenelli. Automatic weapons.

Juan Andromede. Light artillery.

Schwarz. Electronics genius.

Blancanales. The politician. And mechanic. And medic.

Jim Harrington. Marksman.

George Zitka. Scout.

Brave hellgrounders fallen in the good fight, that night twelve years ago, all of them except for Blancanales and Schwarz, who still assisted Bolan from time to time.

The loss of those good men had always weighed heavily on Bolan's heart and soul.

Especially here and now as his past and future collided close to where The Executioner and his War Everlasting had its beginnings.

But it had truly begun for Bolan well before that, when the men of Bolan's Death Squad had plied their grim combat specialties in a strange war eight thousand miles away from home.

In a place called Vietnam....

One

A warm July wind whipped across the tarmac, rattling the wings of the commuter plane. The aircraft sat on the other side of the glass door and observation windows of the terminal's indoor waiting area.

"I wonder where pop is?" Johnny Bolan said, looking around. "He's had plenty of time to park the car and be here by now. He won't want to miss seeing Mack off."

Mack Bolan, thirty years of age, standing tall in freshly pressed, military dress green between Johnny and their mother, did not take his arm from its affectionate hold around the shoulders of his kid sister, Cindy.

He glanced out at the ground crew preparing and loading the twin-engine plane that would fly him to Boston.

"Pop won't miss anything," Bolan said, grinning at his brother. "It's another ten minutes to boarding. Heck, after putting me up, or putting up with me, for the past three weeks under the same roof, pop's probably had his fill of his oldest, anyway."

Both of Cindy's arms were clasped as far around her big brother's middle as they would go. She had to tilt her head way back to look at him.

"Stop talking like that, Mack! You know darn well it's breaking pop's heart to see you off, just like all of us every time we have to say goodbye to you. I..." The lovely youngster paused for a moment with a catch in her voice, as if fighting off tears. "I...wish you didn't have to go."

"Maybe I should go looking for pop," Johnny offered. "Funny, him not being here—"

Elsa Bolan, rested a plump hand on the arm of her younger son.

"Sam will be along," she assured her children. "He's probably just having trouble finding a parking space, that's all."

The Bolan family had arrived at the hometown airport several minutes earlier in the family station wagon.

Sam Bolan, steelworker by trade, had dropped off his family at the closest entrance to the airline ticket counter. Sergeant Bolan had checked in his gear before strolling with his mother, Johnny and Cindy to the preloading area.

Then Sam Bolan had driven off to park the wagon, but had not yet returned for the final farewells to his eldest child. It was the end of a three-week furlough that Mack Bolan had spent with his family before shipping off to his second tour of combat duty in Vietnam.

Cindy rested her head affectionately on her big brother's chest as they stood side by side. She voiced a thought shared by the four of them.

"We'll all pray for your safe return, Mack."

Bolan gave her a hug and put on his best stiff upper lip.

"I hope you continue to write to me, sis," he kidded. "You're going to have a hard time keeping the boys away."

Cindy Bolan had been writing to her soldier brother every night that he was gone, diarylike letters she would mail Mack once or twice a week.

Bolan was something of a hero to Cindy. He could read it in her eyes. He knew that to her he stood for everything: her brother, her pal, her counselor, and Mack did not like the idea of depriving either Johnny or Cindy of any of that, especially at Cindy's age.

Cindy was a senior in high school, an age when Bolan knew most youngsters are at their most impressionable, vulnerable to good and bad influences. Mack felt there were far too many of the latter around for any young person coming of age in the troubled America of the late sixties.

"I think the most difficult thing in life must be to be a soldier's mother." Elsa Bolan spoke softly, and for the first time that day Bolan saw his mother's eyes begin to moisten. "I...just never get used to seeing you off, son. I never will."

"Don't worry, mom. I'll be back pretty soon." Bolan grinned his best cheery smile, one he did not feel.

Nothing in this life was easy, this soldier knew, not the things that matter, especially in times like these. But he did not want his mother to fall apart, not now. She had the strength of character that was her Polish American birthright, but she was a mother, first and last, and no mother in her right mind would ever enjoy sending a son off to war.

He glanced around idly, but his steady gaze was looking for the familiar, ambling form of his father amid the small crowd lolling around the gate, waiting for word that the commuter flight was ready to board.

He spotted mostly businessmen, some with their wives to see them off; a few college student types outfitted for skiing; and the usual assortment of more or less nondescript folks, men and women, awaiting the flight for who knew what reasons.

But no Sam Bolan.

It had been some ten minutes since pop had dropped them off, surely enough time, Bolan thought, for the family wagon to be parked and pop to rejoin them for final goodbyes.

Mack hated the idea of leaving his family behind, and he knew gruff, irascible Sam Bolan felt the same way.

Where was he?

Bolan's mind drifted from the thought when his mother reached up and touched his face lightly, lovingly, with her fingertips.

"I'm sorry, son, I can't help but worry. And you'll get your care packages," she promised in a heroically controlled quaver. "The Polish sausages you like, the cookies...and Christmas is coming. You'll get something special for Christmas, and Thanksgiving. Oh, Mack honey...this is your second tour of duty over in that terrible place. Why did they have to send you to Vietnam a second time?''

"We've been over this, mom." Bolan reached up to return the loving touch. "They're sending me back because I asked. I'm a soldier. Vietnam is where the action is. It's where things that matter are happening. It's where I belong."

Johnny grinned to break some of the sadness.

"Hey, you can't fool me," he said, chuckling. "Heck, mom, Mack just wants to lay eyes on those Oriental beauties again."

Bolan returned the grin and delivered a buddy-buddy chuck under Johnny's chin.

"You know, John, you just might be right about that."

"Save a few Cong for me, guy. I'll be along in a couple of years, soon as I can."

The words rested like a heavy weight across Bolan's shoulders.

"I hope not, John-O." He addressed his brother by the family's pet name for a kid who still thought in terms of dumb adolescent glory. "I hope to God by the time you're old enough, it'll be finished over there. I'll do everything I can to see to it."

Johnny nodded contritely.

"I didn't mean to sound so flippant. I know it's a living hell, what you're going through over there. I'm sorry. I'm gonna miss you, man."

Cindy had not moved from close to her brother's side.

"I...just hope it's worth it, Mack," she said quietly. "Vietnam is so far away. Some of my friends say that what's happening over there doesn't have anything to do with us...that we have no business sending our young men so far from home to risk their lives. Some of my friends at school have staged protests with the college kids, and sometimes, when I tell them my brother is in the service in Vietnam, they call me terrible things and I—I know they're wrong, but I don't know what to say. They say the Army is waging a ruthless, unjust war—"

"The Army is sent to do what our elected officials order us to do, sis," Bolan interrupted firmly, yet gently. "Ruthless? Yes, we have to be that, considering what we're up against over there. Unjust?" He shook his head. "You'll just have to believe me when I tell you that after what I've seen over there, I know we're on God's side."

He had no intention of breaking the mood or giving Elsa Bolan more reason to worry. But yeah, Bolan had devoted time and thought to the *why* of his government's involvement in Southeast Asia.

He had lain awake nights, trying to figure out the reason that the U.S. was sending him and hundreds of thousands of other men to fight and possibly die in some distant hellground that few people had even known the name of before the draft calls started going out; before then it had always been Indochina.

Bolan was a twelve-year military veteran, a "lifer" in the parlance of the armed services, a man of self-discipline and a strong sense of duty, a thinking individualist, a good soldier who also had a mind of his own.

From the beginning he had seriously questioned his government's intention to bring about a satisfactory solution to the complex struggles—military, cultural, ideological—that had been raging throughout Southeast Asia in one form or another for thousands of years.

Bolan knew that the command and the grunts in the field had to wage a war against two fronts, both of them no damn good for morale or getting the job done. The armed forces trying to accomplish their mission in Vietnam were being increasingly, equally snafued by less than full support from the home front.

Both the American people and their elected government seemed unwilling or unable to move in full measure. Add to that the fact that the enemy was virtually indistinguishable from the friendly inhabitants of the land the miltary had come to protect.

The kindly, fragile old woman doing laundry on base could be feeding intel on troop strength and the like straight to the local Vietcong leader.

The teenage kid running errands for the guys in the motor pool could don the black pajamalike outfit of the VC and toss a grenade into that same motor-pool garage during the night, killing those who had trusted and befriended him.

But soldier Bolan's orders had been to go to Nam and fight. And this is what he did. It had been almost impossible for any man with a sense of honor and right and wrong not to become emotionally, gut-level involved after he saw what Vietnam, a land of harsh beauty and delicate culture and wisdom, had on its hands.

Over one million North Vietnamese, mainly Christians, had fled south across the 17th parallel immediately after a 1954 Geneva conference had partitioned the country following the French defeat. The north became a Communist dictatorship called the Democratic Republic of Vietnam, while South Vietnam, below the 17th parallel, was known as the Republic of Vietnam. That told a man something right there.

But the cannibals in power in Hanoi wanted all of it. From Quang Tri just south of the 17th parallel to Quan Long on the southern peninsula, they waged a cruel war of terror perpetrated by the Cong from within the Republic of South Vietnam.

Viet Communist paramilitaries operated in close conjunction with the North Vietnamese army in staging systematic attacks intended to destabilize and bring about the fall of the democratic government of South Vietnam.

As a soldier, Bolan could understand the killing of the military, but the VC specialized in the extermination of civilian leadership and the torture and murder of innocent women and children.

Another case of the strong taking and destroying, unless the weak had help in holding on to what was rightfully theirs. Bolan had quickly seen plenty of proof that the war in Vietnam was not simply an inner conflict in some faraway place; not an internal civil war and nothing else.

In his first full month of active combat duty in the bush, Bolan had come across the bodies of slain Vietcong, Chicom K-50 machine guns, SKS Soviet-made carbines and Czech Communist-manufactured ammunition.

Soldier Bolan did have his personal reservations about whether or not Vietnam was a winnable war, but enough firsthand evidence had convinced him that something profoundly important was being defended there, too.

At stake was a struggling democracy, plagued with no shortage of its own inner strife. And it did matter what happened in Veitnam because of the very principles Bolan's own country had founded itself on.

If one of the last holdouts for democracy in Southeast Asia called for assistance against a hostile aggressor, and if Bolan's government saw fit to send him to help the defenders build their own workable society without threat from the Communists, then by God Sergeant Mack Bolan would give everything he had to this struggle into which fate had thrust him.

He had seen the stomach-turning aftermath of enough VC atrocities to want—to need—to stop it any way he could.

Bolan felt that this farewell to his family was no time or place to articulate why he was going back. But he decided at that moment to begin keeping a journal—he'd call it a war journal—and cut through the bull right from the git-go, yeah.

He would attempt therein to express the way he felt about what he had experienced and what he was returning to. Because as a man Bolan knew he had no choice. And he would rewrite excerpts of the journal as letters to his family, so that they might comprehend the truths he had witnessed in the strange land, the strange war, of Vietnam.

More than anything, Bolan wanted them to understand what compelled him to leave this beautiful existence they shared together, one that he knew so well and cherished, to help those of another race in a foreign land. Indeed, these people did not even speak the same language; but they wanted and needed what Bolan had to give, and he would not let them down.

"Flight seven-twenty-four to Boston, now loading at gate seven."

The public-address announcement sliced through his thoughts.

"There's your father," Elsa Bolan told her children.

Johnny spotted Sam Bolan, and the youth's expression clouded with concern.

"Looks like pop's found some company. Or some trouble..."

Mack stepped aside from Cindy and eased her from him, turning around with an instinctual, barely noticeable step away from where his family stood.

The familiar figure of Sam Bolan, strutting forward, looking every bit as hearty and strong-willed as Mack always pictured him, cut through the milling crowd as travelers and well-wishers began shuffling en masse toward the glass door held open by airline employees.

Sam walked faster than usual, as if trying to out-distance the two men who kept pace with him. The three of them had almost reached where the Bolan family waited.

The duo, whom Bolan did not recognize, had forty pounds each and at least fifteen years on his father.

Mack pedigreed them fast enough, their kind having been in no shortage on the streets of Pittsfield where he had grown up, or anywhere else for that matter, it seemed.

Street punks who thought they were tough guys, complete with black leather jackets.

And they were hassling pop.

The punk on Sam Bolan's left snarled something harsh, close to Sam's ear.

The elder Bolan pretended not to hear and kept walking, and Mack could not make out the words through the babel of the bustling crowd around them.

Then the punk on pop's right reached out and grabbed Sam roughly, a viselike fist clenched around Sam's arm. The punk jerked, pulling Sam off balance.

The elder Bolan emitted a groan of discomfort that did reach Mack's ears.

Sam fell to support himself on one knee, the punk holding his arm.

The other tough leaned down to snarl something else to Sam.

Cindy gasped audibly.

"What's happening?" she asked, looking into the startled faces of her mother and brothers.

"Let's find out," growled Bolan.

He elbowed his way through the crowd as it parted into a circle around the two men roughing up Sam.

There were a few gasps of dismay from bystanders, but Bolan was the only person to act. Onlookers moved aside for the tall man in uniform.

Bolan moved fast, his anger held in check, his every move calculated, precisely executed.

The two toughs and Sam eyeballed Bolan at the instant Mack came in with a powerhouse kick that implanted the spit-shined toe of his right boot deep into the groin of the creep gripping his father's arm.

The hood emitted a choking gasp. His face turned beet-red. The impact of the kick flung the punk into a backward, open-armed fall, his fingers releasing Sam.

The elder Bolan's painful wince turned to surprise. He scurried to the sidelines even as the hood slammed against the glass observation window.

The punk collapsed, grabbing his damaged genitals, dry-heaving, to become a cramped fetal ball moaning into the linoleum.

Mack swung around out of the kick to face the tough who had been about to snarl at Sam Bolan.

This hood unlimbered a leather blackjack from his right-hand jacket pocket and slapped it once sharply into his left hand.

"Okay, soldier boy, come and get it. You just bought yourself the farm."

The punk came in, bobbing, arms out, knees bent in the best street-fighter style.

Bolan gave the jerk some jungle-fighting style.

His left boot lashed up and out in a lightning martial-arts kick that caught the punk's blackjack wrist with enough force to shatter the bone with a sound like a dry twig snapping.

The sap flew from nerveless fingers. The punk started to scream something in pain, surprise and anger.

Bolan bounced in to clip a snappy right punch to the creep's jaw, holding back on what could have been a lethal blow. But there was enough power in the punch to snap jawbone and push back down the scream along with a mouthful of broken, bloody teeth.

The punk stumbled back, stunned.

Bolan followed through, pinning the hood's head roughly up against the wall, supporting the semi-conscious man there with a strong, sure grip.

The crowd started to edge in a little closer.

Bolan looked around, spotting his father and the concerned, stunned expressions of Elsa, Johnny and Cindy.

"Call the cops, pop! These stumblebums aren't going anywhere."

Sam Bolan edged in closer, pitching his voice low, out of earshot of anyone else.

"Mack, please. Let 'em go."

Bolan wasn't sure he heard right.

"Let them go? Pop, what's this all about?"

"Later, son. Thanks for what you did. But, please...for your mother's and my sake, and for Johnny and Cindy...*let them go*."

The thug Bolan held propped up was beginning to regain some awareness.

Sam looked anxious, upset, more scared than before his son had taken a hand.

Mack released his grip on the hood.

The guy collapsed into a sitting position, shaking the cobwebs from his head, the pain returning. He looked up at Bolan and his confusion became naked hate and kill lust, held only barely in check.

Bolan nodded to the other guy who continued to groan and writhe about on the floor.

"Take your buddy and scram, hairbag," Bolan told the toothless one, "and don't come back."

The punk with the busted wrist and broken jaw did his best to coax his incapacitated partner onto his feet.

Together, the two hoods hobbled away without a backward glance.

One of the airline people, a well-shaped blonde, Bolan noted, cautiously eased through the dispersing crowd.

"Should I...call the police?"

Bolan glanced again at his father.

Sam returned a nearly imperceptible headshake.

"Thanks, miss," Bolan told the airline employee, "nothing the police could do to help now. Some muggers after my dad's wallet, I guess."

The airline blonde looked skeptical but she didn't want to get involved, either.

"Whatever you say, then. Nothing like this has ever happened in the airport before...."

She returned to her duties.

The crowd had dispersed, almost as if nothing had happened. Someone had even picked up and walked off with the blackjack as a memento of the ruckus.

The Bolan family drew into a small circle.

Mack saw that most of the airline passengers had already boarded the flight to Boston waiting out on the tarmac.

"Pop, maybe I'd better catch a later flight. What's this all about?"

"It wasn't about nothing, Mack. I'm—I'm sorry this happened."

Sam had recovered most of his natural gruff demeanor but a tremor remained in his voice.

"Who were those guys?" Mack asked.

"I don't know...punks...hoods...too many of 'em around these days."

"You're right about that, pop, but excuse me for saying so, you're also a lousy liar." He looked to his mother. "Who were they, ma?"

"Elsa—" Sam said warningly.

"Oh, stop it, both of you," Cindy broke in. "Can't you see Mack only wants to help?"

"Tell Mack, pop," Johnny added.

Elsa Bolan looked to her son for understanding.

"It's like this, Mack. Your father was sick some time ago and the bills...well, the bills just became too much."

"Okay, okay, I can tell it," Sam growled, and he looked squarely at Mack. "You're right, son. I did lie to you. I'm sorry. I...guess I'm just too damn proud for my own good, like your mother always says."

"If you needed money, you should have told me."

"I know what I shoulda done," Sam admitted. "But there's this guy...he hangs around the parking lot outside the factory. He...helps guys out who need a hand like I did."

"A loan shark," Bolan growled under his breath. "Some friend."

"Times have been hard, son. I'm sure you must've noticed it during your stay with us. You've been too damn decent to mention it. Anyways, I fell a little behind in my payments." Sam indicated the direction taken by the hoods. "Guess they figured they had to come around and remind me, damn scum."

Johnny and Cindy beamed at their older brother.

"Man, that was some job of handling yourself, big guy," Johnny gushed. "Wow!"

"I'll say." Cindy nodded enthusiastically. "You sure can take care of yourself, Mack."

Elsa quieted her two children with a somber glance, then looked to Mack.

"I'm sorry you had to get involved in this, son, I really am."

"I'm not. How much do you owe them, pop?"

Sam shook his head stubbornly.

"I won't take money from my own son."

"Then I'll send it to ma. We've got to stick together, this little family of ours. I owe the two of you more than I could ever repay."

"You're a good son, Mack," said Elsa. "Sam owed those...people...eight hundred and fifty dollars."

"I'll send it to you as soon as I reach Da Nang," Bolan promised. "There's hardly anything worthwhile to spend money on over there, anyway. It'll do a whole lot more good helping you folks out, getting these creeps off your back."

"Final boarding call for flight seven-twenty-four at gate seven," crackled the public-address-system speakers overhead.

Sam Bolan appeared to make a decision. His features relaxed and some of the old good humor returned.

"Well, son, no one can say I didn't try to keep you out of this mess I got myself into. Thanks, Mack. Your mother's right. You're one of the good ones."

"Just do me a favor, pop. Don't ever go to jerks like that again when you need help. Get word to me. Let me see what I can do."

"I'll...try to remember that, son." Then some of the habitual paternal bluster returned. "But right now you'd better shake it, soldier, or that plane out there's going to take off without you."

"You're right about that." Bolan nodded reluctantly. The big soldier stepped forward. Father and son embraced wholeheartedly, unreservedly. "Take care."

"You too, son."

Then it was over almost too fast to register.

A bear hug for ma and Cindy; a handshake and a man-to-man hug with Johnny.

Then Bolan moved briskly through the loading gate and across the tarmac, to board the commuter jet for the flight to Boston, where he would connect with a nonstop flight to the West Coast.

From Travis Air Force Base he would hop the World Airways government contract flight to Da Nang, Vietnam, via Anchorage, Alaska; Atsugi, Japan; and Kadena Air Force Base, Okinawa.

Away from home.

Away from the four people he cared about more than anyone or anything else in the world.

Back to another world where life was too cheap and could be lost without warning, including Bolan's.

Especially Bolan, whose job in the bush was the leader of Sniper Team Able, a combat unit that routinely penetrated deep behind enemy lines for commando strikes.

The tall man with the icy blue eyes boarding the commuter jet in Pittsfield had already scored nearly one hundred official enemy kills.

Bolan experienced a nagging something in his gut that refused to go away. This elusive sensation told the departing soldier that as important and personally rewarding as his hellgrounding in Vietnam might be, he was leaving home to fight an enemy eight thousand miles away when the precious home did not look at all as safe and sound as a son, a soldier heading off to war, would want it to be.

It took the usual amount of time and delay for the commuter jet to taxi around for the runway approach.

The last glimpse Mack Bolan had of his family came as the jet revved forward into its takeoff, picking up speed as it rattled past the loading-area observation window.

Sam and Elsa Bolan, and Cindy and Johnny, stood inside waving as the plane roared past. They were probably unable to make out Mack, but they waved goodbye anyway. He saw the four of them huddled as one, as people do after a departing loved one.

Sergeant Mack Bolan returned a wave of acknowledgment and farewell.

Then the jet was past the terminal, clawing its way into the summer sky toward Boston, carrying him off on the first step of his journey back to Hell.

Bolan could not shake the strangest premonition that he would never see his family again.

Two

Pleiku Province, Vietnam ———————————

The ten-man patrol in camou fatigues and combat gear jogged rapidly alongside the winding, narrow game trail through the August night.

The wilting humidity and stench of jungle rot enveloped them like a heavy, invisible blanket.

The faint clink of their equipment and steady, muted footfalls were the only sounds made by the American soldiers. They moved in low crouches to either side of the trail, through vines and dense undergrowth, between liana-wrapped trunks of ancient mahogany and balsa trees that probed the sky.

Team leader Bolan had split his men to both sides of the footpath to avoid Charlie's booby traps that festooned the infiltration route this near to their objective.

Juan Andromede and "Gunsmoke" Harrington ran point, followed by Bolan and "Gadgets" Schwarz, who toted the radio.

Zitter and Fontenelli hustled along behind Schwarz.

Blancanales and Hoffower pushed their way through the jungle on the other side of the trail.

The men hurried through the dense bush, each man separated from his buddies by ten feet or so. They maintained a loose formation as they humped across the nearly impenetrable terrain near the Viet-Cambodian border where the Vietcong and North Vietnam army claimed control of this primeval countryside that resounded with a symphony of nightlife: insects, bats, monkeys.

Schwarz's radio crackled faintly with the voice of the team's scout, "Bloodbrother" Loudelk, a Blackfoot Indian from Montana.

"Striker, this is Able Three, over."

"Hold it," Bolan whispered to his team. He reached for the handset extended to him by Schwarz. "Able Three, this is Striker, over."

The others held their positions, forming a loose perimeter, each man facing out, hidden in the foliage, their M-16s held ready to fire, the jungle sounds continuing undisturbed all around them.

"We've got it, Striker," came Loudelk's transmitted whisper. The caution in his voice transmitted clearly, too. "About two hundred yards dead ahead. Watch it coming in. The trail ends and it's killzone time with this damn moon on, over."

"Hold right, Able Three," Bolan growled into his transceiver. "We're coming in, over."

"Roger that, Striker, over."

Bolan handed the transceiver back to Gadgets.

"Fan out," Bolan whispered to his men. "Break from the trail. Move it."

They pushed on.

Each man carried an M-16, a .45 pistol, a combat knife and a full array of pouches containing extra ammo and grenades. And the faces of this death squad were blacked out to better camouflage them with the night.

They advanced wordlessly, like one well-oiled machine, and regrouped at the tree line where Bloodbrother awaited them.

The Indian summoned them to him with a muted animal call, a prearranged signal.

Sniper Team Able maintained its defensive positioning while Bolan crept in to crouch beside Bloodbrother.

Bolan gazed at what Loudelk had found, what they had penetrated into the enemy-held territory to find.

Knee-deep elephant grass separated their position from the bamboo-walled perimeter of an NVA outpost.

The little fort basked in the silver, surreal glow of the full moon.

An eight-foot-high wall of sharpened bamboo poles, linked at top and bottom with strong twine, appeared hastily assembled, as Bolan knew this outpost to be.

This North Viet subcamp, operated secretly in the middle of nowhere, was utilized by the NVA and VC as an interrogation center and, of course, to billet some of the personnel charged with the chore of "pacifying" this dangerous area.

The outpost, a 250-yard-by-200-yard rectangle, squatted in the middle of a clearing in the jungle.

A heavily guarded gate at the far corner of the compound appeared to be the only entrance.

The thatched roofs of several structures poked up from inside the walled perimeter.

A twenty-foot-high guard tower, also thatch-roofed, commanded a clear view of the killground surrounding the post. The barrel of a mounted machine gun—Bolan guessed an M-50 from this distance—poked out into the night from the guard tower, and behind the gun Bolan could discern two pinpoints of red.

Security was hardly as tight as it should have been—as it seldom is in the hours between 0300 and dawn when sentries the world over begin experiencing the boredom of an all-night vigil. The time was right for the kind of surprise hit-and-git attack Bolan intended.

The guards in the watchtower were enjoying a smoke and probably some idle conversation to keep themselves awake.

The crew manning the gate would be in approximately the same shape.

Bolan and Bloodbrother hastily ducked back lower in the shadows as a five-man sentry patrol suddenly marched into view from around the far corner of the wall.

Bolan clearly discerned five helmeted, khaki-clad NVA regulars marching the length of the outside wall before disappearing again around an opposite corner of the perimeter.

"I've timed 'em," Loudelk whispered to Bolan. "They pass at five-minute intervals."

"Good work," Bolan grunted.

He motioned Loudelk to pull back with him. He hand-signaled the other men to withdraw several yards deeper into the bush, where they crouched, forming a tight circle.

"Everyone get to eyeball the place?" Bolan asked.

"Could be worse," Juan Andromede whispered. "The sentry patrol will give us the most trouble."

Chopper Fontenelli grunted. "You bring some of that wacky weed back with you from the last leave you took, Flower Child? How the hell do we know how many guns they got inside that flimsy-looking dump?"

"Chopper, Flower Child, save it for the barracks," Bolan admonished. But he recognized the camaraderie that made his team the best there was. He knew the good-natured wordplay was only these warriors' way of setting their minds for the dirty reality of kill or be killed. "Maybe we won't have to deal with the patrol going in. We use Alternate Plan Bravo."

Gunsmoke Harrington nudged Bill Hoffower.

"Guess that means you and me in the fire again, Boom-Boom."

Harrington was one of the few grunts allowed to carry personal weapons into combat. The Texan traveled with two hair-trigger six-guns worn old-west quick-draw fashion, handles forward.

Boom-Boom looked to Bolan.

"Which wall you want me and Smoke to hit, Sarge?"

"Take the west wall." Bolan glanced at the human mountain crouched beside him. "Deadeye, you and I will work our way around and penetrate from the north. That should give both teams four minutes at least with that outside patrol on the east and south."

The big black man grinned his famous ear-to-ear number.

"Gonna use my natural camouflage again, eh, Sarge? I call that hedgin' the bet, dude."

Bolan returned a chuckle, then looked at the shadow-shrouded faces of Blancanales, Zitka, Schwarz, Andromede and Fontenelli.

"Pol, Zitter, Gadgets, Chopper, Flower Child, you guys stay under cover. When you see us making the break for it, pour in that cover fire hot and heavy. Or maybe we'll make it in and out before they know we've hit."

"I just hope to hell our intel is on the money and the chief's wife and daughter are inside," growled Blancanales.

"We all hope that, Pol," said Schwarz. "What about Bloodbrother, Sarge? You left him out."

Zitka grinned.

"You forgetting that tower, Gadgets? Or am I wrong, Bloodbrother?"

Corporal Tom Loudelk unlimbered a crossbow and arrows from where they rode strapped to his back.

"Right for a change, paleface," Bloodbrother cracked without a grin. He wore a small feather in his helmet.

Loudelk began fitting an arrow into the cross-bow, which was a time-honored weapon of silent killing that had fallen into favor with jungle forces of both the north and the south in this war.

"That's it then," said their leader. "Questions? Okay, move out."

The men split up as silently as they had approached.

Those designated as flank men positioned themselves for fire support for the withdrawal or backup if things got hairy.

Gunsmoke Harrington and Boom-Boom Hoffower angled away from the others after watches had been synchronized.

Deadeye Washington and Bolan eased off in the opposite direction to pick their way carefully around the edge of the clearing toward the opposite wall, on the north side of the small fort.

Bloodbrother Loudelk separated from the unit and positioned himself with a clear field of fire on the machine gunners in the guard tower.

Tom Loudelk bellied down softly among the random patches of deep blackness at the edge of the tree line. He chose a spot where the moon did not play its ghostly light, the silver illumination splaying out into the clearing. He set the crossbow and arrows on the ground alongside him, waiting for the time when his expertise would be needed.

He itched for action, but knew it would come to him soon enough.

The crossbow was a new touch. He had practiced with it plenty, but this was the first time he'd carried it into combat.

Loudelk was responsible for sixty-seven verifiable enemy dead; none of those had been from gunshot.

The Indian was an expert self-trained knife fighter; a skill he had picked up for his own personal survival well before Vietnam, in the redneck wilds of Montana. He could break a man's neck with one movement of both hands.

Bolan once told Loudelk he thought him the most nerveless forward scout he'd ever worked with.

Tom regarded this as a supreme compliment from a guy he considered his own blood brother.

The Blackfoot didn't know the life histories of any of his blood brothers in this "dirty job" unit. The grunts talked about home, but the pros out in the bush knew thoughts of home dulled the survival instinct more than the oppressively muggy atmosphere or the paranoia of unseen enemies everywhere.

The anger building inside Tom Loudelk had seethed to the flashpoint back home, and if he hadn't got the hell away from the chains of white men, he knew he would have killed someone.

Loudelk had got the hell out of a country where he knew he'd end up in a death house, and landed in a country that was nothing but one giant death house.

Vietnam.

Shit.

But at least, he had told himself, he channeled his rage into something that put spending money in his pocket. And if his turn came to buy the ranch, he would go down feeding death back at his attackers the way a brave was supposed to die.

He glanced at his watch, hoping the numbers were falling right for Bolan and Deadeye and Gunsmoke and Boom.

The five-man sentry patrol passed once more, then disappeared from sight.

Reflected moon glow from their light-colored uniforms made them easy targets.

This was a special mission for Bolan's sniper team on orders straight from Colonel Winters. A blood debt was being repaid, not for Bloodbrother and his teammates, exactly, but for the men who led them, and that was good enough for Loudelk.

This NVA outpost was HQ for a baby killer named Major Linh. At this moment he was holding hostage inside the walled perimeter the wife and daughter of a Montagnard chief whose tribe had worked closely with Bolan on several previous missions.

The chief, a fierce mountain warrior named Sioung, was the principal unifying force in the guerrilla war the Monts waged against the Vietcong and the NVA with American support.

This was why Linh had kidnapped Sioung's wife and child, in the process massacring a Mont encampment, while Sioung and his men had been out on a mission blowing up a vital supply bridge.

Major Linh left one survivor at the Mont camp massacre to deliver the major's demand: offers of amnesty in return for the surrender of Sioung and his men.

Everyone knew what that meant. Another massacre. And so Sioung had personally entreated Mack Bolan to assist in rescuing his hostaged family members.

Bolan had once lived among Sioung's people during a series of operations codenamed Chimneysweep.

Sioung had saved Bolan's life.

Loudelk didn't know how, exactly, but he did know Sarge had convinced Colonel Winters to send in Team Able. It did not take much convincing, since Major Linh was high on the Viet and Americans' Wanted Dead or Alive list.

Bolan also persuaded Sioung and his men to remain behind, a far more difficult task, but the Meo chief had seen the logic in Bolan's reasoning that to achieve maximum results, his team needed to work unencumbered by extra forces, even Sioung's mountain guerrillas.

Sioung would have been more difficult to convince, thought Loudelk, had it not been for the record of Bolan's team, and for the Meo chief's complete faith in the man Americans and Asians alike had started calling the Executioner.

Loudelk could see the sentry patrol march by again and was surprised to realize another five minutes had passed.

The appearance of the five-man guard detail meant Bolan and the others had not been discovered.

Yeah, Loudelk felt a personal commitment to this mission and not just because it meant something to Bolan.

Loudelk felt a strong affinity with the Montagnard people.

Their name was French for mountaineers, Loudelk had learned.

The appearance, customs, culture and language of the Monts were entirely different from those of the ethnic Vietnamese. They were the outsiders, although they were the ones who had been here first. And the Vietnamese had treated them wretchedly through the ages.

The Montagnards were mainly subsistence farmers with primitive, outdated methods. Every door of opportunity was slammed in the face of these people whose spirituality embraced the land and elements. And though fragmented by tribal rivalry, the Monts kept fighting to preserve a way of life threatened by the Communists' widespread campaigns of genocide that had reached holocaust proportions.

Bloodbrother felt damn glad to be a part of this mission.

He glanced at his watch again.

The action—the killing—would begin any second now.

Major Linh had set a deadline of dawn today for Sioung to surrender, and by now, Loudelk figured, the major would have the idea that there would be no surrender.

And there would be nothing to stop Linh from executing Sioung's wife and child.

Come on, Bolan, thought Tom Bloodbrother Loudelk. Let's do it!

He reached for the crossbow and held it ready to fire from his prone position, like an ancestor poised patiently to observe a herd of buffalo, waiting.

Three

Captain Phuong found Major Linh in the headquarters hut, the most comfortably furnished of the huts in the compound because the major had his private living quarters there. An archway behind Linh's desk connected the major's office with his living quarters.

Through the archway, Phuong had often caught glimpses of the elegant appointments of Linh's private chambers, a distinct contrast to the squalid living conditions of Phuong and his men, and the Vietcong contingent they worked with.

The high command in Hanoi had finally gone so far as to officially sanction the scavenging that had long been a staple of survival for Phuong and his men in this seemingly forgotten corner of the war.

Phuong sometimes wondered if his counterparts in the American Army had it any better. He imagined that it most likely came down to the same thing: the rudiments of survival. The only thing that mattered was staying alive, and often that meant doing what you did not want to do. The rudiments of survival.

Linh looked up from cleaning the disassembled service revolver on his desk.

An SKS Soviet-made assault rifle rested across the desk within inches of the major's hand.

"Yes, Captain, what have you to report?"

Major Linh's slightly sibilant voice dripped breeding and culture.

Traditional Viet music drifted through the archway from the private living quarters.

Captain Phuong, who knew nothing of music, barely heard the muted recording.

"All is quiet, sir."

"I can hear that for myself, fool," Linh snapped. "Has there been no word?"

"No, sir. Not yet."

"How long until the deadline?"

Phuong glanced at the clock on the wall, which Linh could have seen with a slight turn of his head.

"Perhaps an hour to sunrise."

Linh completed reassembling the pistol. He loaded it, his movements crisp, alert, despite the hour.

"I should think we would have heard at least some word by now if they intended to surrender."

"They will not surrender, sir."

The major peered at Phuong, who felt perspiration beading on his forehead that had nothing to do with the stifling humidity of the night.

"You say that with some degree of conviction, Captain," Linh snapped. "Do you find fault with the trap I have devised to rid ourselves once and for all of these mountain vermin?"

The question was voiced as a challenge.

"Er, uh, no fault in your strategy, Major, but perhaps we underestimate Sioung."

"In what way?"

"I suggest this Sioung must suspect that he and his men will be slaughtered when they surrender, despite the offer of amnesty. Sioung must appreciate his own worth, that he is the rallying point of all the mountain tribal resistance against us. He must realize that we simply cannot afford to allow him to live."

Phuong felt nothing but relief when Major Linh nodded as if at some inner thought of his own.

"These savages are ignorant, true, but low as they are on the evolutionary scale, they can reason at a base level. It is sometimes difficult for a man of our, shall I say, breeding, to appreciate that, is it not, Captain? Yes, you may be right. Sioung may sense what you say. But I have his wife and daughter, remember. He will not allow them to die. Even these filthy aborigines have some inkling of familial ties."

"I was speaking only of Sioung and his men surrendering, my major. I did not say they would not come."

Linh's reptilian eyes blinked.

"An attack? They would not dare. They fight with clubs and arrows and the few modern weapons they find. They would be no match for our firepower."

"When has that stopped them in the past?" Phuong asked rhetorically. "Begging your pardon, sir, but they could attack if they had enough provocation, which I believe they do."

"And what else do you believe, Captain?" Linh asked curtly. "You believe you might like my rank, eh? Is that it? Make me look bad, eh?"

"Quite the opposite, sir. We have not considered the possibility of attack before now, because we were so sure Sioung and his fighters would surrender. But now, with an hour until dawn, I only suggest that you at least consider the possibility of an attack, and not only from Sioung and his tribe. There are others."

Linh blinked with genuine curiosity this time.

"Elaborate. Recon reports from headquarters suggest no enemy troop presence in the area at this time."

"The recon flights would have difficulty spotting a commando penetration team, sir, operating under cover of night. And we have received word, you may recall, from one of our paid informants in the Americans' ranks."

Linh's brow furrowed.

"You mean about the man, Bolan, the one they call the Executioner?" The major waved a hand in dismissal. "Yes, yes, we know of the damage he has done. The man shall pay dearly for his crimes against us."

"You will recall," continued Phuong carefully, "that the last word from our informant was that a clandestine action was being launched. Bolan and his men were said to be involved."

"I disregarded that information then, as I do now, as not pertinent to our mission here," the camp commandant countered. "Why should we believe the

Executioner has any intention of staging an assault on this camp, or of trying to effect the rescue of Sioung's wife and child? Ridiculous."

"Mack Bolan is also known throughout the country as Sergeant Mercy," Phuong reminded his superior. "He has close personal ties with Sioung. I have taken the liberty of reviewing Bolan's dossier. Consider the timing of our holding Sioung's family members hostage, the Executioner's sniper team's being dispatched to this area, Bolan's connection with the Meo—he lived among Sioung's tribe, you know."

"Yes, yes, Captain, I am quite as familiar with the exploits of the American renegade as you pretend to be," Linh rasped. "Very well. Awake the off-duty personnel. Double the sentries and send out two recon patrols to see what they can learn. As you know, this is my last bit of business here before I transfer. I want nothing to go wrong."

"Yes, sir."

Phuong saluted and about-faced smartly, glad to leave the glare of those unblinking reptilian eyes. He almost made it out of the hut.

"And, Captain."

Phuong turned, startled.

"Yes, sir?"

"Have the woman and child executed at once. See to it, yourself, to ensure that it is done properly."

"But, sir—"

"Yes, I know. The deadline. Come, come, Captain, you did not really believe we would let the women live, did you? They have only been kept alive

this long in the event Sioung chose to send an emis-
sary to ensure their well-being before coming in to
surrender. Now that we know he will not be coming
in, what is the point of keeping the women alive a
moment longer? Kill them. Immediately.''

Phuong worked up his courage, hoping his voice
would remain steady. He had already pushed this
madman, his commander, far enough, but just because Phuong obeyed orders—Phuong had over-
seen the slaughter of Sioung's camp when the
leader's wife and daughter had been abducted—did
not mean Captain Phuong relished any of it.

He had committed atrocity after atrocity, following the orders of Major Linh, who rarely left the relative comfort of this hut while his troops carried out
his insane commands. But Phuong had just about
reached the end of his own rope, had almost blown
his own brains out after witnessing the slaughter
carried out by his men.

"But, sir,'' he forced himself to say. "The girl, she
is merely a child.... She is only eleven years old.''

"Nonsense, you fool. She is old enough to marry
under these savages' tribal customs.''

"But...could we not spare her? The poor child is
so young...so innocent.''

"Hmmm.'' Linh considered, nodding thought-
fully. "You're quite right, Captain. About the child,
that is.''

"You will spare her, then?''

Phuong was not certain he could believe his ears.

Linh permitted himself a smirk.

"Yes, the little wench shall be spared...for an hour or two, perhaps. As you say, Captain, she is so innocent, so young. It would be worth dirtying myself with the little savage for some respite from the rigors of duty." Linh leered at the man in the doorway. "Don't you agree, Captain?"

"Please, Major—"

"Please, what?" Linh snapped. "I will not share the child with you, if that is your request, though perhaps it might amuse and excite me to have you watch."

"Major, I must protest—"

Linh stood, an impressive figure behind the desk, despite his diminutive build.

It's those eyes, thought Phuong again. I should do something to stop him. *I should do something!*

"I would say you have protested quite enough already, Captain," hissed the sibilant voice, as reptilian as those eyes. "Perhaps if you do not appreciate the work that is carried on here, you would find a firing squad more to your liking. Have I made myself quite clear?"

Phuong nodded, his throat parched dry, but suddenly he did not feel afraid and he was not sure why.

"I quite understand, Major."

Linh resumed his seat.

"How very good for you. Now see to strengthening the guard in the event of attack, kill the woman and bring the child to me. Quickly now, do as I command."

"Yes, sir."

Phuong continued out of the hut into the sweltering humidity of the predawn darkness.

He started across the small compound to awaken the off-duty sentries.

The nagging ache in his soul, urging him to do something, anything, to atone for the horror he had perpetrated, to purge the savage he had become, would not go away.

But what?

He crossed the sleeping compound, noting the sentries in the tower taking a smoke and those at the front gate loitering, lounging.

He felt the most unusual tremor up and down his spine, something like a premonition, telling him what he had known since the massacre of Sioung's villagers several days ago.

This hellhole camp—Major Linh and all those who served under him, thought Phuong—were long overdue for retribution for the evil they had done, especially Captain Phuong himself.

The NVA officer almost wished that his suggestion regarding the Executioner and his death squad planning to stage an attack to rescue the Mont hostages was correct.

The woman and child will die, Phuong thought. I am too weak to save them. I search my soul and I sicken myself at what I have become, but I am not strong enough to stop it.

He collapsed suddenly to his knees, alone in the center of the compound.

He vomited.

When he had finished, Phuong stood and proceeded slowly toward the largest of the thatched huts, where his men slept.

He would awaken them, in case he was right about an attack, then he would proceed to the hut where the Montagnard chief's wife and daughter were shackled, and he would obey Major Linh's orders.

Phuong entered the barracks hut to wake his men, thinking, The woman and child are as good as dead. The Executioner and his men are already too late....

Four

Bolan reached up, supporting himself with one arm against the outside of the NVA outpost's walled perimeter. He used his combat knife to slice through another length of the tightly wound twine used to bind the sharpened bamboo poles together.

He lowered the freed pole to the ground, beside the few others already worked free.

Deadeye Washington stood beside Bolan, the big black man tracking his M-16 back and forth in a steady arc around them, ready to give Bolan covering fire, if necessary. Washington blinked away the perspiration trickling into his eyes.

Bolan swung his own rifle around into firing position. He nosed the M-16's snout through the narrow break in the wall.

He judged that the barricade was intended more to prevent easy escape by prisoners being held and interrogated here than as any serious defense perimeter.

Major Linh ran a low-profile operation, Bolan knew. Linh would depend on the VC or NVA for real protection if things got hairy.

Bolan peered inside the compound.

Several hundred feet in front of him stood a hut from which could be heard the strains of recorded music, a traditional Viet folksong.

A jeeplike NVA vehicle sat in front of the hut.

Another shack some sixty feet to Bolan's left along the inside of the wall showed no more signs of life than the nearest hut.

An elongated barracks against the east wall was separated by the guard tower and gate, from a mess hall building. Beside the mess stood a metal prefab structure that housed the motor pool and munitions dump.

At this moment, Bolan figured, Gunsmoke Harrington and Boom-Boom Hoffower should be penetrating from the southwest corner of the walled perimeter behind those buildings in exactly the same manner as Bolan and Washington did from the north wall.

Bolan could not see the other men's point of entry, because his line of vision was blocked by the motor pool and munitions buildings, but there had been no commotion, no sound at all, from that direction.

Bolan and Washington had separated from Gunsmoke and Boom-Boom several minutes earlier, the plan being for both teams to hold tight until the five-man sentry patrol had passed the west wall a second time after Bolan's men were in position. This would allow Bolan and his men the five minutes it would take while the NVA regulars marched the perimeter of the jungle compound.

Bolan stepped back. He motioned Deadeye through the opening in the wall.

"All clear."

Washington squeezed his hefty bulk through the aperture.

"Looks like that sentry patrol wants to be real co-operative," Deadeye muttered as he passed close by Bolan.

"So far," Bolan growled.

The black man hunched low inside the wall, the M-16 back in firing position, ready to give Bolan cover fire from the inside.

Bolan stepped in after Washington. He dragged the bamboo poles of the wall in after him and quietly, rapidly, propped them into approximately their former positions.

There was no time to rewind the strips of tough twine securing the poles in the wall, but they would do unless anyone looked too closely.

Bolan did not think that would happen in the next few minutes.

He brought his M-16 around from its strap, gripping the assault rifle with both fists, his right index finger curled around the trigger.

He motioned to Washington with the weapon, indicating the nearest hut from which the music emanated.

Washington nodded.

The two soldiers crept quietly toward the hut and when they reached its side, Bolan saw lamplight from inside.

Washington saw it, too.

"Sioung's wife and kid won't be in here," he whispered to Bolan with a nod toward the shack. "Looks like the big boy's crib." Deadeye glanced toward the hut in the moon-washed area between the lighted hut and the barracks structure. "I say we find 'em next door, Sarge. Linh wouldn't keep the hostages with his troops, and that leaves out the mess hall, too."

"You're right," Bolan agreed, "but let's take out the major anyway, if he's home. Cover me."

"Goes without saying," Washington said, chuckling.

The black human mountain positioned himself next to the entranceway of the lighted hut, out of the line of vision of sentries stationed at the front gate or the watchtower across the compound.

The heavy night air filtered vague voices conversing idly from that direction.

The sentries on the ground had lit up smokes like the guards in the tower.

Bolan shoulder-strapped his M-16, then unsheathed his combat knife.

He burst into the hut, finding himself in an office.

Empty.

He cat-footed across to the archway from beyond which emanated the recorded music. He peered in.

Linh's private living quarters.

Also empty.

Damn.

He considered a quick search of the major's files, ut Bolan's command of Vietnamese included the spoken language, not the written.

There was a file cabinet against one wall of the hut, but there was no time to look anyway, not with Sioung's wife and daughter held hostage in this compound. With Major Linh out and the hour this close to dawn, the deadline when Sioung's family members were to die, Bolan had to move fast.

He knew enough from scanning Linh's dossier back at the base that the NVA cannibal would not be above rushing the deadline if it suited him.

The Executioner felt an ache of apprehension grab his gut. He hoped like hell that he and his men were not too late.

He sheathed his knife and hurried outside to rejoin Washington.

Deadeye glanced at him inquiringly.

Bolan shook his head, then indicated the next thatched hut down the line.

As they hustled in that direction, Deadeye whispered, ''I was watching close for Smoke and Boom-Boom while you were inside. No sign of 'em. And Linh's got a four-man guard posted around the munitions dump.''

Bolan started to reply that no sign of Harrington and Hoffower meant the two were probably doing their job. Bolan froze before speaking. He motioned Deadeye to do the same.

Lights flared inside the barracks across the compound, beyond the hut toward which Bolan and Washington were heading.

The Americans faded back closer to the base of the perimeter wall.

Voices drifted to them from inside the barracks, most of the voices grousing. Then someone spoke in a sharper, more authoritative tone, silencing the others. An officer issuing orders in Vietnamese, Bolan thought. Then came a more orderly sound from the barracks: sleepy-eyed Vietcong grumbling to life under the riding of their noncoms.

"The heat's on now," Deadeye growled. "Two minutes and this compound will be crawling with VC."

"So let's do it," Bolan grunted.

The Executioner angled from the shadows of the wall toward the hut several hundred feet away.

Washington kept pace, not making a sound despite his considerable size.

Bolan froze again when they had about one hundred feet to go, close enough for both Americans to discern a low, moaning, a strange lament above the tropical night sounds.

"Someone's crying." Washington listened harder. "A woman. Bingo."

"And checkmate," growled Bolan.

Washington followed the Executioner's line of vision. He realized that Bolan had not halted their progress because of the crying.

"Sheeit," Washington muttered with feeling.

An NVA officer—Deadeye spotted the North Viet's rank as captain when the man passed beneath a light above the door of the barracks—left the hut.

The officer started walking toward the shack near which Bolan and Washington crouched. The NVA officer did not see the two Americans, who darted the rest of the way to cover behind the hooch.

Bolan and Washington positioned themselves in such a way that they could both peer secretively around the hut toward the approaching NVA captain.

The officer should have reached them in the short span of time it took the Americans to seek cover, but they spotted the Viet standing midway between the hut and the barracks structure he had just come from, having roused the regulars and VC attachment.

The officer stood, wasting matches trying to light a cigarette, but his hands shook so badly, he kept dropping the matches at his feet while he glanced around to see if anyone was observing him.

"Someone's got a job he doesn't want to do," Bolan guessed aloud in a whisper to his buddy.

"Take him?" asked Deadeye. "He's in our sights, Sarge, and we know where the women are."

"We wait on Boom-Boom and Gunsmoke," Bolan decided.

"There'll be plenty of that," Washington grumbled grimly.

The Viet officer seemed to make up his mind about something. He threw away the unlit cigarette and strutted determinedly toward the entranceway of the hut from behind which Bolan and Deadeye watched his advance.

As he approached the building, they saw the officer reaching for something on his hip.

TI BAHN, WIFE OF SIOUNG, renewed her efforts to free herself of the handcuffs clasping her wrists together behind her back. Her arms were secured in place around a thick bamboo pole that reached from the dirt floor to the domed roof of the thatched hut that was her prison.

Ti Bahn's daughter, Tran Le, was similarly bound to an identical pole several feet away. The child slept in an uncomfortable sitting position, a fitful sleep tormented by the frightened murmurings of nightmares.

The child had not awakened to the whispered pleas from her mother.

Ti Bahn did not want the Viet savages soldiering here to be drawn to this hut.

It had happened once before.

Three North Vietnam army regulars, drunk, had stumbled into the hut where the hostages were kept unguarded, so confident was Major Linh of his facilities.

The intoxicated soldiers had taunted the women and begun to fondle the young girl. Ti Bahn had feared the worst and did the only thing she could think of in her helpless state. She emitted a blood-curdling scream, which brought the officer, Captain Phuong, who reprimanded the soldiers and ordered them away.

But it could happen again, Ti Bahn knew, and the man, Phuong, might not be around.

Or he might be among them, next time.

Ti Bahn trusted none of these pigs.

She twisted and pulled at her shackles as she had throughout her captivity, her wrists slick with blood.

And still they would not slide through the cuffs.

Ti Bahn had kept count of the days since the animal, Linh, gloated to her that first day about why she and her daughter were being held captive, and what would happen to Ti Bahn and Tran Le if Sioung did not surrender.

Ti Bahn did not fear for herself. She had led a full life, accompanying her husband in the fight for their people's freedom—for the Montagnards' very existence.

Ti Bahn remembered better times when the savage beauty of her beloved mountain highlands had been at peace, when life had been good. She knew she would never see such times again, but it was for her daughter that Ti Bahn brutalized herself in what she knew to be vain attempts to free herself, to escape.

The hope of peace belonged to the future, to the young, or so she thought.

Ti Bahn sobbed in anguish and frustration. She stopped chafing her wrists.

Her daughter awoke with a frightened start when the figure of Captain Phuong appeared without warning at the entrance of the hut.

The mother's eyes dropped to the pistol the officer held in his right fist, then she looked to his face, which she could not see in the shadows.

Ti Bahn did not need to see her executioner's face to know that the end of everything for her and Tran Le was but heartbeats away.

"BETTER NOT WAIT TOO DOGGONE LONG, Sarge," Washington whispered tautly.

"I've got a feeling about this guy," Bolan said.

He inched around the hut, closer to the entrance, a split microsecond after the officer disappeared inside.

Bolan motioned Deadeye to remain where he was.

Washington nodded, concern plainly etched across his features, watching Bolan and continuing to eye the still-deserted compound.

The barracks across the way rattled with the men rising, getting dressed, preparing to fall into formation for further instructions in front of the building.

Deadeye figured another minute or less and everybody's shit would be in the fan.

Bolan positioned himself close enough to the entrance to see only part, but enough, of the tense scene unfolding inside the hut. He hugged the deepest shadows where the thatched roof of the hut overhung the walls slightly. Here he could maintain cover of night and be within firing distance of the man inside if he was wrong about the feeling in his gut.

He could barely make out the terse exchange of hushed Vietnamese from inside the shack's open entrance.

The soft crying sounds of the young girl continued unabated.

The mother snapped at the officer, "Captain Phuong...the time has come to kill us?"

A long pause.

"I...cannot kill you," Phuong said as he moved deeper into the hut.

Bolan heard the barely audible twin clicks of shackles being undone.

The daughter's frightened sobbing ceased.

The woman gasped.

"This...is a trap! Your men will slaughter my daughter and me when we step outside."

"Not a trap," Phuong replied, a rising note of desperation in his low voice. "I will go with you. I shall defect, anything. Quickly, we must hurry. I—I've had enough—"

Bolan squatted farther back into the shadows an instant before the officer emerged warily from the hut, one fist grasping a pistol, the other reaching back to hold the hand of the squat, coarse-featured woman in soiled mountain garb.

Sioung's wife allowed herself to be led from the hut by this unusual NVA officer. She in turn led a scared-looking youngster, a kid who might have been lovely under the grime and fearful expression, thought Bolan, though it was impossible to tell in the gloom.

The three of them—Phuong and the two women—glanced hesitantly, furtively, left and right, not seeing Bolan or Washington.

"Follow me," Phuong whispered to Ti Bahn. "Hurry. I know a way. If we are caught—"

A new voice from inside the hut—a male voice just behind Phuong and the women—hissed sibilantly with barely controlled rage.

"You have been caught, Captain Phuong. Drop your weapon, please, or I shall be forced to execute you on the spot."

The three leaving the hut halted as if stopped by invisible wires, the woman pivoting frantically, eyes flaring with new fright.

Captain Phuong looked around more slowly, as if half expecting what was happening, but not sure of how to respond.

"Major...this is not right. I beg you to reconsider—"

"Silence, fool," snapped the unseen voice from inside the hut. "Right has nothing to do with it. Drop your weapon. I would prefer to see you sweat and squirm under a full military court-martial. Or would you prefer to die right now with these savages?"

In the shadows, Bolan's muscles tensed as the big man prepared to execute a forward dive that would land him before the entranceway of the hut, between Captain Phuong and the women and the cannibal inside who had got the drop on them.

Washington held his position on the opposite side of the entrance, remaining unseen by any of the other principals in this tense tableau.

The big black soldier crouched like a panther ready to spring, his M-16 trained on Phuong just in case.

The world seemed to explode in the instant before Bolan could launch his body at the still-unseen Major Linh.

The motor pool and munitions dump erupted into a sense-shredding, thunderclapping fireball that burst outward in a reddish orange flash and roiling black smoke.

The explosion hammered the night apart, shattering windows, shaking the ground, spraying the darkness with fiery, whizzing shrapnel. Human debris, chunks of building material and hurtling automotive parts sliced the air like flying guillotines, the force of the blast slamming Bolan and everyone else off their feet like rag dolls.

Five

Bolan recovered from the blast before anyone else, the powerful concussive effect of the eruption having hurled him against the hut, then forward to the ground.

The loud rumble of the explosion diminished into the banging tattoo of secondary detonations from the munitions.

The chatter of automatic rifles peppered the night from the other side of the flames and explosions.

Harrington and Hoffower sewing up the loose ends, was Bolan's first lucid thought after the milliseconds it took for his senses to right themselves.

The Montagnard women regained their bearings after the blast had deposited them near Deadeye Washington, who was trying to gather his wits together. Captain Phuong was shaking his head to clear it while waving frantically to Sioung's wife and daughter.

"Run for your lives!" the captain urged the women, his revolver tracking toward the hut. "I will—"

"You will *die*!" a voice snarled with fury from inside the hut.

Bolan resumed his pounce toward the entrance.

Phuong's eyes widened with fear as he realized he had not reacted fast enough.

A single pistol shot stung the night from inside the hut, the report almost drowned out by the bursts of chain-reaction explosions thundering from across the compound.

Captain Phuong made a resigned grunt when a lead projectile cored open his forehead, the impact pitching him backward into a spread-armed deadfall.

Bolan hit the ground, landing on his shoulder in front of the entrance to the hut at the same moment he heard Phuong's body pitch to the earth several feet behind him.

The warrior triggered a hammering burst of rifle-fire into the hut, pumping 7.62 mm bullets, raking everything in sight under a blistering volley.

At that moment Washington darted from his cover to intercept the two Mont females, who were dashing away with no sense of direction, driven by pure panic.

The barracks building already spewed out a running stream of semidressed VC and NVA regulars toting assault rifles.

The soldiers were shouting frantically to one another, their full attention focused on the flaming ruins that moments ago had been the motor-pool garage and munitions depot.

The fire from the blasted rubble and secondary explosions spread to ignite the mess hall. Tongues of flame licked the night sky.

Billowing black smoke blocked out the moonlight, throwing the compound into a deeper gloom, except for the raging fire flicker and the light over the entrance to the barracks and from inside.

The Mont women reacted to the sight of Washington's American uniform with more confusion than relief, but they stopped.

Deadeye tracked his M-16 toward the commotion around the barracks as the NVA noncoms restored some order over there, and men began cautiously edging toward the heat of the flames.

There was still plenty of chaos and yelling back and forth in excited Vietnamese, but no one was reacting to the shooting around the hut where the women had been kept prisoners.

And from the other side of the compound, the sounds and confusion of Boom-Boom Hoffower's demolition work swallowed the gunfire near the hut.

Washington held his fire on the men pouring out of the barracks, not wanting to give away his position.

He motioned to Ti Bahn and Tran Le to seek cover behind him, behind the hut, and after they hurriedly obeyed his mute instructions, he motioned them to the ground.

Wide-eyed, the women obeyed, their faces like masks of terror.

Deadeye tracked his attention and his M-16 back toward the men across the compound.

At that instant, Washington heard more hammering M-16 fire cutting loose from the southwest corner of the outpost. Must be Hoffower and

Harrington, Deadeye guessed. They were firing on the unsuspecting regulars inching closer to the flames, mowing down VC and NVA soldiers who shuddered wildly, toppling under the salvo of riflefire.

Washington triggered a burst at the windows of the barracks, blasting out the lights inside and the one over the entranceway, and in the process putting out the lights of several running men still inside the building.

The compound grew darker without the barracks lights, adding to the panic of those lucky enough to have survived the ambush thus far.

Soldiers scampered everywhere, bumping into one another, stumbling over bodies of the dead and the moaning wounded. The grisly scene was barely illuminated by the unworldly golden red shimmering from the flames and the strobelike flashes as some of the men held their ground, returning fire at targets they could not see.

Washington dodged to a new position and started unloading into the frenzied panic of those darting for cover and on those brave enough to stand their ground and die. And still more assault rifles yammered from across the killzone as Harrington and Hoffower cut down several others.

Two loud thumps could be heard amid the sounds of battle.

That'll be the two machinegunners falling from the watchtower before they could fire a shot, thought Washington, Bloodbrother working out with his bow and arrow.

Deadeye slammed another clip into his M-16, turning to make sure the women were okay. Then he rushed over to where Bolan had disappeared into the hut moments earlier.

INSIDE, BOLAN FOUND THE HOOCH empty, the interior devastated by the burst he had fired before entering.

No sign of Major Linh.

In the earthen floor, Bolan spotted a trapdoor.

It had been concealed by a mat, which had been flung aside when the trapdoor had been used seconds earlier.

Bolan charged over to stand above but several feet away from the wooden cover. He stooped, reached out with his rifle and slid the snout through the circular metal handle attached to the wood of the square lid, keeping an eye on the entrance of the hut, though he trusted Deadeye to keep them secure for a few moments.

The reports of Deadeye's M-16 outside the hut told Bolan his teammate was on the case.

Bolan caught the metal ring of the trapdoor just right with the barrel of his rifle on the first try. He pried the door upward a half inch or so.

Three sharp pistol shots punched up from the hole beneath, impacting hard enough to slam the door open and tug the rifle in Bolan's grip.

Bolan heard the rapid footsteps of someone scurrying away down there.

Washington filled the front entrance of the hut, concern taut across his broad, glistening face, a tendril of smoke curling lazily from the barrel of his M-16.

"You need help?" he asked Bolan, drawn by the shots, his eyes on the escape hatch.

"That's how Linh got the drop on his captain," growled Bolan. "This countryside is swarming with networks of these caves."

Bolan could see Sioung's terrified wife and daughter huddled behind Washington.

"Where d'you figure it leads, Sarge?"

"Any number of places. His hut down the way, maybe. Another branch could take him out of here."

The gunfire out in the compound had died down.

The VC and NVA regulars crouched behind their barracks building, watching their ammo dump and mess hall flame away; they could also see the bodies of their dead and wounded scattered everywhere.

An NVA noncom started snarling orders, but none of his men was brave enough to be the first to obey.

"Sounds like Smoke and Boom-Boom have stopped firing, Sarge. They're pulling out." Washington nodded toward the yawning hole in the floor. "How bad you want this Linh dude? I can go after him while you escort the ladies out."

Bolan shook his head. He started out of the hut.

"Thought of that. Linh could sit at the other end of that tunnel and pick off whoever comes after him with no trouble. No, we'll save Linh for another time. Let's pull out."

Washington broke out with the famous Deadeye grin.

"I hear you, Sarge, all the way."

He grabbed the hand of the Montagnard girl with his left hand while he fanned their backtrack with his M-16. He hurriedly led the way from the hut, back toward the loosened poles where he and Bolan had gained entry.

The Mont girl stumbled along after Deadeye.

Her mother followed.

They moved fast, goosed into more speed than stealth by the sight of a dozen or more NVA regulars and VC finally yielding to their noncom's shouted commands.

The soldiers were warily venturing out from their cover behind the barracks, advancing toward both the dying fires and the hut where the hostages had been held.

The presence of the intruders and escapees had not yet been discovered, but those troops would find Captain Phuong's sprawled body within seconds.

Bolan moved along toward the wall, picking his targets, holding his fire. They reached the loosened poles.

Washington tossed the poles aside, stepping through. He motioned to the women to follow him out.

Ti Bahn and Tran Le rushed through to join him.

Bolan followed, pausing only long enough to unhitch a grenade from his webbing. He yanked the pin and straight-armed the explosive.

It scored a direct hit, landing beneath the jeep parked in front of the major's hut. The vehicle shuddered under the explosion, tipping onto its side, smoking, blown tires spinning unevenly.

"Move, move," Bolan urged the others.

It looked as if they would make it.

Washington gained the midway point up the sloping embankment through the expanse of elephant grass to where the tree line began on higher ground.

The Mont women scampered up the embankment, their breathing ragged from this heady exertion after so many days of captivity.

Washington covered the left flank, Bolan covered the right, as the small group hurried through the humid darkness.

The daughter tripped and fell to her knees with a small, sharp cry of dismay.

Bolan passed by and scooped the girl up onto her feet without slowing his own rapid stride.

An exchange of gunfire stuttered from south of the fortress, from the outside.

"Sounds like the sentry patrol's meeting up with Chopper and the boys," Deadeye growled, panting.

The women reached the tree line and scampered into the wall of foliage.

The jungle received them into its claustrophobic, muggy embrace.

Bolan discerned a lone sentry approaching them from the northwest corner of the perimeter, opposite from the firefight between Bolan's men and the rest of the guard detail on the other side of the compound.

This sentry charged in at a run, then eyeballed Bolan and Washington starting into the bush with the women. The soldier stopped short in surprise and tracked his rifle up toward Bolan.

Bolan's M-16 pounded out a 3-shot burst, greasing the sentry, then the Executioner darted into the jungle after Deadeye and the females.

Moving through the dark, they angled back south along the route they had come, parallel to the tree line on the ridge. Several hundred yards to the southeast the firefight sounded as if it might be dissipating, the gunfiring from the front of the outpost tapering off to nothing.

Bolan raised a hand and motioned for his little group to halt, after they had traveled some two hundred yards through the bush.

Gunsmoke and Boom-Boom materialized from Bolan's right, on schedule.

"Glad y'all could make it," Harrington said, grinning. The habitual sneer on his narrow face did not disguise the genuine relief in his Texas twang. He gallantly tipped the brim of his cowboy hat to the women. "Ladies," he said, nodding politely.

Bolan and Harrington shifted to point.

Hoffower fell in, trotting along with Washington, the women book-ended in the middle for maximum protection as the six of them continued to hustle along.

Bolan heard shouts in Vietnamese and several bursts of autofire as men unloaded at shadows inside the compound.

The billowing tar-black smoke parted long enough for the moon to illuminate the corpses of four sentries, who had fallen where they'd been forced to fight. The front gate of the compound was left locked by the panicky lookouts inside, the slain guards a testament to the combined firepower of the rest of Bolan's dirty death squad.

Bolan's group linked up with the other members of the Executioner's team beneath the curving rim of terrain that formed the jungle tree line, where Schwarz, Andromede, Loudelk, Fontenelli, Blancanales and Zitka had poured in fire on the little fort.

The men regrouped in the gloom, avoiding a close-in cluster.

"Bloodbrother, recon to the north," whispered Bolan.

"North it is."

Sniper Team Able's scout jogged off ahead, disappearing from sight.

The jungle forest erupted to the slamming of the heavy-caliber machine gun from back in the guard tower.

The machine gunner had nothing to shoot at, but the earthy thudding of nearby ricochets off the other side of the ridge made everyone in Bolan's group hunch lower.

The facial expressions of Ti Bahn and Tran Le said they understood they were not safe yet. It was far from over.

"Chopper, Flower Child, take the point."

Bolan motioned for the team and the women to continue along in the direction taken by Bloodbrother Loudelk, the group moving by twos deeper into the bush toward the game trail, back the way they had come.

Six

Major Linh retraced his course through the tunnel, moving as quickly as the confined space would allow. He scurried, hunch-shouldered, gripping his revolver.

The earthy smell and his own sweat made the short tunnel trip back to his hut most unpleasant.

Linh usually did not mind the tight restrictions of the tunnel, but at the moment he felt trapped and he knew it was because of a human devil named Bolan.

The major was returning from having crouched, waiting to kill, beyond the mouth at the other end of the tunnel, one hundred yards beyond the wall of this outpost.

Linh had hoped that the man, who could only be Bolan, would give chase after unleashing the burst of gunfire into the hut that had missed Linh by fractions of inches. And Linh knew he had escaped death only because he had seen the Montagnard women react after he executed Captain Phuong.

Linh had flung himself to the floor of the hut and scrambled back down into the tunnel, yanking the trapdoor shut after him beneath the deafening thunderstorm from the Executioner's fire.

Linh realized that he was one of the very few lucky ones even to have been fired on and missed by the American fighter who had attained such a reputation in this war.

Bolan had been smart enough not to give chase into the tunnel after Linh, depriving the major of any chance at picking off anyone appearing through the opposite opening of the tunnel. But Linh had opted, nonetheless, to remain at the far end of the tunnel until the sounds of battle had ceased in and around the compound.

He hoisted himself out of the tunnel and into the private quarters of his hut. He quickly brushed away as much grime from his uniform as he could, then dashed outside, relieved that none of his subordinates had seen him emerge from the trapdoor. His actions could have been misconstrued as cowardice, he realized: the commanding officer seeking refuge until the shooting stopped.

He emerged from his hut to find smoldering ruin, tendrils of smoke eddying skyward from rubble where the motor pool and munitions dump had stood.

The mess hall blazed out of control despite efforts of men scrambling everywhere, trying to douse the flames with buckets of water.

The major's jeep was a devastated, overturned wreck.

He saw dead bodies everywhere.

He glanced around several seconds before discerning a narrow, gaping space in the bamboo wall.

Linh nodded to himself, cursing heatedly under his breath.

Sergeant Thi, Linh's ranking noncommissioned officer, hurried over to intercept the major, from the direction of the activity around the fire destroying the mess hall.

"Major! We feared you were lost! Captain Phuong has been killed."

Linh indicated the hole in the wall.

"I spotted them escaping and gave chase. They lost me, but not for long. Phuong, dead? Poor devil."

"It was not the Montagnards, sir. These men who attacked us...fought like...superhumans! They've destroyed all our vehicles!"

"It was Mack Bolan, Sergeant."

"Bolan? The one they call—"

"The same. They cannot have got far. They will have one of their infernal helicopters coming for them."

"There are not many spots near here with clearing sufficient for one of their Hueys to land," Thi said.

"Except for the commune two kilometers north of here," Linh snapped decisively. "The paddies! That will be their helicopter's landing zone, Sergeant. Come with me. Call your best men. We shall give chase! On foot."

"My best men...are dead, my major."

"The best you have then, imbecile! Hurry, damn your eyes. We have a hope yet of catching up with them before their copter lands. My final day of command of this wretched base will not end in failure!''

Linh's heart pounded against his rib cage as if trying to escape.

Sergeant Thi joined his commander in hurriedly gathering the disheveled survivors of Thi's group.

After Bolan.

The Executioner.

And anyone else they could kill.

THE FIRST DIRTY GRAY SMUDGE of false dawn caressed lush-green, cloud-haloed mountains to the east.

Sniper Team Able slogged their way forward through the jungle undergrowth, bulldozing a course due north toward the village of An Chanh.

The settlement was less than one-half of a klick ahead, where the communal rice fields and livestock grazing area provided the only suitable LZ close enough to Major Linh's outpost.

The choppers were on call not far to the east, waiting for a quick, low-level contour buzz in and out to pick up Bolan and his crew, the same way the Executioner's team had got in. Getting out, though, would be a whole other ball game, as usual.

The motor pool back at Linh's camp had been leveled for a good reason; there would not be much around for anyone to give chase in even if Linh did figure out where the LZ would be.

Bolan knew cannibal Linh by reputation. He did not underestimate the snake.

Which is why Bolan urged his group to hump so fast through the jungle: the darkness of night around them was taking on the hint of bright green that would soon come full with the daylight.

Bolan's heart pounded against his rib cage as he and his men and the two Mont females pushed on, drawing nearer and nearer to An Chanh and the predesignated LZ.

These were the most vital moments of any mission, the toughest on even the most experienced hellgrounders, because the final numbers of a mission meant the last chance for something to go wrong.

Everyone knew of short-timers who would not leave their bunks for the last week of their tours of duty, and of the poor bastards with one or two days left who got zapped or lost legs or more to a Charlie booby trap.

Bolan would not feel right until he got his men and these civilians into that chopper and off the ground.

Bloodbrother's muted voice crackled over the radio that Gadgets toted on his back.

"Striker, this is Able Three. Do you read me?"

Bolan grasped the transceiver extended by Schwarz. He responded to the scout as he and the group continued forward without slowing their pace.

"Go ahead, Able Three, over."

"I'm at the LZ," Loudelk reported. "All clear this end, over."

"Roger, Able Three. Coming in, over." Bolan handed the handset back to Schwarz. "All right, Gadgets, call in our ticket out of here."

The rescue choppers were hovering close enough to buzz in during the time it would take Bolan's group to reach the landing zone outside the village.

"Hallelujah," Gadgets said with a sigh. Then he spoke into his radio transceiver. "Samaritan One, Samaritan One, this is Striker. Striker, over."

Several things happened at once.

Bolan's team and the women pounded through the bush, struggling forward with a muted intensity through a jungle growing lighter by the second with the encroaching dawn.

Then Bolan sensed more than heard the rustle of near-distant hot pursuit, running men trying to stay quiet, the clank of equipment....

"Take cover," Bolan called to the others. "Trouble closing in from the rear."

At that instant, automatic riflefire opened up on them from the semigloom well behind them.

The air and overhead leaves of banana trees zinged to the whistle of incoming projectiles randomly spraying the jungle.

From close behind, Bolan heard the nasty, unmistakable *thwap* of a heavy bullet slapping into human flesh.

And the gasping grunt of pain as someone in his team stumbled to the ground.

"WE SHOULD HAVE HEARD from them by now, is it not so, Colonel Winters?" Sioung inquired.

The mountain fighter's softly spoken query, so typical of the stoicism of his people, was uttered with a steely concern that "Howlin'" Harlan Winters similarly felt.

Winters and Sioung were waiting in the colonel's "office" at Special Forces Camp A-105—Code Name: Three-Niner-Bayou—in the central highlands of Vietnam. The camp was situated at almost the halfway point between the US and ARVN bases in and around Pleiku and the Cambodian border.

Three-Niner-Bayou boasted a full complement of Monts and Special Forces personnel and a Medevac unit.

And almost nightly harassment from VC mortar fire.

Winters sat behind his desk.

Sioung paced like a caged tiger, unable to remain seated.

A radio receiver on Winters's desk crackled with static.

For some inexplicable reason, this had been a quiet night in the jungle for the personnel of Camp A-105.

No Charlie mortar attack.

But Harlan Winters's gut was an uncomfortable ball of worry.

He gave the guerrilla leader his best look of confidence.

"Uh, it's always a mistake to hold these operations too close to schedule, Sioung."

Sioung paused in his pacing to stare steadily at the man behind the desk.

"You and I both know Mack Bolan, Colonel. If anything, the Executioner would have contacted your choppers ahead of schedule."

Winters broke eye contact with Sioung. He had no reply because he knew Sioung was right.

Colonel Harlan Winters was Mack Bolan's commanding officer, and he felt like this any time "his boys" went into the bush on a mission as dangerous as the one Sniper Team Able was on that morning. He always waited up for Bolan and his men to return, like a father worried about his sons staying out late.

He glanced at the warm, muggy red haze of dawn.

Too late, yeah.

Then, a voice crackled from the radio.

Winters recognized the voice of Gadgets Schwarz, Bolan's radio man, sounding harried, worried, summoning the choppers meant to ferry Sniper Team Able out of their hot spot.

"Samaritan One, come in and get us," came Schwarz's plea to the chopper pilot. "And make it fast, dude. One of our men is hit, over."

"Striker, this is Samaritan One," answered the chopper pilot's voice with sounds of static. "Coming in, over."

Nothing else.

Winters glanced again at Sioung.

The Mont tribal chief did not turn from peering out of the window at the gathering light of a new day. Sioung said nothing, and yeah, Winters knew just how the guy felt about this mission to rescue his wife and child, because the CO of the Executioner's death squad felt the same way.

Colonel Harlan Winters tried hard not to reflect too much the last words of Schwarz's transmission.

One of our men is hit!

Which man of Sniper Team Able had been hit?

And how badly?

Winters stifled a curse of frustration.

He reached for his pipe and packet of tobacco for something to do.

Sioung was right.

There was no sense in talking. Not now. For the next nerve-racking thirty minutes or so there was nothing to do, period, except wait.

And pray.

CHOPPER FONTENELLI GROANED IN PAIN.

One moment the American grunt was keeping pace with the full-steam pullout through jungle foliage that had begun to thin as Bolan's team drew nearer to the paddies of the village of An Chanh.

Then the riflefire had opened up on them from behind.

Fontenelli felt the bullet's impact and everything went black for him except for the sensation of falling, arms outflung. The M-16 flew from his fingers as he pitched face-forward into tangled vines and slime on the jungle floor, his soul plummeting into nothingness....

ANOTHER SHORT, TENTATIVE RATTLE of autofire stung at Bolan's group from back there, then another.

Everyone, including the women, slouched low, continuing, moving.

Bolan and Schwarz were the closest to Fontenelli when he took the hit and went down. Bolan reached him first.

Zitka and Blancanales rushed to either side of the two men, tracking their weapons around, peppering the backtrack with a blistering volley of return fire, quieting things down for a few seconds at least.

Bolan knelt beside Angelo. The Executioner grabbed his buddy by the shoulder and rolled Fontenelli over.

More gunfire opened up from the semidark backtrail, and withering fusillades of projectiles whistled in everywhere, too close. Yammering weapons unleashed a hail of bullets that made dull *plop* sounds when they whizzed off ground and flora.

"Ugh!" snarled Zitka. "I'm hit! Rotten bastards!"

Zitter sprawled backward, landing several feet away.

Bolan glanced over his shoulder.

He saw Zitter working his way back to his feet.

Zitka rested the butt of his M-16 against his right hip and triggered a blast that muted the stream of obscenities he fired off with the savage gunburst. He had taken the grazing wound high in his left arm. A lucky nick.

"Move out with the others," Bolan told Zitter. "I've got Chopper."

Zitka fell ahead to keep up with the other men of the team, but he hurried, moving backward, not taking his trigger finger off his rifle, blazing angry death along the backtrack.

Gadgets reached Bolan and the wounded Chopper Fontenelli on the run.

"Is he alive?"

"Barely."

Facing Fontenelli, Bolan shifted his M-16 to his left hand and slid his right arm under the wounded man's right arm to pull him up.

Gadgets tossed away the extra equipment that only slowed him down.

He assisted Bolan and together they hoisted Fontenelli across Bolan's back.

Bolan reached around behind and grasped Chopper, supporting the unconscious team member.

Angelo looked like hell. Crimson rivulets trickled from both corners of his mouth. The wound was in his right side and it appeared serious, but Bolan discerned the faint, ragged beating of a pulse.

Schwarz pulled back.

Bolan commenced humping on across the final distance of bush before the clearing of the rice fields began.

The LZ could not be hotter than it was right now.

Gadgets and Pol Blancanales laid down a fiery carpet of riflefire along their backtrack. And again the fire from Linh's position subsided into shouting in Vietnamese while men were frantically diving for cover and others died on their feet beyond the veil of creeping morning mist.

Bolan hustled to catch up with the others, traveling as fast as he could with the added deadweight of Angelo Fontenelli.

Blancanales and Schwarz scurried in low trots once Bolan and the wounded man had enough of a start.

The panicky Viet shouting from way behind dissolved into more firing that began advancing.

Bolan with Fontenelli reached the others of his team at the evenly trimmed line of the clearing.

Sioung's wife and daughter hid low in the jungle growth while Bolan's squad, who had all reached the clearing, opened up covering fire over the heads of Bolan and his load, and Pol and Gadgets.

Above the cacophony of the dawn fight, Bolan faintly heard the clattering motors of approaching freedom birds.

He hoped like hell those gunships would make it in time for Fontenelli.

In time for all of them.

Seven _____

Major Linh also heard the clattering rotors of approaching helicopters.

He cursed into the dank, unpleasant jungle floor upon which he had flung himself for cover when the men of the Executioner's team opened up with return fire.

The man next to Major Linh caught a bullet and collapsed into a back-ended flop without uttering a sound.

The major pressed himself tighter against the ground and tried to conquer the paralysis of fear threatening to overcome him. He gripped only his pistol, which he knew would be useless at this range.

NVA regulars and VC cried out and died all around him, the fallen wounded shrieking in hysteria, shock and pain.

Everyone else dodged for cover, shouting under the brutal incoming hail of automatic riflefire from the Americans beyond the shifting veil of mist that played tricks on the eye.

"Return the fire, you cowards!"

Linh heard himself screaming at his men, hoping they could not hear in his voice the terror that consumed him. He held his own fire, hoping to make himself a lesser target against the putrid, swampy earth.

His men resumed firing at the Americans, the clammy dawn deafening with the hellish violence and more screams of pain.

Sergeant Thi struggled through the foliage to toss himself down alongside his commander.

"Their helicopters come for the pickup, sir." Thi was out of breath. "They won't land close to the tree line. Too much danger of a rotor clipping something and taking them down." Thi glanced toward those who carried mortar setups. "Set up your mortars as soon as you reach the paddies!" he yelled to them above the thunder of exchanged battlefire.

Linh reached across and grabbed Thi's sleeve urgently. He knew Thi could see it was panic that controlled him, but Major Linh did not worry about that now.

"You must stop these Americans, Sergeant! And bring back those women, damn their souls. They shall pay dearly for this!"

Sergeant Thi ignored the cowardice he read clearly in Linh's face. The NVA noncom wiped sweat from his eyes.

"We will stop them, sir."

"Uh...see that you do, Sergeant. Quickly!"

Gunfire, from the direction taken by the Americans, tapered off.

To his men, Thi ordered, "After them! Try to take out the helicopters! *Kill them!*"

Thi led his motley crew of twenty in a sweeper movement, drawing closer to the paddies of An Chanh. He heard the throbbing rumble of approaching copters, and now he could see the cursed aircraft circling in from the east for a landing in the clearing several hundred meters ahead.

Linh held back until the last of his men ran past him. Then the major cautiously gained his footing and proceeded after his force, well to the rear.

Linh cursed his luck, cursed a traitor named Phuong, and most of all cursed a blacksuited demon from hell named Mack Bolan.

BOLAN BROKE FROM COVER of the jungle tree line, hurrying after the others toward the Hueys descending into the center of the clearing. The clearing was one of many that made up a network of dikes and paddies in a design unchanged for centuries.

Bolan slogged forward, mustering as much speed as he could with the added weight of the unconscious, wounded man straddling his back, his M-16 ready in his left fist.

The mists began to dissipate with the increasing heat of the morning sun, shrouding the upper reaches of the elongated An Chanh valley, but clearing near the ground with a ceiling of several hundred feet.

Gunsmoke Harrington and Deadeye Washington shifted to cover their trail, allowing Pol and Gadgets to reload on the run. The "gunfighter" soldier and the crack rifleman cut loose nonstop bursts as they trudged backward, staying as low as possible against

incoming gunfire from the straggled line of VC and
NVAs advancing in hot pursuit.

The noisily rotoring Hueys hovered into sight,
materializing and descending through the ceiling of
mist, like giant predatory insects.

The doorgunners on the two choppers were raking the enemy with M-60s mounted on pylons to
either side of both gunships, the machine guns unloading nonstop until the barrels began to glow red.

A streamlined Cobra, one of the two-man-crew
jobs, buzzed in the fast deathbird zipping in the direction of Major Linh's troops.

The Cobra's pounding miniguns and rocketfire
added destruction to the hellfire din, attempting to
clear the landing zone.

The pilots set their Hueys down on the nearest
paddy dike.

Bolan saw the doorgunners continuing to fire over
friendly heads toward the oncoming tide of VC and
NVA less than two hundred yards behind. The crew
chief and copilot of each chopper began tugging
aboard the Mont women and Bolan's point men before the copter skids had even touched down.

The pilots kept the choppers idling, the rotors
spinning in a low, weird hum, ready for a double-
time takeoff the instant everyone made it aboard.

Bolan heard bullets smack into the Hueys.

Someone, Bolan couldn't tell who at first amid the
swirling hellfire, snarled an oath and splashed forward into the ankle-deep water of the paddy.

As he slogged along with the weight of Fontenelli
across his back, Bolan saw Flower Child and Boom-

Boom stooping to pick up a felled Gadgets Schwarz, the radioman appearing more angered than injured from what looked to Bolan like a leg wound.

Hoffower and Flower Child hoisted Gadgets gingerly onto the deck of the closest Huey.

Several idle water buffalo one hundred yards away observed the unfolding human drama with indifference.

Bolan and Chopper had less than two hundred feet left to reach the nearest chopper and the beckoning, frantic arms of those already aboard, when Linh's force opened up with mortars. Devastating explosions began chomping up the earth in eruptions of earsplitting blasts that clouded the scene with dirty smoke and dirtier death.

The Cobra buzzing the VC position suddenly disintegrated into an exploding fireball that pitched into the jungle.

Bolan carried Chopper Fontenelli between the blamming explosions of impacting mortar fire. He deposited Fontenelli through a side door, onto the deck of the closest Huey.

Boom-Boom and Flower Child scampered onto the other chopper.

Through the all-encompassing shaking and rough shimmy and racket of the Huey's overhead rotor mechanism, the copilot hurried back to strap himself in, shouting into the mike of his flight helmet, "Let's go, let's go, let's go!" to the pilot. "This is a hot LZ, dammit! We're taking hits!"

The pilot yanked the collective stick up.

The Huey lifted, then the skids of both choppers left the paddy dike together.

The doorgunner and crew chief of both helicopters continued pulverizing Major Linh's force on the ground below.

The Vietnamese troops returned heavy parting fire after the choppers during the final seconds before the Hueys could gain enough altitude in the safety of the rapidly dissipating mist.

The doorgunner nearest to where Bolan gripped the frame of the Huey for support stopped firing and flew across the deck already slimy with Fontenelli's spreading pool of blood. The chopper's crewman spasmed from the impact of bullets from below that pulped his chest into red horror; then his twitching stopped.

Bolan swung around and positioned himself behind the vacated grips of the M-60. He had only heartbeats before the pilot took them high enough out of range, but he had to do something.

He slammed off a burst in the direction of Linh's troops, and was rewarded with the sight of figures down there death-jigging under the lethal impact of the M-60's fire, human targets toppling into the turbulence of the chopper's backwash.

Then the ear-hammering rumble of the Huey's accelerating rotor speed was the only sound left as Bolan lifted his finger from the trigger.

The pilots commenced evasive actions, both choppers banking sideways sharply and higher to a cruising altitude in the hazy rays of the new sunrise, the ground mist becoming clusters of cotton balls from fifteen hundred feet.

The pilots, aces both, aimed the Hueys into that sun and opened their birds up at 110 knots, like homing pigeons heading back to Camp A-105.

The copilot of the chopper carrying Bolan was already busy raising Three-Niner-Bayou on the tacnet that they were coming in.

Bolan turned from the M-60 to check on Fontenelli.

SERGEANT THI TRACKED HIS RIFLE skyward on the lifting Hueys. He started to shout an order to his men that Linh, standing next to Thi, could not hear above the racket of the choppers and the inefficient parting fire from his force on the ground.

Linh turned to ask Thi to repeat himself, experiencing a profound inner relief that at least this killing in such close proximity would soon be at an end.

Major Linh had lost his taste for pursuit.

The major suddenly realized they were being fired on from the side of the chopper into which Linh had seen Mack Bolan disappear moments earlier.

At that moment, Major Linh also registered the sinking, sickening realization that Sergeant Thi was dying, shuddering grotesquely, bloodily, close enough for his blood and brains to spray across Linh's uniform.

Linh squealed and again flung himself groundward as more of his men collapsed beneath the parting fire of the choppers.

A few brave troopers continuing firing at the Hueys even after the rising mists had swallowed the copters' deafening ascent, taking them out of range.

"Cease firing," Linh screamed at his troops. "They are gone! We have lost them!"

The sporadic riflefire from the shaken survivors of his command trickled off.

Then Linh heard the receding echoes of war grumbling like an angry giant through the valleys and peaks of the highlands, accompanied by the pitiful, agonized shrieks of the wounded and the crackling of flames from the smoldering pile of rubble that had been the Cobra gunship and its crew.

Linh averted his eyes from the carriage and scowled at his soaked, soiled uniform.

Then he raised his eyes to the lifting mist, in the direction taken by the helicopters carrying Mack Bolan's team and the Montagnard hostages to relative safety.

The disjointed postcombat sounds, shock and human suffering hardly concerned Linh, who was already busy gathering his wits.

He stared off into the distance for a long time after the vanished Hueys.

"Next time, Bolan..." he whispered softly to the tropical morning. "Next time the odds will all be on my side."

Eight _____

The pilot eased forward on his cyclic stick when the Huey reached three thousand feet, maintaining that altitude on a northeasterly course toward Three-Niner-Bayou.

The mountainous jungle green of the highlands blurred into a labyrinth of hills, valleys and waterways speeding by beneath the twin gunships.

Ten minutes into the flight without incident.

The fuel gauges read low, making the birds light, giving them more speed.

The pilot nodded to the man riding the armored chair on the other side of the dash.

"Your turn."

The copilot nodded and took over the controls.

The flier breathed a sigh that felt as if it came all the way from his bootlaces. He massaged tired, aching eyes for a moment, then looked around the back of his seat to survey the scene on deck between the open side doors.

One stretcher case.

One dead.

Damn.

The dead was Smitty, the doorgunner.

Double damn.

The pilot tore his eyes away from the bloody remains of a buddy who had been telling him off-color jokes only a couple of hours ago over chow at Pleiku.

Then his attention shifted to the big soldier sitting on the bench next to the rushing wind of the chopper's open doorway.

He sat hunched with his back to the pilot, who could not see the guy's features, nor could he tell the man's rank.

These dudes did not wear their rank: SOP on classified operations in the bush.

The pilot knew nothing of what these men had been up to back in those treacherous highlands. His orders were to pick up, ferry back to Three-Niner-Bayou, end of mission. But a man cannot take fire with others and not want to know something about them or at least wonder. The pilot knew one thing for sure.

The soldier in the opening was a leader; *a* leader, *the* leader of this team, whoever he was, whoever they were.

The pilot sensed this even without seeing the big dude's face.

He didn't figure the guy as an officer. The man had the body language of a grunt, plain and simple, yet the pilot also sensed an aura of command even through the frantic, noisy atmosphere of the chopper in flight.

The team leader looked the epitome of the eternal American fighting man, his M-16 cradled on his right knee, left arm reaching down, strong fingers vising the good shoulder of the unconscious grunt of his team, who was sprawled across the chopper's mud-and-blood-spattered deck.

An emergency field dressing had been plastered across the man's wounds, but the pilot, the soldier in the doorway, and the crew and other passengers all knew the wounded guy was hanging on to life by a very slim thread.

The pilot turned back to the controls.

"I've got it," he told the copilot. "Tell 'em we're coming in with one serious wounded."

He coaxed another ten knots out of the Huey while the copilot raised the Special Force Camp on the radio.

Less than five minutes later, the two Hueys touched down on the sun-splashed tarmac of Three-Niner-Bayou, the thrown-together, raggedy-ass structure inside the perimeter reflecting gold from the rays of the rising sun.

The pilots set their birds down two rotor diameters from each other to the frantic reception of a sea of corpsmen double-timing from the direction of the emergency room, wheeling gurneys toward the choppers.

The pilot, who had lost a friend named Smitty, watched the big team leader assist the medic crew in hanging a portable IV bottle and hooking the wounded man up while the unconscious guy was quickly, professionally lifted from the chopper onto the gurney.

Two corpsmen took off with the gurney at a run toward the ER.

The pilot had flown enough Medevac dust-off flights in and out of hot LZs to know how to help and when there were enough men on the job, like now.

He clicked off the bird; the rotors and engine winding down their eerie hum.

The copilot climbed from his seat and started aft.

The pilot took his time unstrapping himself from the armored chair. He did not want to have to look at what was left of Smitty. He glanced out at the scene on the tarmac.

His role in the mission was finished.

The other men of the team were debarking and the pilot saw the two Mont women, whoever they were, emerge from the other Huey.

He had to look around some before he spotted the big soldier.

Of course.

The guy was running along with the corpsmen wheeling the gurney with the badly wounded soldier toward the ER.

He had never seen the team leader's face, and now of course he never would.

The pilot would hike over to the operations tent, turn in his flight record and mission report. Then, he knew from experience, he would be ordered back to Pleiku for whatever this day held for him next.

He watched the corpsmen wheel the gurney through the arch of the emergency room, and the team leader also disappeared from his sight.

The pilot emitted another sigh from the bootlaces and got up to join his crewmen to take care of Smitty. When they got back to Pleiku, this pilot intended to find himself a bottle and a woman, in that order, to lose himself in both.

To forget his latest descent into Hell. And yet he knew, as tough as his job was, there were guys in this man's war with tougher jobs, yeah, like leading their men to their deaths and having to survive that and be tough enough to do it again and again when their duty demanded no less.

That was the kind of man this sniper team leader was and that was why this pilot respected the guy like hell without ever having met the hellgrounder or having seen his face.

The pilot, a warrant officer named Grimaldi, wondered who the big man was.

He wondered if their paths would ever cross again.

BOLAN HAD SEEN the makeshift emergency room of Camp 105-A many time after patrols were ambushed.

He had witnessed the wounded, the dying, brought in en masse, the plywood-frame ER shrill with the moaning and screaming of human suffering, doctors and nurses scurrying from stretcher to stretcher making hurried, superficial examinations to decide who should be operated on first.

This early in the morning there was no such activity. This was only a field MASH unit. Men were either patched up here and sent to Pleiku to recover, or airlifted immediately to a definitive care unit at the 71st Evacuation Hospital there.

The ranking MASH officer, Jim Brantzen, and a nurse were waiting to begin work the instant the corpsmen rolled Fontenelli through the doors into the ER.

The nurse, like the males, wore fatigues, flak jacket and helmet. She went to work with practiced economy of motion, using scissors to cut Chopper's uniform off to examine the unconscious man's wound.

Doc Brantzen injected a quick shot of morphine.

"GSW Tandt in the left shoulder," the nurse said to the doc without glancing up from tending Fontenelli. "Blood pressure 80 over 50, pulse 150."

The others of Bolan's team straggled into the hut.

Flower Child and Gunsmoke supported Zitter, who continued to curse a blue streak, concerned about the flesh wound he had sustained.

Gadgets Schwarz limped in, leaning on Boom-Boom Hoffower and Deadeye Washington for support.

Medics hurried to care for both men.

Bolan stayed with Fontenelli.

The Executioner knew the cool-as-ice nurse caring for his buddy.

Her name was Shawnee.

They were the best of friends; not lovers, but she knew Fontenelli too, and she knew Bolan's soul.

Their eyes met briefly as she glanced toward the doctor.

"Get another IV into him," ordered Jim Brantzen, another friend. "Type and cross him for fifteen units. After we have him in Operating." The MASH guys grabbed the gurney and started wheeling it toward nearby double doors.

As she passed him with two other medics also rushing to save Chopper's life, Shawnee's fingertips brushed lightly against Bolan's hand and the look she passed him told Bolan she knew what he felt.

Then Shawnee and the men, and the grunt would work to save, disappeared into Operating, where Bolan knew he would only be in the way, much as he wanted to accompany them, to stay at Chopper's side.

He went instead to see how his other men were doing.

The medics were busy hovering around Zitka and Schwarz, who had been stretched out on raised cots.

The MASH shack had been vacated, most of Sniper Team Able ambling in the direction of their hooch for some much-needed sack time.

Deadeye waited for Bolan at the doorway.

Bolan joined Washington outside the ER hut. He accepted the cigarette Washington offered him and the light.

They could hear a rising in the decibel level of Zitter's cursing from inside as a medic went to work on him, Zitka's yapping more indignant than anything else.

Bolan and Deadeye cracked tight, fleeting grins at each other, part wind-down release, part respect for Zitter's spunk and the luck that had made his and

Schwarz's wounds only superficial. But the break in the tension did not last long.

"You think Chopper is gonna buy it?" Deadeye asked grimly.

"Too soon to tell. Where are Sioung's wife and daughter?"

"Bloodbrother and Pol walked them over to the colonel's hooch for a reunion with Sioung, and here you are ducking the applause."

"Screw the applause, Deadeye." Bolan could not get the image of a wounded and bleeding Fontenelli out of his mind. "Sometimes this war is too damn dirty."

"I hear you, Sarge," growled Washington to Bolan's back as his team leader strode across the compound toward Colonel Harrelson's headquarters. "Yeah, bro, I hear you real loud and clear."

Big Deadeye Washington made no attempt to wipe away the solitary tear he felt roll down his cheek.

Damn.

Nine

First Lieutenant Pete Fletcher, USMC, intel officer assigned to Special Forces Camp Three-Niner-Bayou, braked the jeep one-half klick short of the rendezvous point.

Sp5c Ray Corbett rode shotgun.

Corporals Gary Robbins and Cleon Murphy, rode in the back of the open vehicle.

The rough-hewn jungle terrain crackled and screeched with the animal activity of a new day.

The mist had lifted, the sun a smoldering blood-red ball in the humid white sky, as if seen through layers of gauze.

The jungle simmered like a steam bath turned up too high.

The jeep was painted jungle camou.

The American servicemen, togged in sweat-stained fatigues that matched the jeep's camou paint job, wore .45 automatic sidearms and toted M-16s locked and loaded.

Murphy, a black man, used a sleeve to wipe perspiration from a flat-featured face highlighted by a jagged, knife scar that ran from his left ear to twist the corner of his mouth into a permanent sneer.

"This is a hell of a way to earn some spending money. Must be damn near a hundred in the shade."

Fletcher was busy eyeing their surroundings, listening. He saw and heard nothing to worry him.

"You're being paid enough to take it and shut up," he snapped.

"I ain't been paid yet, cracker."

Fletcher ignored that.

"The heat is the least of our worries."

"You mean the dink colonel?" Robbins said with a sneer.

Fletcher also chose to ignore the blatant lack of respect for his rank.

This was hardly a military operation.

"I mean Colonel Quan, yes, and whatever ace that sneaky gook son of a bitch has up his sleeve." Fletcher glanced at the man beside him. "What time is it?"

Corbett looked at his wristwatch.

"We're early. 0740."

"We're right on goddamn time," growled Fletcher. He looked back at the two in the rear. "All right. Get out here. You know what to do."

Robbins chuckled, patting his M-16 affectionately.

"I've got a pretty damn good idea. The only good dink is a—"

Murphy paused before climbing from the jeep.

"Fuck that," he interrupted Robbins brusquely. He leaned close to Fletcher so his thick lips were a fraction of an inch from Fletcher's ear. The snout of Murphy's M-16 poked Fletcher in the ear. "You listen up and listen good, Lieutenant. Everything better go according to plan when you meet up with the dink. I wouldn't want me or Robbins to have anything happen to us…by accident, know what I mean?''

He roughly nudged the M-16's snout deeper into the officer's ear for emphasis.

Fletcher tried to keep his voice steady.

''I don't know what you mean.''

''I think you do, cracker. Just don't fuck up…Lieutenant.''

Murphy alighted from the jeep.

He and Robbins left the jungle road and moments later disappeared into the thick foliage out of sight of Fletcher and the Sp5c, who watched them go.

''That boy Murphy is good at mind reading,'' commented Corbett.

Pete Fletcher spit in the direction taken by Robbins and Murphy.

''He won't be nothing for long, Ray. He won't be nothing but a dead smartass. Bet on that. Being careful ain't going to help those two worth a damn.''

''And Gary?''

''Robbins? What the hell do you think?'' Fletcher studied the man beside him. ''You're not going soft on me, are you, Ray? I laid it out to you when you bought in. We need those two right now but we won't in a few days when the stuff is on its way back to the States.'' Fletcher chuckled appreciatively. ''I gotta hand it to you, man. Coming up with the idea of shipping the shit back in bodybags marked 'Remains Unviewable.' That was a stroke of genius.''

"It wasn't my idea. I know more than one guy in my position doing the same thing."

"Yeah, but I needed your connection in Saigon and back in The World to make this happen."

Corbett studied Fletcher long and hard.

"Is that why I'll outlive Gary and Cleon? Do you always kill what you don't need?"

"I destroy what threatens me," snarled Fletcher. "Punks like Robbins and that spade are too dumb to keep their mouths shut. They get drunk or get their hands on the shit we're getting from Quan and they start yapping, and you and me are up for life, old buddy. You, I can trust. You've put money in this, too. Uh, speaking of which—"

Corbett patted his pocket.

"Right here. We'd better get rolling, Pete. Quan might be too nervous to wait around. I, uh, guess you're right about Gary and...about both those guys."

Fletcher cranked up the jeep.

"You're damn right I'm right. Stay with me and hang tough, Ray, and I'll make us both rich."

Ray Corbett looked away, nodding, saying nothing, but Fletcher could see the Sp5c's mind working too much.

Fletcher slipped the jeep into gear, continuing along the dirt road toward the rendezvous point with Colonel Quan.

There was no ensuing conversation with Corbett during the remainder of the drive, for which Fletcher was grateful. It gave him time to think. He had to be absolutely certain of how to play the confrontation about to happen because there would be no way to correct an error, not when it came to killing.

It was starting to look to Fletcher as if this thing with Quan and Corbett and body bags shipped home full of heroin would have to be a one-time thing, lucrative as it had promised to be.

Corbett showed all the signs of getting religion and it would get worse after the two rummies, Murphy and Robbins, were out of the way, Fletcher knew. So he would have no choice but to take out Corbett too, and that would be the end of the body-bag pipeline.

Fletcher also had his suspicions about Colonel Quan, whom he had never dealt with before.

The lieutenant slowed the jeep on the approach to the final curve leading to the rendezvous point, considering whether or not there might be too damn many complications all around for him to continue at all in the black-market drug trade.

So far Lieutenant Peter Fletcher had filled a Swiss bank account to bulging during the year and a half he had served his country in Vietnam.

His assignment as intelligence officer gave Fletcher unlimited resource capability for tracking the Vietcong heroin traffic that came down the Ho Chi Minh Trail; the profits used to support guerrilla activities.

Fletcher had devised an as yet fail-proof system of tracking down the distributors among the VC and ARVN, using the resources at his disposal. Then it was always an easy second step to confronting regional distributors.

Fletcher was already a millionaire, though of course no one knew this. When his duty was up he intended to retire to a life of ease and pleasure forever.

But yes, he decided as he wheeled the jeep over the hump of terrain, rounding the curve, a winner knows when to cash in his chips before risking everything, and a guy could only spend so much money in one lifetime, anyway.

It was time to pull out of the drug thing, but Fletcher knew he could not stop now and he thought no more about it.

He braked the jeep nose to nose with a sedan sporting official Viet markings.

Two rifle-toting Viets stood on either side of the sedan, each man resting the butt of his rifle on his hip, finger on the trigger, weapon pointed skyward.

A third Vietnamese in fatigues waited near the sedan. He observed the jeep pull to a stop. He started forward, toward Fletcher's side of the vehicle.

Fletcher had never met the man approaching him, but he knew the Viet well enough from the man's files channeled to him in his capacity as intel officer at Camp 105-A.

Colonel Quan, district chief and commander of the National Police Field Force, was no taller than the average Viet male, but the beginning bulge of a little potbelly evidenced the good life of a prospering drug dealer.

Quan nodded curtly to the driver, barely acknowledging the presence of Corbett.

"Lieutenant Fletcher."

Fletcher nodded.

"Colonel. I suggest we transact our business as expeditiously as possible."

"Of course. You have brought the money?"

Fletcher mirrored Quan's expressionless eyes, which reminded the American of polished black marbles.

"You have the merchandise?"

"Naturally. I should like to see the money, please."

Fletcher maintained eye contact with a man he did not trust. He wanted to grab the M-16 that rested between his and Corbett's seat, but he knew it was not time yet—not according to plan.

"Ray."

Corbett reached into a pocket and withdrew a rubber-banded roll of American currency. He handed the packet to Fletcher.

The lieutenant gestured with the money in his hand.

Quan smiled like a cat that has just eaten the canary. He stepped back.

And Fletcher knew his plan was about to go to hell.

Quan murmured, "Excellent," and snapped his fingers.

The two Vietnamese standing on either side of the sedan lowered their rifles into firing position and aimed from twelve feet away at the Americans in the jeep.

"Sonofafuckingbitch," Corbett muttered.

Fletcher kept his cool. His years in the drug business in the States before the Marines had taught him never to show fear, especially not to a man killer like Quan.

"This is not very smart, Colonel. I'd had hopes of a long-term association highly profitable to both of us."

Quan's shit-eating smile stayed right in place.

"You will toss that money to me, please. Then perhaps I will allow you and your friend to leave here alive."

A vague movement from a ridge of high ground across the road behind Colonel Quan caught Fletcher's attention.

The colonel and his men did not see it.

Fletcher registered a tight smile.

He hoped Corbett saw Murphy and Robbins angling into place along that ridge.

The ball was back in Fletcher's court.

"Go to hell, you double-dealing gook bastard."

Quan's expression flared into rage. He started to snap a command to fire at his men.

Twin autofire opened up from the ridge.

Quan's shout spasmed into shock and death as a stream of bullets exploded into his back, bursting most of his chest and what was inside all over Fletcher's jeep.

Fletcher and Corbett tumbled over each other as they piled to the ground on the opposite side of the jeep away from the incoming fire.

Corbett hit the ground muttering Hail Marys.

Fletcher landed to track his rifle around on Quan's Viet on the same side of the sedan as Fletcher.

The Viet saw his buddy on the other side of the car slam into the sedan as projectiles from the ridge blasted life out of the guy.

The remaining man ducked behind the sedan to escape the incoming fire Murphy and Robbins strafed into the Viet army vehicle, the armor plating stopping any penetration.

The surviving Viet looked around frantically, not bothering to return fire, only wanting a way out. Then he saw Fletcher's smiling face over the barrel of the M-16. He started to scream a plea not to fire.

Fletcher squeezed the trigger.

A long burst splattered the Viet's head into mist as red as the morning sun.

The two men on the ridge ceased firing.

Corbett ceased praying.

Fletcher did not lift himself over cover of the jeep.

"All clear down here," he called to the men on the ridge. "Let's move it. Hurry! Someone's going to investigate all this noise."

Fletcher waited until he saw Murphy and Robbins appear and advance.

When they were out in the open where he could keep an eye on them, Fletcher handed the money back to Corbett.

"Here. Snap out of it, Ray. Never figured you for a Holy Roller. Turn this jeep around while I look for the stuff."

Corbett pocketed the money. He got to his feet, looking dazed.

"Uh, yeah, right. Uh, sorry, Pete. First time I ever took fire. Guess I, uh, sort of lost it."

"The jeep, Ray."

"Yeah, right."

Corbett climbed into the jeep and did as he was told.

Fletcher did not take his eyes from the advancing Robbins and Murphy, nor his finger from the trigger of his M-16.

He made a quick search of Quan's pockets and various hiding places: the dead man's boots; his crotch.

Fletcher found a billfold bulging with piasters and pocketed the money.

He found no heroin.

The two troopers from the ridge reached the road.

Corbett completed backing the jeep around for the getaway, the engine idling.

Robbins and Murphy confronted Fletcher as the intel officer finished a hurried feel search beneath the seats and in the glove box of the Viet's car.

Fletcher looked up to see a barely concealed belligerent sneer across Cleon Murphy's face.

The black trooper palmed a fresh clip into his M-16.

"Mighty smart of you and Corbett, ducking behind the jeep the way you did, sir." He emphasized the last word with no respect whatsoever. "Woulda been a real shame if you'd a caught a couple slugs by accident."

Fletcher tried his best not to bloody his hands as he made a search of the other two dead Vietnamese.

"I was thinking the same thing when you and Robbins were coming down that ridge just now...*boy*." Fletcher felt good at the anger that caused a flash point of rage in the black's eyes. Fletcher continued quickly in a different tone before he pushed too far, drawing Corbett and Robbins into the conversation. "We were suckered, gentlemen. I thought maybe our friend the colonel might have brought along the shit anyway, but it was a setup all the way. He figured to make himself a quick bundle and leave a couple of ambushed American soldiers for someone else to explain."

"Where do we go from here?" Robbins asked.

"This doesn't change a thing," Fletcher snarled. "Matter of fact, I've got an idea."

Cleon Murphy glared at the dead bodies sprawled around them.

"Better be a damn sight better than this idea."

"I've got another connection in Pleiku," the officer told them. "I went with Quan because he offered us a better price. I see now why he thought he could afford to. I've dealt with the man in Pleiku before."

Corbett looked anxiously from the jeep.

"It won't mean more...killing, will it?"

Robbins and Murphy both thought that was funny.

"Hey, chickenshit, there's a war going on," Robbins said, snickering. "People get greased all over the place."

Murphy nodded agreement. The black turned to Fletcher and most of his belligerence was back under wraps.

"Okay, cracker boss, I'm in. I've gone this far."

"We've got the money," Fletcher said persuasively to Corbett, "and we've got your pipeline set and ready to go. I've covered our absences, everything. We just realign the picture a little bit, that's all."

"We better start realigning by hauling ourselves the fuck out of here," said Murphy. "Shooting ain't so common that nobody's going to come and not find these dead dinks."

Fletcher knew inside that everything was back on the rails again. Corbett, Robbins and even Murphy eyed him to tell them what to do next.

He strode to the jeep and shoved Corbett into the passenger seat, taking the wheel himself.

He pretended not to notice Murphy grab Corbett's shoulder and roughly force Ray into the rear with Robbins.

"In the back, motherfucker. We need a man up here on the j-o-b, not a prayer boy."

Robbins thought that was funny, too.

Corbett, as usual, said nothing.

Fletcher popped the vehicle into gear and got them away from there.

Toward Pleiku.

He knew he would have to kill Murphy before the black killed him, but that was not the time.

The time would come soon enough, but there could be more wrinkles before this last thing was played and Pete retired, and if things got hairy he could make good use of a homicidal animal like Cleon Murphy.

Corbett would be a problem, too, but Fletcher felt confident again, driving the jeep toward Pleiku.

When they got closer, he would turn the wheel over to one of the enlisted men, as befitted Pete Fletcher's rank.

He hoped there would be no more snags and felt especially confident with the knowledge that the one man he particularly considered a threat was nowhere around—a do-gooder bastard from hell named Mack Bolan, whom Pete Fletcher did not wish to tangle with even if he had ten Cleon Murphys.

Fletcher had witnessed enough of Bolan around the camp's headquarters to size up the ST leader as a man to avoid if you were in the business Fletcher got rich on.

Thus far, he had avoided Bolan and this suited Peter Fletcher just fine, especially on what he had decided for sure would be his last tap.

He was close enough to getting back to The World and into the fortune he'd already stashed away, and it only made sense to exercise extreme caution this close to the payoff.

Before leaving "on patrol" with these three enlisted men, Fletcher had confirmed that Bolan and his ST had been sent by Colonel Winters on a particularly dangerous mission into the heart of VC-controlled territory.

Fletcher did not know the details of the mission and he could not care less. He only hoped Mack Executioner Bolan would catch a fatal bullet from

Charlie, though he knew it wouldn't happen that way.

Bolan had shown an uncanny knack for staying alive.

As the jeep sped over the bumpy road, Fletcher reflected that killing was always easier once you got started. He would take out Murphy and good riddance.

In fact, he had decided he would kill *anyone* who got in his way this close to the finish, this close to his days of living as a king forever. He felt he could take on even Mack Bolan, the way things were clicking back into place again, the way he had planned.

Yeah, thought Fletcher, that would be the perfect topper to a brilliant career as businessman in the drugs his old buddies eagerly awaited, ready and willing to pay through the nose for it back in The World.

Nothing would stop the show now, Fletcher thought.

If Mack Bolan took a hand, the Executioner would be more than welcome to his own damn funeral.

The craggy highlands bowled into a valley.

Fletcher pulled the jeep to a stop and ordered Murphy to take the wheel and Corbett to resume his former position in front.

Murphy telegraphed hate strong enough to feel, but did as he was told, avoiding Fletcher's eyes.

He knows who the boss is, thought Fletcher.

The black soldier steered them toward the highway to Pleiku, through an area that Fletcher knew to be relatively pacified, again thanks to his capacity as intelligence officer.

The only thing that mattered now was pulling it off fast enough for it to work.

But one thing still troubled Fletcher. With Murphy's ruffled feathers more or less soothed and Quan out of the way, those bodies left behind could put someone wise to what Fletcher had been doing all along. In that case, Mack Bolan would damn well take a hand and if that happened, Fletcher predicted only one sure bet.

Fate alone would decide who would live and who would die when an Executioner came for blood.

Ten

Bolan felt a weariness creeping through every inch and fiber of his being as he crossed the compound toward the Old Man's bunka.

The big soldier had experienced the sensation before: the postcombat wind-down when the body begins to register the abnormal stress to which it had been subjected, but for Bolan it was only a weariness of the body.

His mind was wide awake, as it had to remain until the mission windup was complete, his men taken care of and Colonel Harrelson briefed on the mission report.

It was all part of Bolan's job. Then he could allow his mind, his whole being, to relax.

Until the next mission.

Or the next attack from Charlie.

He reached the command hooch just as his CO emerged from the hut into the morning sunlight. Accompanying him were the Meo leader, Sioung, his wife and daughter, and Pol and Bloodbrother, who looked every bit as worn as Bolan felt.

Special Forces Camp 105-A bustled with morning activity, personnel moving here and there, everyone maximizing energy with a sense of purpose.

Camp Three-Niner-Bayou was a quarter-mile by quarter-mile perimeter of concertina wire decorated with empty beer cans, so that any attempted penetration would rattle an alert to the sentries.

The perimeter boasted much more security: 81 mm mortars, 3.5 rockets, M-79 machine guns and 30-calibers facing a 450-foot killing area separating the perimeter from the jungle.

Bolan did not salute Colonel Winters.

Enlisted men did not salute their officers in frontline field operations like this. The trees and hilly terrain beyond the clearing could host any number of snipers at any given time despite the most thorough of security measures.

Charlie loved to pick off the officers first, disrupting the chain of command, and so there was no saluting outdoors to keep these snipers from knowing who was who.

Instead, Winters exchanged a firm handshake with Bolan.

"Good work, Sergeant. Sorry to hear about Fontenelli. Any word on his chances?"

"No, sir. Too soon to tell. It's pretty bad."

"Zitter and Schwarz?"

"They'll be out of action for a bit, not too long."

Sioung stepped forward, his wife and daughter flanking him, one of his arms around each of his women.

Ti Bahn and Tran Le both looked relieved, exhausted, in mild shock as they clung to their man.

The guerrilla's features stayed expressionless, but his eyes spoke volumes.

"You have returned what is more dear to me than life," Sioung intoned solemnly to Bolan. "I am in your debt, Sergeant Mercy."

"I want only your friendship, Sioung," Bolan replied.

"You have that," the hill fighter assured him. "And now I would accompany my women to your infirmary."

Bola nodded, trading glances with the females who looked too shaken up to speak.

"You've got tough women here, Sioung. Things could have gone worse if they had panicked."

Sioung nodded.

"They are Meo. Thank you again, American. Sioung's heart knows joy and I cannot recall the last time this was so."

The Mont fighter stepped past them, leading Ti Bahn and their daughter toward the MASH bunker.

Bolan stood in silence for a moment, watching Sioung and his small family stride across the bustling compound.

The Meo warrior and his women disappeared through the doors of the ER.

Bolan again felt the knot of concern tighten like a fist on his gut for a brave man named Fontenelli who did not deserve to die....

He turned to Bloodbrother and Pol, who stood covered with the accumulated grime, minor bruises and filth of the battlefield, their fatigues muddy and in disarray.

Loudelk's native American eyes were sharp as ever, the little feather worn in his helmet was right in place, and Pol looked ready also to wade back into blood river if ordered to do so.

"You did one hell of a good job, guys," Bolan told the men.

Blancanales looked around from having watched Sioung lead the women away.

"Seeing those three reunited almost makes me feel good, if it weren't for Chopper."

Bloodbrother rested a hand on Pol's shoulder.

"It was worth it, man. Chopper'd be the first to say so."

Pol looked at the ground.

"Would he? And if he dies, what difference will it have made? What glory is there when a guy loses his life in an armpit jungle eight thousand miles from home?"

"Glory has nothing to do with it, Pol," Bolan countered. "There's a woman and child over there who were about to be raped and murdered until we showed up and stopped it and brought them home to safety. Maybe you can cut something like that more than one way. I can't. Chopper did what he had to do."

Pol looked up.

"You're right, Sarge. But damn, if Chopper buys the damn farm...shit."

"Easy, Pol. You and Tom head back to the hooch."

"Best idea I've heard all damn day." Loudelk turned toward the direction of their hooch. "Come on, Pol, let's hang it up for a little while. Stay hard, man."

Blancanales nodded.

The two soldiers strode off.

Bolan turned to Colonel Winters.

"Ready to deliver the mission report, sir."

Winters shook his head.

"Later, Sergeant. The results speak for themselves. Right now, I have a choice to offer you."

"A choice?"

"We've got a break on the Fletcher thing."

Bolan felt a spark of interest cut away at the tiredness.

"What sort of break?"

"I said I had a choice for you," the CO reminded Bolan. "It's against my better judgment to bring you in on something right on the heels of what you and your men have just been through."

"If it's Fletcher, sir, I want a piece of the action. I've been on this thing since the beginning. I feel I'm entitled to be in when the payoff comes."

Winters grunted.

"Figured you would. Major Po wants you in on it too, of course. So do I, for that matter, if you want to know the truth, but damn it all, Sergeant, I am not about to order you into action of this nature unless I have your assurance that you feel up to it.

"Hell, son, don't go heroic on me and get yourself killed. You're a helluva lot more useful to me alive. We stand a good chance of nabbing Fletcher with his fingers in the jar this time, but there are other men for the job.''

''I feel more than up to it. I'd like nothing better.''

Winters eyed the noncom speculatively for several seconds, then grunted.

''Okay, guy. That's your choice. Shower up, see to ordnance and be back here on the double. This one's for you alone. Your team has earned its rest.''

''I'll be back here in fifteen minutes.''

BOLAN MADE IT BACK into the sandbagged HQ hut in ten minutes, freshly showered, in clean fatigues, his M-16 exchanged for a shoulder-holstered .45 automatic.

He felt better and ready enough to go after a soldier gone bad named Pete Fletcher who needed going after.

The base command bunker was a labyrinth of activity. Orderlies, officers and ranking enlisted men bustled here and there, relaying this report just in from the field, conferring on that report of enemy strength buildup. The headquarters of a wartime military operation was in full swing.

And the day was only beginning.

Bolan knew his way through to the colonel's office. He could have found his way blindfolded, so often had he followed this route to report on the outcome of combat missions.

This time, though, there was a difference from the standard debriefing.

Colonel Winters had a visitor.

A man Bolan knew slightly and had worked with on one former occasion.

Major Po, head of internal security in the Viet government's National Police Field Force, had the standard slight build of men of this part of the world. He sported a dapper mustache and goatee, and his shrewd, alive eyes and precise military bearing suggested a quiet inner strength, tempered with the cordiality of his smile.

He stood from his chair near Colonel Winters's desk at first sight of the soldier who appeared in the doorway of the makeshift office.

"Sergeant Bolan. It is most pleasant that our paths should cross again," the Viet major intoned in that pleasant lilt a Viet accent gives to English. "I was sorry to hear of your man being seriously wounded."

Po's handshake was strong, like the man himself, Bolan thought.

Bolan and Po had joined forces several months before in the matter of three Green Beret A-Teamers gone sour.

Floyd Worthy, Jim Hinshaw and Angel Morales had joined the Army only to escape the hot breath of the law back in The World.

Bolan got a bad taste in his mouth just thinking about those three punks.

They had taken their street-hood ways from the States to the jungles of Vietnam to exploit this war as a means of personal profiteering.

Bolan knew the three were far from the only ones, both in Nam and in the States; soldiers, civilians and politicians, twisting what was happening over here to fatten their own purses.

It happened in every war and Bolan loathed such men as much as he hated the enemy for trying to conquer and crush this beautiful land, though as a grunt in the field there was little if anything he could do concerning the evils of profiteering.

Until Hinshaw, Worthy and Morales.

The trio had instituted a campaign of terror and intimidation against the inhabitants of the region at another base where Bolan's ST had been stationed, not far from Three-Niner-Bayou. Viet civilians were forced to pay "insurance" premiums or face arrest on charges of collusion with the Communists.

Those who did not comply paid with their lives, and in the confusion that is war behind the lines, the three rotten grunts had got away with it for a while.

Until Bolan showed up.

He and one of his men, a flanker named T. L. Minnegas, no longer with the unit, had caught Morales, Hinshaw and Worthy in the act of murdering three unarmed villagers.

Bolan's intervention had resulted in the indictment of the three profiteers, who presently occupied cell space in the stockade at Da Nang, awaiting their court-martial, at which Bolan would testify as the prosecution's star witness.

Bolan had met Major Po during that investigation. The three rotten Americans had paid off National Police Field Force officers to look the other way.

Po had gone on to ferret out and break up the bribed bad apples in his own barrel in such a way that told Bolan that Po was one of the good ones.

Bolan turned from Po's handshake to salute Colonel Winters, who returned it. Then Bolan turned back to Po.

"Should have figured you'd be in on the Fletcher thing sooner or later, sir."

An orderly came in carrying a tray with three cups of coffee. The soldier set the tray on the colonel's desk and departed.

The three men sat, Bolan and Po in chairs facing Colonel Winters.

Bolan reached for a coffee cup, the other two reached forward also.

"Was kind of hoping all of these would be for me," Bolan cracked the conversational ice. He could feel the coffee infuse him with further awakening. "If you gentlemen have been waiting on me, I'm ready."

Po smiled.

"It would seem that such is your natural state, Sergeant Bolan." He set his cup down and stood. "The sergeant is quite correct, Colonel. We can explain the particulars to him on our way."

Winters nodded. He and Bolan both stood, set down their barely touched coffees and started toward the door with the Viet, who was armed with a flap-holstered pistol at his hip similar to Winters's side arm.

"You figure they'll move up the contact?" Winters asked Po.

The trio filed out of the office into the buzzing labyrinth of the command area.

"Anything is possible with Hieu Dai, Colonel. I should have thought of this sooner."

They exited the hut and strode toward the chopper landing pad nearby.

"We just got the word on Quan and his men two minutes ago, Major," countered Winters. He looked at Po. "So don't go blaming yourself for anything." Winters turned to Bolan. "Quan is a National Police Field Force district chief. The major's unit has been fixing to bust him."

"How does it tie in with Fletcher?" Bolan asked.

"I didn't want you distracted from what you had to do, getting Sioung's wife and child back," said Winters, "but Quan's latest hook is our boy, Fletcher. We were preparing to make the bust this afternoon."

"What's changed?"

"The report that just came in says Quan and two of his men were found ambushed at the spot where the bust was planned, not ten klicks from here. They moved up the schedule, the bastards. Fletcher is playing for keeps."

A chopper started revving its rotors when the waiting pilot saw Winters, Po and Bolan approaching.

Po lifted his voice to be heard above the engine sounds but the lilt of his accent crept through.

"They moved the schedule ahead with Quan, which is why they will do it the same with Hieu Dai."

"Who's that?"

"The next link in the chain," Winters explained. "It seems Fletcher has been doing business with Hieu Dai, who has quite a reputation in the drug under-world in and around Pleiku. But Hieu Dai has the power and the bucks to establish a near foolproof system for getting away with it. Major Po hasn't been able to get the goods on him except to put a few dents in Hieu Dai's operations."

"Which has already resulted in the death of two of my people," said Po. "Hieu Dai must be stopped. I will stop him, with your help."

"After what happened to Quan," Winters briefed Bolan, "we figure Fletcher will go through with a meet he's already set up for two hours from now in Pleiku with Hieu Dai. Fletcher's got some men with him. So will Hieu Dai, if he shows."

"He will show," said Po.

Bolan glanced toward the ER hut.

A movement in white from that direction caught his attention.

"Begging your pardon, Colonel," Bolan ad-dressed Winters, "request permission to check on the condition of Fontenelli before we leave."

Winters considered briefly, then nodded.

"Make it fast, Sergeant. We'll wait for you in the chopper."

Bolan saw the curt nod of approval granted by Po, who understood.

Winters and Po continued on.

Bolan hurried over to where Shawnee, fresh blood staining her white smock, came forward to meet him midway in front of the medical area.

"How is he?"

"Doc Jim has done his best, Mack."

Bolan felt the bottom of his gut drop out.

"Not—"

"No," she added quickly. "Not yet...I mean...oh, *hell*!"

He stepped forward to lightly touch her arms with his fingertips, not a hug, just a touch, but an embrace of sorts nonetheless.

Shawnee looked ready to come apart at the seams, but Bolan knew she wouldn't. He had seen her show her mettle often enough under fire. He and this woman knew each other in every way except one— some said the most important—but it had never seemed to get in the way of the communication and rapport between them.

Shawnee and Mack Bolan were just friends. A cliché come true. She shared Bolan's anguish.

"I've got to leave," he told her briskly. "I'll check with you the minute I get back. Take care of him, lady."

"I will, Mack. So will Doc Jim. He wanted to speak with you."

Bolan squeezed her arms briefly, then broke contact.

There was no more time.

The chopper was waiting.

Jim Brantzen had patched countless nicks, cuts and minor injuries for Mack and the members of his team, and more serious operations like this one with Fontenelli, so that a very special bond had grown between Bolan and Brantzen.

At least Bolan knew Chopper was in the best of care, and he hoped like hell that would be enough to pull Chopper through.

"I've got to go."

He turned toward the waiting chopper and broke into a jog to make up for lost time.

The soldier did not look back.

He was thinking about busting a punk named Fletcher, in more ways than one.

He did not hear Shawnee's parting words, whispered as softly as a kiss.

"God speed you home safely to me, Sergeant Mercy."

She stood there for several moments watching the receding figure of Bolan, which still looked imposing even from a distance. Then the Executioner climbed into the waiting Huey to join Colonel Winters and Major Po.

Shawnee watched the chopper lift off and bank to the east.

Toward Pleiku.

She turned and made her way back into the emergency-room hut.

Shawnee had been under no illusions, prior to arriving in Vietnam as a combat nurse, than her tour of duty would be anything short of endless, awful horror.

"You don't have to die to go to hell," one of her instructors had told her back in The World before shipping out.

That truth was hammered home day in and day out as she witnessed the endless stream of dead and dying that came through the ER doors; brave young men forever cheated of the normal life that should have been their birthright in great America.

Instead they were shipped to war overseas to fight for a cause, Shawnee sometimes thought in her darker moments, possibly not worthy of their bravery and sacrifice.

It did not pay to dwell on such things when you had a job to do, she knew, and anyway, there was Mack Bolan to counter the dark depression that always seemed to lurk nearby, trying to grab hold.

At times like these, Shawnee would think of Bolan and his towering strength, and she would somehow draw on some of that strength for herself. She suspected that many also did, who knew the warrior they called the Executioner.

Shawnee preferred to think of him as Sergeant Mercy, though she felt both appellations fit Mack equally, a man she knew to be anything but a "green machine" robot blindly following orders.

In her mind, Bolan was a thoughtful, aware, peaceful man, as strange as she knew that sounded. And yes, she did know soldier Bolan well enough, she told herself, to realize there was much about that incredible guy to draw strength from, not the least of which was that the big guy saw his duty and carried it out with little concern for the considerable personal sacrifices always involved.

Shawnee had learned from Bolan that man, or woman, is not whole without goals, dreams, that sense of sacrifice—or call of duty, be it to ideals, career, whatever—necessary to strive to make those dreams and goals into reality.

Mack Bolan was a peaceful man, yes.

He also happened to be a soldier by profession.

Thus a peaceful man fought, saw his friends maimed and killed, and yet somehow always found that inner strength of sacrifice. He kept on fighting, holding fast to his dream of a peaceful world, because duty demanded no less.

These were the things Shawnee had learned from Bolan, not that the big guy ever spoke of such things.

She tried to concentrate on them and not on Mack because she knew he was tired and concerned about his buddy, Chopper.

She wished Mack had not taken off immediately with Colonel Winters and Major Po for whatever matter had been so urgent to send them to Pleiku. But what she had seen in Bolan's steady blue eyes, eyes that could be so warm and alive one moment, like chips of ice the next, told her that Bolan would have preferred to stay near until he knew something about the progress of Angelo's condition.

But there was work in Pleiku from which Executioner Bolan could not turn away.

This Army nurse understood war.

And she understood Bolan.

Duty, yes.

Eleven

The building where the bust was supposed to go down was a one-story structure on a narrow side street that connected two of the busier arteries of Pleiku.

The town's usual population of 23,000 had doubled during the recent past, burgeoned to overflowing with war refugees, two armies and the wide-open free-enterprise chaos all this fed.

There had been no way to hurry the drive in from the air base after Bolan, Po and Colonel Winters landed at the nearby U.S. facility.

The streets of Pleiku were awash with curb-to-curb traffic—little, if any, like the jeep Bolan drove.

There were mostly bicycles, jostling pedestrians, motorcycles and countless rickshawlike contrivances, some taxiing human passengers.

Others wound precariously through the sea of mass confusion, baskets of noisy farm animals, pigs and chickens on their way to market, Oriental faces mixed with some Anglos, a nonstop, tumultuous babble everywhere one looked.

From the air as the chopper approached the base on the outskirts of Pleiku twenty minutes earlier, the

town had appeared to sprawl amid the heavily culti-
vated rolling countryside of varying shades of brown
and green. Roads and canals crisscrossed numerous
mazes of flooded rice fields in every direction.

Down on the ground, away from the air base and
in the overcrowded middle of the town, Bolan steered
the U.S. Army jeep inches at a time through the
surging mass of human misery that clogged the main
thoroughfare.

He picked his way carefully, fighting the frustration he felt at their snail's pace. He could sense the
raw defeat and fear, strong enough to be palpable, of
the rabble in the crowded street.

Everywhere he saw piles of trash and garbage,
heaped indiscriminately in vacant lots, between
buildings and on street corners, picked at by children, stray mongrels and some adults.

And lounging against the doorways were the
whores, discernible because of their gaudy Western
clothing, not the traditional Viet *ao dai* worn by re-
spectable Viet women.

Vietnamese females had for centuries been called
the Flower of the Orient—small, delicately boned,
straight of back.

The Americans in the crawling jeep elicited offers
in fractured American slang, which they ignored.

Bolan steered the jeep into a narrow alley mid-
block away from the address Po had given him.

The side street, lined with shabby structures
shaded by arrack palms and other small-leaved
semitropical trees, was residential, decidedly less
traveled than the main artery.

There was a trickle of pedestrian traffic that paid scant notice to another U.S. Army jeep in this town.

Bolan shut off the ignition and turned to face the men in the vehicle with him: Major Po beside him, Colonel Winters in the back seat.

The shade of the alley was like an oasis after the drive from the air base. The occasional civilian crossing either entrance to the alley did not cast even casual sideways glances at the three men sitting there, the art of minding one's own business having been perfected in South Vietnam.

Passersby appeared to be residents of this side street, the women in *ao dais* on their way to shop, the males, elderly, too old for military service in the ARVN.

The flowing river of noisy humanity on the main thoroughfare, scant yards from the men in the jeep, could have been a million miles away, so effectively did the walls of the alley buffer the outside world.

"The building where your Fletcher and Hieu Dai are to meet has only two entrances," Po told Bolan and Winters. Po unholstered his pistol, checked it. "It would be best to split up and come in from both sides."

Bolan and Winters made final checks of their weapons.

"And if the meet between them hasn't been moved ahead?" Bolan asked. "We run the risk of queering the bust for later."

Po's expression clouded.

"Queering?"

"Sorry, Major. Slang. If Fletcher isn't there yet, we get Hieu Dai possibly, but the man we want gets wind and never shows."

"They will have moved ahead the time of their meeting," Po said confidently. "After what happened to Colonel Quan, Hieu Dai would never risk remaining in Pleiku a moment longer than necessary. He lives in the country, you see.

"And yet it is my estimation of the man that he will not pass up the opportunity to again deal with Lieutenant Fletcher, especially since the lieutenant represents a considerable expansion in the market for the goods Hieu Dai can supply."

Bolan climbed out of the jeep.

"The remains of men who've died for their country, used to smuggle heroin back to the States. Yeah, you told me, Major. Let's nail these slime."

Winters and Po debarked from the jeep, reholstering their pistols as Bolan did.

"Just wish we had some backup on this," Winters groused. "I don't mind killing a few vermin, but the one thing we don't have is an accurate accounting of Hieu Dai's firepower inside that house."

"Had we brought reinforcements with us," Po reminded them, "we would not possess the small chance we do of breaking Hieu Dai's operation. He has too much money for graft, too many connections."

"Which is why a major, a colonel and a lowly sergeant are making the bust," Bolan said. "What about the layout of the house? Where in it would Hieu Dai and Fletcher be meeting?"

"As you saw before you turned into this alley, it is a small structure of only a few rooms," said Po. "The two entrances are connected by a hallway that runs the length of the house along the south wall. The house has been used for such meetings twice before by Hieu Dai as a contact with others in his operation. He uses the sitting room, in the center of the hallway, through an archway."

"Your undercover operative, the one who fed you this," said Winters. "Is he in that house now? Can we count on him for help?"

"Our agent was a woman," answered Po quietly. "She posed as Hieu Dai's mistress. Her body was found three days ago. She had been slowly tortured to death."

"Let's hit 'em," Bolan growled. He looked to Winters. "If it's all right with you, sir, I'll take the hallway just ahead of you and Major Po."

"Blowing each other away in a cross fire wouldn't do at all," Winters said. "If that's the way you want it, Sergeant, you've got it, but I'm not going to sit out there and let you be blown to bits, either." He glanced to Po. "There's no other way into that house?"

"The windows are barred," Po replied, adding, "and we must hurry, gentlemen."

"The hallway it is," Winters agreed, nodding, but not sounding a damn bit happy about it. "When the shooting starts, Sergeant, I'll give you a five count, then come in low, so watch for me."

They synchronized watches and separated.

Winters and Major Po rounded the opposite end of the alley a moment before Bolan emerged into the sun-baked side street.

He strode along the hot pavement toward the small house built flush against the street. Identical structures sandwiched the tiny residence, their vaguely European architectural lines remnants of the period of French colonization.

Bolan knew that more than just the very real concern of a security leak had brought along a man of Colonel Winters's rank to an in-the-streets bust like this one.

The Executioner's commanding officer and Major Po shared a deep-rooted hatred of what the men in this house were up to, and felt, like Bolan, that there was no sin worse than a soldier selling out.

Right now, Fletcher was dealing his white powdered death for the inner-city ghetto streets of America. That was bad enough. But in his capacity as intelligence officer during his tour of duty in Nam, how many other bum moves by this lieutenant had resulted in hampering U.S. military interests over here?

Bolan wondered how many American and ARVN casualties had resulted from Fletcher's corruption. The warrior knew corruption to be pervasive when it grabbed hold of a man, and Bolan thought Fletcher's sins were hardly limited to desecrating the remains of fallen American servicemen.

He approached the door of the designated house on the numbers prearranged with Po and Winters.

He paused an additional heartbeat to allow a cluster of yapping, dirt-encrusted urchins filter by— the children of war—laughing, playing games among themselves as they scampered down the side street and turned a corner, disappearing from sight.

There was a lull in the sparse pedestrian traffic.

No one had given the GI a passing glance.

Bolan, back against the wall, unleathered his .45 automatic, holding it up, arm bent, ready to fire.

He leaned forward, ever so cautiously but with no wasted movement, and tried the door handle.

Somewhat to his surprise, the latch clicked almost soundlessly. Unlocked.

He thrust the door inward and followed it through.

PETE FLETCHER NEVER GOT OVER how much Hieu Dai looked like the pictures of Dr. Fu Manchu on the covers of the paperback novels Fletcher had read as a kid. The ancient mandarin-robed Viet drug boss always had the same effect on Fletcher that Fu had on the characters in those books, too.

The lieutenant experienced a chilly, unpleasant kind of feeling across the surface of his flesh and could barely restrain himself from upping and running the hell out of this house. He had met the drug boss here once before when, Fletcher recalled, he'd felt an identical revulsion from Hieu Dai.

The Viet stood unusually tall for an Oriental; he was lean, with a bald head, and a drooping Fu Manchu-like mustache enhancing the sinister effect of slitted eyes that seemed to glow.

Fletcher drew little comfort from the knowledge that Robbins and Murphy were waiting in the hallway just beyond the archway entrance of the room where he stood facing Hieu Dai. He did feel good knowing Corbett sat in the jeep out front, its engine idling for a quick getaway.

Hieu Dai had allowed Fletcher, Robbins and Murphy to retain their firearms in the house, but their protection was offset by three armed bodyguards who belonged to the drug dealer. The three hulking behemoths—they looked like Mongols to Fletcher—stood near Robbins and Murphy just beyond the archway.

Fletcher felt none of the confidence he'd experienced following his dealing with Colonel Quan several hours ago, after which Fletcher had contacted Hieu Dai, who had demanded this meet be moved ahead.

Hieu Dai and Pete Fletcher confronted each other across the width of a plain wood table, the sole piece of furniture in the room. Heavy draperies shut out the sunlight, making the room dim, giving it the clammy coolness of a tomb.

Hieu Dai finished counting the currency that his aristocratically long fingers had plucked from the table, then the bills disappeared into the drooping sleeves of his garment. The robed Viet folded his arms, slipping both hands into the sleeves.

Another Fu Manchu gesture, thought Fletcher.

The American placed a parcel, which he had just finished inspecting, into a wrinkled grocery sack containing several items boasting the Viet lettering of a local food store.

The innocent-looking bag would earn millions when the smack hit the streets at the other end of Fletcher's pipeline.

A sense of relief that the transaction was coming off so smoothly replaced the uneasy apprehension that had plagued Fletcher since he had stepped into Hieu Dai's presence less than five minutes earlier.

"A most satisfactory transaction," the Viet purred, his voice pure Fu Manchu. The Oriental nodded dismissal. "Until we meet again, Lieutenant."

Fletcher saw no sense in telling Fu Manchu that this would be their last transaction. The lieutenant had no intention of pushing his odds after this pipeline was set and running smoothly. He forced himself to nod in curt response and tried not to look too eager as he grasped the shopping bag and turned toward the archway to leave.

Hieu Dai's voice froze Fletcher in his tracks.

"A pity, was it not, about poor Colonel Quan of the National Police Field Force being ambushed this morning."

Fletcher did not know what to do or say.

And then the situation hurtled entirely out of his control when noisy gunfire erupted from the direction of the hallway.

BOLAN EXPLODED into the shadowed, low-ceilinged hallway of the house, assuming a shooter's stance in the doorway. He knew he was silhouetted into a target for the men he expected and found inside. But still he tracked the .45 on the weapons-toting figures in front of the archway.

Now the warrior was certain that the meet between Fletcher and Hieu Dai had to be taking place, which accounted for the heavy-duty firepower.

The gunners reacted to the intrusion by tracking their rifles and pistols in Bolan's direction in the heartbeat before Bolan started snapping off rounds. The .45 automatic roared, and spearing pencils of flame felled selective targets.

The three giant Mongols in the hallway stumbled every which way into death sprawls, as .45 caliber projectiles zapped heads one, two, three, splashing the walls with surreal swirls of red and gray.

The sight of bodies tumbling like bowling pins temporarily distracted two American troopers—one black man, one white, neither of whom Bolan recognized—in the instant it took the Executioner to sidestep into deeper shadows. No longer a target from the sunlit street, Bolan straightarm-aimed the .45 at the two GIs who abruptly aborted their reactions.

The street door at the other end of the hallway smashed inward.

Howlin' Harlan Winters came through to assume a shooting stance like Bolan's, the colonel's automatic also aimed unwaveringly at the two Americans in the hall before the archway.

"Don't even think about it, guys," Winters warned. "Drop 'em real slow or you're deader than hell."

The GIs dropped their weapons.

Bolan rushed the archway, casting a quick glance outside the doorway behind Winters.

Major Po held a drawn pistol aimed at another American serviceman. The Viet colonel shoved him into the hallway to join the first two captured troopers.

Bolan slammed a fresh clip into his pistol as he reached the archway.

"Cover 'em, Colonel!"

"You got it, boy!"

Winters held a steady bead on the apprehended members of Fletcher's gang.

Bolan stopped at the archway long enough to crouch and eyeball the scene inside the room, his .45 tracking in well below where anyone waiting to fire would have expected, mere seconds having elapsed since they had stormed the house.

The men inside the room were caught without time to react; they had been involved in some unfriendly exchange of their own, Bolan sensed, entrusting their security to the goons in the hall.

Lieutenant Fletcher stood slack-jawed with surprise at how fast everything could go wrong, his side arm flap-holstered, his gun hand grasping what looked to Bolan like a sack of groceries.

The lieutenant hurled the sack at Bolan in a frantic attempt to reach his side arm, but thought better of it when the cold-eyed soldier in the archway tracked his .45 to level on the spot between Fletcher's eyes.

"Don't, Lieutenant," warned the figure in the archway. "I'm looking forward to testifying at your court-martial. I'd hate to cheat myself of the opportunity to send you away for life. Take out the pistol by the fingertips of your left hand. That's it. Drop it. Now get over there with your rummies in the hallway. You're under arrest.''

Bolan kept Hieu Dai under cover. The Viet drug dealer had not moved from where he stood, arms folded inside the sleeves of his mandarin robe, beside a wooden table in the center of the room.

Bolan had kept the ancient Oriental in sight during the moments it had taken to get the drop on Fletcher. He now centered his full attention on the Viet drug boss.

Fletcher faded to the periphery with his hands upraised, stepping over to where Winters kept all four of the Americans under cover in the hall, directly beyond the archway.

"*You* can try anything you like, Hieu Dai,'' cold eyes and .45 invited. "You, I've got no stake in.''

The hint of a humorless smile pulled the corners of the Viet's thin, cruel mouth upward.

"I have no reason to resist, foolish American. I will not spend one hour in a Viet jail. Do you not comprehend the extent of my power?''

"Don't talk me into it,'' Executioner Bolan cautioned without joking.

Hieu Dai started to say something. He stopped when Major Po stepped into the room.

A strange emotion that Bolan recognized as fear flickered in the gleaming slits of Hieu Dai's eyes. He tugged his arms from his robe and held them up. Suddenly he started babbling something, frantic, beseeching, but before he could utter a sound, Major Po lifted his pistol, aimed and fired, the report somehow muted as if muffled by the dimness of the room.

Hieu Dai caught the bullet through his open mouth, the impact toppling him against the table, which overturned when his corpse sagged into a sitting position in the corner.

Po holstered his pistol and looked past Colonel Winters covering Fletcher and the three GIs. The major looked at Bolan and explained in an emotionless deadpan, "The undercover operative who posed as Hieu Dai's mistress, the woman he ordered tortured to death, was my sister."

There was nothing to say to that.

Bolan picked up the sack Fletcher had thrown at him and plucked out a package wrapped differently from the others. He inspected the package.

Heroin.

He turned to confer with Colonel Winters, leaving Po to stand silently over the man he had killed.

Bolan had accepted some harsh truths during his time spent in this land of war.

The late Hieu Dai had been right.

The drug boss would have spent no prison time at all in atonement for the horrors he had perpetrated.

Sometimes a man has to make his own justice to get justice.

Vietnam had taught Executioner Mack Bolan that sometimes a man has to face the cannibals on their own damn terms.

Twelve

Sunset is the most beautiful time of day in Southeast Asia, not only because it brings promise of sometimes up to a ten-degree drop from the sweltering daytime temperatures, but also because the red ball easing beneath the horizon tints the clouds, mist and muggy atmosphere with brilliant hues of red, providing a spectacle of nature.

Bolan and Shawnee had returned once again to their private spot at the Special Forces Camp, the flat roof of Bolan's hooch or sleeping quarters, one of the ramshackle wooden buildings interspersed with the metal Quonset huts and bunkers.

The privacy of night cloaked soldier and nurse, man and woman, relaxing side by side on the little rectangle of roof. They propped themselves on their elbows, drinking, a soda for Bolan, a beer for Shawnee.

Each time they came up here, they had to dust away the ever-present red powder that seemed to cover everything in this country. But still, the roof was a private haven for these two friends, a place where they could find some solace and talk as human beings, removed, however temporarily, from around-the-clock hell.

Lieutenant Fletcher and his cronies—Murphy, Corbett and Robbins—had been unceremoniously thrown into Three-Niner-Bayou's makeshift stockade.

At this moment, Bolan knew, Colonel Winters was overseeing the paperwork, making the arrangements necessary to transfer the four arrested GIs to the stockade in Saigon. A Special Forces base camp was no place to hold prisoners.

The colonel regretted having to assign two troopers to guard the bad apples even this one night.

Bolan was thankful his own work brought him into a minimum of red tape run-ins with the green machine.

Bolan and Winters had left Po, with the reinforcements the Viet major had called in to clean up the bust, to make their way back from Pleiku with the sullenly silent prisoners. The colonel had again offered to process a promotion for Bolan, and he and Colonel Crawford before him had tried to do repeatedly. And again Bolan had declined the offer as he figured Winters, by this time, expected him to.

After they returned to the base and turned the prisoners over to an armed guard, Bolan took his leave of the colonel and headed straight for the ER.

He had been unable to speak with either Jim Brantzen or Shawnee, however, both of whom were swamped, working with other medics and nurses to treat the dying and wounded that a dust-off chopper brought in from a skirmish during Bolan's absence.

Bolan returned to the hooch he shared with members of his team.

Boom-Boom Hoffower informed him that Chopper Fontenelli remained on the critical list but with a stabilized condition. Chopper had been airlifted to Saigon, where he would receive better treatment than the base field facilities or Pleiku could provide. Hoffower told Bolan that Zitter and Schwarz would be fine.

Boom-Boom added, "And you look like shit, Sarge, if you don't mind my saying so."

Which was what Colonel Winters had told Bolan a few minutes earlier upon ordering Bolan off duty for the rest of the day.

Bolan took one look in the mirror in the latrine to confirm that he did indeed look as bad as he felt.

He shed his fatigues and climbed into the shower, standing under the spray that scalded his skin and opened clogged pores until he lost track of time and started to feel clean again. Then he let the frigid water close his pores again to reawaken his senses.

He returned to the six-by-ten cubicle with the pale green walls and the smell of mildew that was everywhere and the bunk and footlocker that were home for this soldier.

He settled on the bunk and entered in his *War Journal*:

The colonel offered me a promotion again today.

I don't want a promotion. It isn't that I can't handle the responsibility—I can.

My place is out on the firing line, helping these war-torn people. I cannot turn my back on the innocents struggling for survival when the VC savages are eating them whole. I would be less of a man if I did.

War is hell, yes.

But I have a duty.

AS DUSK DEEPENED and nightfall claimed the rugged silhouette of mountain jungles beyond the base perimeter, a kind of silence blanketed the countryside that Bolan, survivor of enough Charlie mortar and rocket attacks, had come to regard as the calm before the storm until proved wrong; yet there was serenity about the moment just the same.

The ever-present distant sounds of choppers—C-130s, "spooky" helicopters, circling the skies on the lookout for VC—and the occasional hint of conversation were the only sounds to be heard from the rooftop sanctuary of Bolan and Shawnee.

They had not spoken for the past thirty minutes, a mutual, undeclared respect of the other's need for solitude by two people who cared about each other.

The chatter of natural jungle nightlife commenced from beyond the perimeter, while human nightlife inside the camp's walls made its presence known. Someone in one of the hooches cranked up the volume on a Jimi Hendrix album and an unrecorded, in-the-flesh voice let loose from the same direction. Off-duty grunts were letting off steam with a rebel yell that brought a chuckle from both Bolan and Shawnee. The mood of introspection between them shifted gears. Sort of.

"It's amazing," Bolan said, finishing his soda. "A few normal sounds can almost make you forget you're here."

Shawnee chuckled at that, too.

"You're a strange one, Sergeant Mercy. You're probably the only lifer I'll ever know who thinks Jimi Hendrix is a normal sound. I thought you were a Peter, Paul and Mary man."

"I mean normal, comparatively speaking," Bolan amended with a wink. "Compared to guns going off, Jimi sounds just fine. How are you doing, lady? Rough one, wasn't it?"

"No rougher than yours. But...I don't want to talk about that, Mack. None of it. Not now."

He could respect that too, just as he respected the lady.

Sassy, intelligent Shawnee. She of the fluctuating weight, a good soul, a brave plump NFG—New Fucking Guy, in Army vernacular—who had evolved before his eyes over the months they had known each other into the tough, shapely, raven-haired go-getter beside him now on this roof in the semidarkness.

The muggy climate was no good for stargazing or starlight. Indirect lighting from the base around them cast Shawnee's strikingly beautiful features in an almost candlelike glow.

These two had never been lovers, no, but in this setting, which was almost romantic, Bolan could not help but wonder briefly if his platonic relationship with this woman had evolved that way because sex would only have complicated a good friendship, or because circumstances in a war zone hardly lent themselves to budding romance.

She was fighting hard for control after working six hours in a battlefield emergency room.

"Let's talk about home," Bolan suggested quietly, near her but with his M-16 nearby, too.

Shawnee smiled but Bolan could tell that her strain did not disappear far beneath the surface.

"My home or yours?" she kidded.

"Got a letter from home," he said. "Ma says, 'hi.' She told me to ask you if you're such a smart girl, what are you doing befriendin' her oldest who she knows for a fact won't take orders from a woman, end quote."

Shawnee smiled a real smile this time.

"I'd like to meet your mom someday, Mack. Your whole family sounds so nice."

"The best," Bolan agreed with feeling, but he realized even as he spoke that talking about his family did not really ease him the way it should have.

The memory of his last moments with ma and pop, Johnny and Cindy, in Pittsfield Airport that warm July day, came flooding back to him. He recalled the punk loan-shark hoods who had roughed up his father, and the uneasy ominous premonition he had experienced as his flight left home. As much as he had tried he could not dismiss the inexplicable sensation that he would never see his loved ones again.

He had tried to pass the premonition off as the effect of being surrounded for too long by the human misery and suffering everywhere he looked in this land of death.

Every paycheck he sent to his parents was more than he had sent before he learned about their troubles with loan sharks, and though ma was always appreciative, neither she nor Cindy ever mentioned the hoods or the scene at the airport in their letters and, of course, Sam and Johnny did not write.

Bolan told himself that everything on the home front was okay again, but all the while he felt in his heart of hearts that such was not the case. And he continued to fight the frustration that there was nothing he could do to help his family because he was fighting this war.

Bolan found himself tugged from these ruminations by the woman beside him.

She suddenly seemed to lose all pretense of trying to keep it together and he imagined that somewhere inside Shawnee the emotional dam broke.

From grim experience he knew that a person, any person, even the best or the toughest, can only take so much. Bolan watched as she began to shake uncontrollably in spite of her attempts to keep it wrapped, and the tears came rolling down those high cheekbones like pearls glinting in the lights of the base.

Without really thinking, his heart told him to wrap her in his arms. She came to him willingly, desperately, her muffled sobbing bordering on hysteria as she nestled against his shoulder, as if to seek warmth.

"I'm...just so...so tired, Mack. S-six hours of trying to save the mangled bodies of young boys...*children*! I can't take any more of the *pain*! God forgive me for my weakness, but all I see is ugliness...emptiness. Oh, God, Mack...*I feel like I'm dying inside!*''

It was a plea, and what happened next blossomed into gently paced spontaneity born of two people's need to affirm their humanity. They shared that very special intimacy, experienced only by a man and a woman, and it did not surprise Bolan, though he had not expected it.

Both Bolan and Shawnee knew there was nothing romantic in what they were about to do. Nothing romantic, at least, in the accepted sense. It was simply an exercise in need.

For one heartbeat in this continuum, they needed each other, physically. Surrounded by death and the ravages of war, they agreed, tacitly, that they could draw strength from each other and, in the process, enrich their friendship.

For Shawnee's part the big man astride her body, stroking her ego, represented a kind of security.

He mitigated all the conflicts, it seemed, the inner ones that Shawnee harbored about sensitive things like her weight problem and her place in American society—she was Indian, after all—and the outer ones, like her place in the Vietnam conflict.

For Bolan, there were no promises to this woman beneath him, and he was making none. He could promise nothing, with Fate taking potshots at everyone.

The big guy knew that they could both lose it on the rooftop of this Vietnamese shack. All the same, he was going in with the special kinship he felt for Shawnee, one that could only be strengthened by the act of love. And let Fate play her deadly game.

Mack Bolan and Shawnee made love quietly for the sake of necessity and propriety, but also because the special feeling between them on that roof in the middle of a Special Forces base camp in the highlands of Vietnam, communicated something that had to be private and theirs alone.

He and this young woman were well matched in their first sexual encounter for Bolan in more than a year, since before his first tour of duty in Hell.

Bolan and Shawnee took their time with each other. The holding nearness became kisses, soft, then intimate but still soft, and no words passed between them.

Their movements were slow in the darkness, not a mad uncontrollable passion but an uncharted magic that could not be rushed or forced.

Shawnee gasped in delight beneath him, and after a few moments her body arched, and he felt the tightening of her embrace as she emitted tiny whimpering sounds.

The self-disciplined warrior played the gentleman and remained still, letting the lady ride out her orgasm. She sighed and relaxed, Bolan giving her time to bask in the afterglow of her release.

Shawnee forced down intimate loving woman sounds as she teethed his ear, and the hot expulsion of her sigh in his ear was all it took for Bolan to feel his own being in blind flight into a cresting wave of physical release.

He bit his tongue to stem the growl if pleasure he emitted into her tangled, damp hair. In a few more moments, it passed and man and woman relaxed on the roof of a hooch in the middle of a war zone. But the way Shawnee held him, her arms wrapping him to her, her legs entwined with his, their perspiration and heartbeats mingling, told Bolan that she did not want it to end just yet.

He nuzzled her neck, kissing her lightly there, and she murmured as an awareness of where they were slowly regained hold of their senses: the lights in the near distance, the sounds of the jungle night and the camp around them.

And with awareness of where they were came the realization of what had happened between them.

Bolan knew Shawnee was feeling it too when he lifted his head to look down into her eyes, which wore an expression he had never seen there before.

"Shawnee," he whispered into those eyes. "I'm...not sure what to say—"

"I know," the lady whispered back. "I don't know what to say either, Mack. So...let's not say anything, okay? Can we just...hold each other?"

He slid his arms around her torso as he rolled onto his side, drawing her with him, pressing snug against him, a knee curved across his legs, her head nestled in the crook of his arm in the timeless embrace of lovers in the moments after.

Her musky natural scent tantalized his senses, and his fingers traveled restlessly over her body.

The lady was right, of course, he told himself. There would be time later for talk.

He fought a pleasant temptation to drift asleep.

The abrupt, high-pitched whistling from overhead disrupted everything, snapping Bolan alertly into the combat consciousness that was his natural state.

"Incoming!" he snarled, flinging himself as a human shield across the startled lady.

Shawnee tried to gasp something as Bolan rolled atop her, pinning her this time with only survival on his mind. He clawed at his fatigues with one hand in a frenzied effort to dress himself, his other hand seeking his M-16.

A deafening explosion shattered the evening as a rocket exploded nearby, shaking the ground and the hooch where the lovers were caught in darkness. The blast flared into reddish-white somewhere inside the base perimeter.

Another rocket zapped in, then another, and within the heart-tumbling moments it took Shawnee to gather her clothes and scramble down the ladder at the back of the hooch, aided and guided by Bolan, a blistering barrage hammered the Special Forces base camp.

And everywhere the sharp blasts of thunder, lightning, destruction and hellfire of a Vietcong rocket and mortar attack rocked the night!

Thirteen

The night crackled with strobelike horror as blossoming fire balls of incredible intensity illuminated the dark Asian night. Earsplitting detonations erupted one after another, the deafening booms cascading like thunder across the lowlands. The blaze of return fire from mortars and machine guns answered the blistering attack as men hurried, yelling to one another to be heard above the hellish din.

Incomings impacted scurrying figures of soldiers inside the perimeter, spewing up ground and hurling human bodies into the flaming night.

A mortar hit the mobile home that served as the camp chapel. The vehicle tilted off the ground, bursting apart into flame.

Structures were taking direct hits, blurring into fire and smoke and flaming debris.

Bolan and Shawnee touched ground behind the hooch, and with a parting wave they separated without words, two professionals knowing their jobs.

Shawnee darted low in a run of gazellelike grace toward the ER structure. She did not waste time dodging from cover.

Destruction, bedlam and battle blazed everywhere, randomly.

Shawnee knew she would be needed with the other MASHers.

Bolan mentally wished her godspeed but did not wait to see if she made it.

He dashed to the front of the hooch he shared with his team members and came face-to-face with Hoffower, Loudelk and Andromede. They tumbled out of the hooch, sleepy-eyed but ready, each steadying his helmet with one hand, gripping assault rifles as they pulled up short, sliding chin straps into place.

Colonel Winters rushed over to them, shouting to be heard amid the sense-shredding cacophony of madness swelling around them.

"I've called in an air strike! Harrington, Pol and Washington are beefing up the ER," Winters shouted to Bolan. "Take your men to the—"

Winters was interrupted by an abrupt ringing silence that befell the night.

The explosions stopped.

The answering fire stopped.

An eerie quiet reigned that seemed every bit as deafening as the din that it suddenly, totally blanketed.

"We'd better reinforce the perimeter," Bolan snapped. "Charlie cuts a rocket and mortar attack this short, it means only one thing."

He was already turning to hurry toward the nearest stretch of perimeter, Winters nodding to the others to follow their team leader, when the 50-calibers resumed hammering the night with their chugging snarls.

Viet voices shouting battle cries, screaming up their courage, poured from positions from beneath the canopied foliage of the jungle line, one hundred or more charging, rifle-firing wraiths in the night, a black-pajama-clad human wave striking across the 450-yard killground in a suicidal assault.

The 50-caliber and other concentrated fire from inside the sandbagged base perimeter commenced toppling dozens of the shadows before they got anywhere near the defenders.

Some of the enemy force reached the concertina wire before bullets caught them, splaying tumbling bodies across the wire.

The claymores began detonating, eating up more VC in eyeball-searing explosions that leveled dozens of enemy attackers.

Andromede, Hoffower and Loudelk hustled after Bolan toward the nearest bunker.

Bolan counted six dead U.S. troopers, their blood still pumping across the ground where they had caught bullets while firing on the attackers.

The men of Bolan's team spread out to join the remaining men who covered this stretch.

Bolan, Hoffower, Loudelk and Flower Child opened fire across the sandbagged bunkers. They were rewarded with the sight of more VC toppling into the dust, but the fallen were instantly replaced by a seemingly unending suicide charge of VC.

The ones in front were firing as they braved the nonstop fire from the defenders, the bodies of the fallen utilized as makeshift bridges over stretches of concertina wire.

Someone ordered the explosives planted throughout the wire to be ignited, and the HE punctuated the flashes of machine-gun fire with more fire balls and tumbling, airborne bodies as VC were hurled backward by the blasts.

And still they kept coming.

Bolan, like the men near him, kept his M-16's barrel white-hot, triggering burst after burst, hardly needing to aim.

Incoming projectiles zinged their song of death, claiming another behind Bolan. Other bullets ricocheted off the ground everywhere, slapping into the sandbags.

And the attackers were closing in on the perimeter from every direction.

SP4C BILL HOFFOWER would have felt a damn sight more comfortable lobbing HE at the shadowy mass of advancing Vietcong, but the demolitions expert of Bolan's team hadn't had time to get his hands on any high explosive and so had to make do with the rifle with which he hammered death into the incoming assault.

Boom-Boom stood elbow to elbow with Bolan, Bloodbrother and Flower Child.

The three sniper-team members saw it happen at the same time when this battle corkscrewed into a deadly new twist.

VC attackers were pouring into the compound from two points where they had mustered the firepower needed to break through. The Communists stormed over the bodies of their fallen comrades across the wire.

Black-clad Cong guerrillas landed inside, shrieking crazed screams as they began unloading at Americans inside the perimeter.

These Charlies weren't all that brave, Hoffower knew. They'd been ordered into this suicide charge and would have been massacred by their NVA superiors had they refused; it had happened often enough, Boom-Boom knew from intel reports passed to the Executioner's team.

Then a new sound from overhead joined the insanity of war.

Two U.S. aircraft jetted in low for the air strike, jellying this mass of attackers outside the perimeter with napalm. The scorching agony did its awful work instantly as some of the attack force broke up amid the screams and the stench of burning flesh that filled the air.

Then the Vietcong bastards were busting through just a couple of yards down from Boom-Boom!

As if by silent agreement, Flower Child and Bloodbrother continued pouring on the firepower, holding secure this stretch of the perimeter. Bolan and Hoffower rushed toward the point where Communist terrorists were starting to trickle across a portion of the undefended barricade near the bodies of fallen American servicemen.

Boom-Boom and Bolan, affixing bayonets, came upon the first few VC who thought they had a clear path until Bolan and Hoffower gutted them, slashing in and out and turning to take out two more.

Three VC almost had enough time to track their rifles on the Americans before Hoffower and the Executioner turned them into three good Communists with twin blasts of autofire.

More were coming in.

Boom-Boom did not know how long he and Bolan could hold this stretch of perimeter as they crouched down to deliver more death to the attackers. Gunfire raged all around them, the screams of the dying, the attacking, the defending swallowed by the free-for-all of weapons, explosions.

Hoffower palmed a fresh clip into his rifle, realizing it was his last clip.

PETE FLETCHER, CLEON MURPHY, Ray Corbett and Gary Robbins had been baiting the troopers assigned to guard them since the attack began less than five minutes earlier.

The makeshift detention structure was modeled after the "cages" of the American Old West, a sturdy, three-walled rectangle, with the open bars of the fourth side securely latched to either end and chained and padlocked in the center.

Murphy appeared not to notice the attack raging around them. The black stood with both giant hands grasping the bars, snarling at the troopers on the other side of the bars who looked as if they would rather be on the perimeter defending their base.

"C'mon, let us outa here," Murphy yelled at the nearest soldier. "Looks like you dudes could use all the help you could get."

At that instant, several VC, who had breached the perimeter, ran yelling and screaming toward the center of the compound.

The soldiers outside the cell opened fire, toppling the VC.

Pete Fletcher, next to Murphy, worked hard to keep the nervousness he felt inside from showing, especially to the black prisoner.

"Forget it, Murph," he growled. "Bolan and Winters worked too damn hard to put us inside these bars to let us out that easy."

Robbins and Corbett sat on the narrow bench connected to the wall behind Fletcher and Murphy.

Robbins stood and joined them, shouting to be heard above the shooting and yelling from outside.

"And they know what we'd do if we got out of this damn cage," he snarled, trying his best to act tough. "But I wouldn't lift a finger to help the cruds who threw us in here. If I get anywhere near that goddamn Bolan, he's gonna be one fragged sonofabitch!"

Murphy sneered derisively.

"Big talk. You—"

A sudden pinging sound made the three of them duck as projectiles riddled the cell, too high for any hits. But the prisoners remained in a crouch.

Fletcher looked over his shoulder at Corbett, who had not budged from where he sat on the bench. Corbett's features looked blank, expressionless in the flickering illumination of fighting from outside the cell.

An exploding grenade blammed somewhere nearby.

The troopers standing guard outside the cell spun in the direction of the blast, starting to track their rifles toward the sound, when an identical explosion shattered their senses. It seemed to originate from inside the cell, it was that close.

Fletcher's world came apart, and then everything pinwheeled and tumbled for a few seconds that felt like an eternity as reality became unglued.

The cagelike structure shuddered and tilted forward under the power of the blast, and the cage slammed into the two sentries, knocking them to the ground. The impact stunned both guards.

Fletcher shook the numbness from his ringing head as he tried to stand. He saw Murphy getting to his feet a few inches away, Corbett and Robbins groaning themselves back into consciousness but not as quickly as Fletcher and Murphy.

The two sentries were struggling to extricate themselves from beneath the cell. Their M-16s had landed halfway between the suddenly freed prisoners and the two troopers who were now almost out from under.

All Fletcher could think about now was getting his hands on one of those rifles. He grabbed one; and as he felt its welcome weight, he saw Murphy snatch the other fallen weapon.

Together the two men tracked the M-16s around on the soldiers as both troopers finally clawed their way out from beneath the cell structure.

"No!" one of the sentries had time to cry out.

Murphy and Fletcher fired into the two soldiers; short, vicious bursts that flung the men across the overturned cell.

Murphy spun and triggered his M-16. Four stealthily advancing VC were bloodily pulped into oblivion, their weapons flying from dead fingers.

Robbins had fully recovered. He dashed over and picked up one of the rifles, a Soviet SKS carbine, and extra ammo pouches from one of the dead VC. Robbins looked back and forth from Fletcher to Murphy, not sure now whom to address as leader.

"What the hell do we do next?"

"We blast our way off this base," Murphy snarled. "Best chance we got is on our own."

Fletcher nodded agreement.

"But first we go to my hooch."

The intensity of the fighting continued along the perimeter, only a handful of VC actually penetrating inside the compound.

No one had yet noticed the jailbreak amid the swirling confusion of battle.

"Your hooch?" snarled Murphy. "What the hell for? Those VC aren't going to work as a distraction too damn much longer! I say we bust our way through them and—"

"*After* my hooch," Fletcher insisted. "Trust me, f'chrissake! I've got a passport out of Vietnam for all of us!"

Robbins looked toward Corbett.

"What about him?"

Corbett was kneeling where he had been thrown by the deflected blast of the grenade. He looked sick. He pulled his gaze from the bodies of the two slaughtered sentries, toward the three rifle-toters standing above him in the swirling haze of battle.

"Shock," Fletcher growled.

"I—I can't do any…anymore." Corbett's hollow voice mirrored his empty eyes. "Leave me…I—I'm staying right here…."

"You got that right, asshole," Murphy said with a snicker.

He triggered a burst that flipped Corbett over backward. The man's body somersaulted into a puddle of his own life forces, blown out his back from the ripping bullets.

Fletcher held himself in check from swinging his M-16 on Murphy.

"You crazy sonofabitch! Why—"

Murphy glared at Fletcher, swinging his own rifle and hate-filled eyes, and Fletcher knew if he tried to trigger on Murphy now, Murphy would return the fire and they'd both die.

"I don't carry deadweight," the black snarled. "You gonna make something of it, Lieutenant Honkie?"

The sounds of battle were dying down, still plenty of shouting and gunfire but no more VC rampaging through the compound, the tide of battle turning.

Robbins hurried over to where Murphy and Fletcher confronted each other.

"C'mon, you guys! Another minute and some-one's going to see what's happening here."

Fletcher backed away from the confrontation.

"Murphy, can you hot-wire a jeep?"

"With the best. Why?"

Dumb shit, thought Fletcher, but he had no choice at all now. He knew he needed these two morons more than ever.

"Find one. Robbins, cover him. Get over to my hooch and pick me up on the fucking double!"

Robbins started off, but Murphy halted him with a grip on the arm and a speculative look back at Fletcher.

"What the hell's so important in your hooch?"

"I told you. Our passport out of this armpit country," Fletcher snarled. "Now get a move on, goddammit! You want to be caught and tossed into another cell? Or do you want your chances out there with me?"

"I'll take my chances out there," Murphy growled, turning to leave with Robbins. "And so will you, *boy*."

Fletcher turned and hurried toward his hooch. He met no one, the base occupied with the fighting. As he ran, he cast a glance through the swirling smoke of battle-shrouded gloom.

The attack was being repulsed.

Fletcher saw dozens of sprawled U.S. soldiers, some dead, some groaning with the pain of their wounds. Fletcher ran past a fallen trooper whom no one had come to help yet.

The man lifted pain-racked eyes and extended an arm as Fletcher ran past.

"Please...help me..." moaned a weak voice.

Fletcher did not stop.

He reached his hooch and dashed inside, going straight through the low hallway to his cubicle. He hurried to his bunk and knelt on it, setting his rifle down and pawing at a small square of the paneled wall adjacent to his bunk.

The renegade lieutenant worked open a loose portion of the partition, all the while conscious that the gunfire from outside was tapering off to sporadic exchanges as the defenders apparently drove back the assault. He also tried to remain aware of any movement from inside the hooch, but he had the structure to himself, his fellow officers seeing to the defense of the base.

He reached inside the small space he had hollowed out behind the strip of mildewed wall.

He withdrew a folded sheet of onionskin typing paper from where he had hidden it, neatly folded.

He folded it again and slipped the paper into his tunic as he spun to retrieve his rifle and bolt out of his quarters into the narrow corridor leading to the exit.

He almost made it when the doorway filled with another officer hurrying inside; one of Fletcher's hoochmates.

First Lieutenant Tim Shiner pulled up short, startled on his way into the hooch for something, not expecting to find Fletcher standing before him.

"Pete, what the hell?" Shiner asked, puzzled. "They let you out to help fight?"

"Not quite," Fletcher said.

He opened fire with a short burst that pulverized Shiner, slamming him backward out of the hooch.

Fletcher did not spare the burbling corpse a second glance. He hoofed out of the shack, sidestepping Shiner's body and the pool of blood spreading beneath it.

The battle had tapered off altogether.

The VC attack was over, the echoes of battle rumbling across the mountain darkness beyond the perimeter, men shouting for medics, crying out in pain, calling back and forth to one another in the immediate aftermath of the attack.

A jeep driven by Cleon Murphy careened around the far corner of this stretch of hooches. Murphy drove full speed to where Fletcher emerged from his hooch. The jeep thumped over the fallen body of a dead soldier.

Robbins held onto the jeep's frame for dear life.

Murphy braked to a stop so abruptly, the vehicle nearly flipped over its front end.

Fletcher leaped into the rear.

"Gun it out the south gate," he snapped at Murphy. "That's our best bet."

"Hey, what are you men doing?" a voice from behind shouted.

Three troopers advanced on the run toward the jeep, not sure of what was happening but investigating anyhow.

Robbins triggered off a burst from his SKS, cutting down the approaching troopers like a scythe slicing through wheat.

Murphy gunned the jeep, rocketing away from there before the dead troopers hit the ground.

The jeep swerved wildly into a skidding turn, Murphy upshifting, flooring the pedal to the metal, the jeep on a high-speed run toward one of the gates.

Fletcher hoped the element of surprise would be enough.

The defenders along the perimeter had their attention centered on the far side of those gates.

Fletcher braced himself against the frame of the vehicle in preparation for the smash when Murphy rammed through the gates.

FLOWER CHILD SPOTTED IT FIRST and pointed for Bolan and Boom-Boom to look.

"What the hell?"

Bolan and Hoffower turned in time to see the U.S. Army jeep juggernaut through the front gate of the camp, the speed of the vehicle flinging the wood-frame-and-barbed-wire gate into every direction along with the body of one soldier who had survived the attack from the Cong.

Traveling without lights, the jeep exited the compound and sped off into the night along the dirt road that led from the camp.

Andromede shook his head.

"Not at all a groovy thing to do, least till Charlie's had a chance to fade."

Loudelk palmed a fresh clip into his smoking M-16.

"If that's who I think it was, dodging Charlie will be the least of their worries."

Bolan nodded, shifting his attention from the direction into which the jeep had disapepared into the night. He surveyed the smoking panorama of carnage and suffering that was the inside of Camp Three-Niner-Bayou.

"There's only one bunch who'd want out enough to risk dodging VC."

Pol hurried over to them through the confusion of the battle's aftermath; men regrouping, others assisting medics, helping the wounded.

"Colonel Winters wants you right away, Sarge. Big trouble."

Flower Child looked as if he wished he had a joint.

"If it's bigger than Charlie, it just might be too fucking heavy for me," he bitched. But he kept pace with Bolan, Boom-Boom and Bloodbrother as Pol led the way through the compound cluttered with debris and bodies, toward the overturned pile of ruin that had been the holding cell.

Colonel Winters stood with a few other men near three bodies.

Winters turned to meet Bolan and his men with none of his usual heartiness. He nodded to the dead troopers.

"They killed these two men. And Fletcher killed Lieutenant Shiner over at their hooch. Shiner must have surprised Fletcher in the act."

"Looks like they left one behind," Boom-Boom noted.

He spit in the general direction of Ray Corbett's bloody remains.

Bolan did not take his eyes from the dead American servicemen who had been entrusted with guarding Fletcher and his men.

Then he looked up to meet Colonel Winters's grim eyes.

"I've got to go after them, sir."

"I know you do, Sergeant. And for more reasons than you think. You want Fletcher because now he's dirtier than he ever was. Any man with an ounce of decency would have helped us defend this base, if anything. Fletcher, Murphy and Robbins killed their own, then deserted. Yeah, Sarge, you're going after those three, all right. Let's take a briefing. There's a lot you don't know and there isn't one damn second to lose. Fletcher and his two punks have got the outcome of this lousy war in their hip pockets, and I do not mean figuratively."

Bolan indicated his men to remain behind to help with the cleanup while he strode with Winters toward the bunker.

He was glad for the brief rest and recreation he'd had earlier in the day when he'd had time to himself after the hit to rescue Sioung's wife and child from Major Linh, and the bust in Pleiku.

He was especially grateful for the time spent with Shawnee. He felt his inner batteries were recharged in spite of the unanswered questions left hanging when their intimacy had been so rudely interrupted.

Bolan wondered how Shawnee was doing, if she had escaped those VC rockets and the Cong who had breached the perimeter for a while.

The night was quiet again, but the human sounds of recovery and pain and the stench of smoking rubble bore testimony to what had happened here.

Bolan knew it would be a while before he got another chance to "grab five."

Lousy war, yeah.

About to escalate even hotter for Bolan and the men of his team, according to Colonel Winters.

Without one damn second to lose.

The fire was heating up.

Hell was about to get hotter.

Fourteen _____

"Fletcher got his hands on a list," Colonel Winters began. "As you know, we've had a close watch on him for some time. We didn't think he'd had any opportunity to be near classified data on his own during the past few months. We always made sure someone was with him, someone we trusted, which includes nearly every man on this base."

Bolan nodded. "You didn't want to tip Fletcher that we were trying to bust him for the drug deals. He'd have bolted."

"Right. But the slippery bastard did get his hands on something, anyway," Winters grumbled. "Don't ask me how. I thought we had that boy under around-the-clock observation, but somehow he managed it."

"Another accomplice?"

"Besides Murphy, Robbins and Corbett? Possibly, but Fletcher would be smart enough to know that every additional accomplice means another weak link in his chain. He probably hated having Murphy or the other two wise to his activities, but a man in his racket needs the muscle."

"What list does he have?"

Winters deferred to the man sitting with them in the colonel's makeshift office in the Special Forces base command bunker.

The bunker buzzed with the aftermath of the repulsed Vietcong attack.

"As intel officer," the third man in the room told Bolan, "Fletcher somehow managed to get his hands on a copy of a top-secret classified list of fifty of our most highly placed, deep-cover people working in the North, who feed intel to U.S. and ARVN forces."

Lee Tuttle, age forty-seven, stocky, salt-and-pepper crew cut, clad in fatigues, was Camp Three-Niner-Bayou's CIA control.

"Fletcher has the list with him now?" Bolan asked.

"Affirmative," Colonel Winters said. "That's what I meant before by saying the outcome of the war, Sergeant. Elimination of the fifty people named on that list would totally collapse our handle on enemy troop movement, VC strategy, everything that's given us what little edge we've managed to gain."

"Fletcher could only have gotten his hands on a copy of that list during the past twenty-four hours," Tuttle said. "It was discovered missing just hours ago and Fletcher's time is pretty much accounted for ever since he left the base this morning to, uh, take care of Colonel Quan."

"Any idea where Fletcher's headed?" Bolan inquired.

"We think he intends to connect with someone you may care to renew acquaintance with," Winters replied. "Your target who got away this morning. Major Linh."

"Linh was trasnferring today from that stockade where they were holding Sioung's family," Bolan recalled.

Winters nodded.

"Ten klicks inside Cambodia, almost due west of here."

"Fletcher and his crew would have the balls to walk up to Linh and try to sell him that list," Bolan agreed.

"We have an idea that Fletcher may have been filtering out secret information all along," Tuttle said. "We've been playing that boy, feeding him nothing but misinformation for the past few months, keeping him away from the real stuff, and some enemy patterns could be interpreted as having been motivated by the poop we gave to Fletcher. We just didn't have the proof. And now he's playing us."

The field phone sounded on the colonel's desk.

Winters grabbed it, growled a few words, listened, then replaced the receiver and looked grimly across his desk at Bolan and Tuttle.

"They made it through or around those dispersing VC. The jeep was found where the Route 6-B road ends."

"Which confirms our reading," the CIA man asserted. "Fletcher and his men are heading for that NVA base. Damn. Linh is due to arrive and assume command there some time tonight; probably already has."

"They had to ditch the jeep once they made it past the VC," Bolan said. "That NVA base is in the middle of some of the most rugged terrain in the area."

"The mountains and jungle will slow them," Winters agreed, "but Murphy and Robbins are seasoned pros. They'll make it unless we stop them in time. Those are your orders, Sergeant Bolan."

"I should be after them now," Bolan growled, getting to his feet. "I don't think I should take the whole team with me on this one, sir."

Tuttle nodded approvingly.

"I'm glad you appreciate the, er, delicacy of the situation, Sergeant. Cambodia is supposedly neutral, the lying bastards. They've allowed the NVA to set up artillery only yards inside their borders at some points and we're not supposed to touch them while they blow us to hell. Nonetheless, any obviously U.S.-related incident must be avoided at all costs."

"I'll take three men with me," Bolan said, pausing on his way out, "and I'll need the exact coordinates of Linh's base."

"At least you're moving by night," Winters said. "It's going to get damn hairy out there, and after you cross the frontier into Cambodia. Which is why we've taken an added precaution, sending along a special guide with you on this mission." Winters looked toward the doorway behind Bolan. "Come in, Sioung."

The Montagnard guerrilla leader stepped into the office, clad in dark camou, carrying an M-16.

Sioung addressed the question in Bolan's eyes.

"Ti Bahn and Tran Le are safe because you and your men risked your lives, Sergeant Mercy. I have spent my life in the mountains where the savage, Major Linh, awaits to receive the list your lieutenant has stolen."

"It will be good to have you along," Bolan said. He had spent enough time with the Mont fighter on previous missions to know Sioung could track a mosquito through the jungle frontier of the Vietnam-Cambodia border. He glanced to Colonel Winters and Tuttle. "I'll get two men and prepare to move out immediately then, gentlemen, if that's it for the briefing."

"Good luck, son," Winters said, returning Bolan's salute.

"And don't endanger yourself or any of your men needlessly in trying to bring Fletcher back alive," Tuttle advised. "The only thing that matters is that the list not fall into Linh's hands. Fletcher dead or alive makes no difference."

"It makes a difference to me," was Bolan's parting shot.

After he was gone, Tuttle nodded knowingly to Howlin' Harlan Winters.

"And we both know what that means, don't we, Colonel? Fletcher ain't coming back alive this time." The Company man stared out the doorway through which Bolan and Sioung had exited. "I just hope Bolan and the men going with him make it back. That is one damn near impossible mission we've just handed that soldier."

"If there's one soldier I'd pick to take on those odds," Winters replied, "you can damn well bet it wouldn't be anyone else but Mack Bolan."

Tuttle reached toward the chest pocket of his fatigues for a cigar.

"And I hope to hell you're right, Colonel, because as it stands right now, that Executioner of yours *is* the only chance we've got."

BOLAN HAD TO CHUCKLE at the heartfelt disappointment registering across the faces of Boom-Boom Hoffower, Flower Child Andromede and Pol Blancanales when they heard that they were not invited along on this mission.

"Man, that's some heavy shit across that border," Andromede reminded them. "The team's going to need one another more than ever, Sarge!"

Pol nodded emphatically.

"Just you, Gunsmoke, Deadeye and Blood-brother? Penetrating behind their lines? Sarge, you are gonna need firepower and plenty of it."

"Not to mention a little boom-boom," Hoffower added.

Gunsmoke Harrington confidently patted his two holstered six-guns. They nestled in their customary handles-forward position in quickdraw leather low on his hips.

"A little faith, pards, if you please," he drawled. "Linh and his doggies'll be the ones requirin' reinforcements after the Texas Twister gets through with 'em."

"And don't forget Sioung," Deadeye added with a nod to the Mont fighter, who waited patiently outside the hooch. "Sioung knows this country better than any of us, including Major Linh."

Bolan started out of the hooch.

"Let's go," he instructed Deadeye, Gunsmoke and Bloodbrother.

Bolan was togged again in camou fatigues, like the three men he had chosen for this mission.

The Executioner toted his M-16 and was equipped with the standard commando accoutrements for a night mission: a Gerber Mark II knife, the handle positioned for fast cross draw at upper chest level, plenty of extra ammo and canteens full to avoid sloshing noises. Each man carried a small supply of rations. Bolan and Gunsmoke wore facial blackout for additional night camouflage.

Pol, Boom-Boom and Flower Child accompanied Bolan, Gunsmoke, Bloodbrother and Deadeye outside the hooch where they joined up with Sioung. Then the five-man unit started toward the front gate of the compound.

"Sarge, one last time," Pol said as their small group strode through the base, which had more or less recovered from the attack of thirty minutes ago. "At least let me and the guys cover your ass up the road to the point where Fletcher and his fellas ditched their jeep."

"Pol's right," Flower Child agreed as they reached the gate. "You guys should at least have wheels to travel in. Humping after those cats sounds like a real downer."

"The jeep Fletcher left behind was only a couple of klicks from here," Bolan said, "and Charlie is waiting around out there to pick off the first vehicle that comes through."

"And Fletcher and his boys could have used up all the luck there is tonight getting through those VC," Washington said.

"Haven't met a VC yet who could tag *us* coming through," Bloodbrother added to Pol, Flower Child and Boom-Boom. "Sarge is right, guys. It'll be safer for us and we'll make better time on foot, especially with Sioung to guide us."

The Mont nodded.

"If your objective is to avoid VC and capture the man, Fletcher, it shall be so. Sioung would rather kill all VC!"

"Our mission is to stop Fletcher, Murphy and Robbins," Bolan reminded them. "And to stop that list from falling into Linh's hands."

"*And* to get back with our asses in one piece," Gunsmoke tacked on. "Let's not forget the most important part of this rodeo!"

The sentries at the gate unbolted the clasps and swung the gate inward just wide enough for Bolan and his men to exit single file.

Other troopers near the gate aimed their rifles out to fan the darkness beyond the perimeter. Nothing seemed to move, but every man knew hostile eyes were watching from out there beyond the killground.

Bolan was well aware that his small group's only hope lay with their speed and night camouflage. The commandos would dart from the perimeter to the relative safety of the jungle line without the VC even getting wise to the fact that anyone had left the camp.

No sweat.

If it worked.

Bolan looked to Hoffower, Andromede and Blancanales.

"This is it, then. Hang tough here. Tell the truth, I feel better knowing some of the team are staying behind to keep an eye on Zitter and Schwarz and all those nurses. Keep 'em out of trouble, guys."

"The nurses or our guys?" Gunsmoke cracked.

Before Flower Child, Pol or Boom-Boom could reply, Bolan led his group out through the opening of the gate, vanishing from sight of Bolan's team who remained behind.

They turned to prepare for the eventuality of another Cong attack this night, though every grunt on the base knew it was highly unlikely considering the enemy losses from the assault repulsed thirty minutes earlier.

American casualties had been light, the compound cleared of wounded and dead, the smoldering fires extinguished.

Blancanales reflected that since he had not seen Bolan, Harrington, Washington, Loudelk or Sioung within heartbeats after they had left the base perimeter, then it stood to reason that the spying eyes of Charlie from somewhere out in the night had missed seeing them leave, too.

Pol hoped so.

THE EXECUTIONER PAUSED and whirled just short of the jungle tree line, swinging his M-16 around to cover Sioung, Dead Eye, Gunsmoke and Bloodbrother as they gained cover of the wall of the jungle.

The only illumination came from the near-distant lights of Base Camp 105-A behind them.

There had been no response from the VC, which Bolan knew were scattered all around them.

The Communist SOP after an attack like the one launched against the base tonight was for the Cong force to disperse, more or less disintegrate, into the surrounding jungle, village and hamlet.

This was perhaps the most frustrating aspect of this strange war, Bolan reflected, suspicious of the eerie nighttime stillness that enveloped the natural insect and animal sounds of the bush.

The American military was attempting to wage a war against an invisible enemy that could materialize, strike, then dematerialize with such stunning speed that it invariably dead-ended retaliatory action.

The NVA forces stayed safely inside Cambodia and Laos except for their own lightning strikes at American targets.

The VC were only around, it seemed, when they were seeking blood; at other times they were that farmer tending his rice fields or the teenage girl pedaling along on her bicycle or the old man or woman sitting in front of their hut watching the passing scene of military occupation with unreadable countenance.

It was this about the war in Southeast Asia that made Bolan suspect, from a purely realistic standpoint, it could well prove to be an unwinnable conflict as far as the U.S. and Saigon governments were concerned.

He remained in low combat crouch for a few seconds after his men faded into the murky cover of the jungle behind him. He tracked sharp eyes and a steady M-16 along their backtrail, along the jungle line merging with the night to either direction.

When he was sure there had been no apparent VC response to their pullout from the camp, that they had made a clean getaway thus far, Bolan backpedaled the last few paces and lost himself in the humid, smothering closeness of the bush to join his team. Then, without pausing, he signaled them to follow.

Bolan led the way, followed closely by Sioung.

The small unit forced their way farther into the bush, angling toward the point where the jeep abandoned by Fletcher had been reported, toward where Sioung would pick up the trail.

Then the chase would really be on.

Unless Fletcher decided to hold back and try to ambush his pursuers.

Bolan had warned those men traveling with him that the VC and NVA forces were not their only enemies this night.

He willed himself to concentrate solely on the dangerous mission ahead, but he could not help wondering how Shawnee was doing.

She would be busy at the ER with the wounded after the assault...if she had escaped injury herself.

Bolan wasn't sure what to make of the tryst between him and Shawnee in those stolen moments on the roof of his hooch just before the attack.

He forced himself to stop thinking about it and push on.

Deeper into this night of danger where hell burned hottest.

Interlude
_____

Southern Death stalked away from the guest house that was, in fact, the bunkhouse for Kenny The Kid Ensalvo's off-duty Mob hardmen.

Five hundred yards to the main house.

Through the darkness of this wet night on an outjutting of California coast near Balboa.

Executioner Bolan traversed the distance with the ghosts of his past, a blacksuited nighthitter drawing closer to the three-level mansion. Inside, a marked cannibal named Kenny The Kid had gathered together the warring hoodlum factions bickering for control of the illegal billions to be skimmed from Southern Cal.

Targets for the Executioner.

He gained the midpoint between the guest house, where he had planted the timed plastique, and the south corner of Ensalvo's home, when one of the two-man patrols rounded the far corner of the residence.

Bolan eyeballed the two within fractions of a heartbeat, thanks to his NVD goggles.

The night penetrator flung himself to the damp ground, the moisture of the earlier rain not penetrating the special material of his black combat suit. From the ground he tracked his Ingram on the two sentries.

The approaching hardmen had not noticed the subtle shift in the nighttime gloom when Bolan landed flat, for they did not wear NVD goggles.

The Mafia soldiers patrolled the south wall of the house, their audible footfalls evidencing the street habit of walking as loudly as they cared to on pavement, not realizing this had become a killzone where a jungle combat vet could kill by sound as well as sight.

Bolan could have taken these two out easily but he stayed his finger on the Ingram's trigger.

It was not yet time for this hit to go hard.

Another minute or less, hell, yeah.

But first he had to make it to that house where Ensalvo and the real targets were—not to mention another half dozen guards.

And so he watched the Mafia street soldiers, imported by Ensalvo as added security for this parlay, as the two-man patrol walked by, clearly delineated through the infrared night-vision goggles he wore.

Bolan utilized the seconds it took for the patrol to move past his position by looking back across the sloping terrain toward the gate house. He could discern the second two-man foot patrol still inside the guardhouse beyond the bulletproof glass where they jawboned with the hoods stationed at the front gate.

The shotgun-toting sentry team near the house marched into the damp, dark distance, away from Bolan's cover.

He was up and moving, conscious that his timing over the next few seconds would play a large part in the effectiveness of those explosives about to go off at the bunkhouse.

He reached the main house, and froze momentarily at the base of the wall for a final quick visual recon. Then he edged along toward the oak double doors at the front of the residence where soft lighting from an old-fashioned, wrought-iron lamp limned the front stoop of the house.

The homey, golden glow did not extend beyond more than a dozen feet in any direction.

The coastal breeze nipped sharply, damp, salty, but it felt good, clean, pure, to the shadowy figure with the Ingram who was about to reign such hellfire upon these environs.

He paused again, hugging the ground along the house beneath a row of darkened windows, calculating adjustment to the falling numbers of this hit to accommodate the delay with the sentry patrol.

Twenty-four seconds to the blowup, by Bolan's count.

Then the killing would begin.

There came to him the click of a door being unlatched, then one of the front doors opened and a nondescript hardguy armed with a rifle stepped outside onto the front step, closing the door behind him.

Bolan did not move, maintaining his position in the darkness just beyond the pool of light. He had intended to take those front doors, and the hoods he knew would be inside, in one smooth roll-through upon the detonation of the planted explosives.

The hardman, obviously a ranker, patted his pockets, came up with a cigarette and lit it, but the hood's rifle stayed ready as he scanned the night, not seeing Bolan.

Bolan did not recognize the man's face to come up with a name from the Executioner's extensive mental mug file.

The shadowy wraith that was Death stalking this killzone, remained motionless in the calm before hellfire stormed, counting off the final heartbeats to the anticipated explosion.

KENNY THE KID ENSALVO tried to keep his mind off Mack Bolan and on the infighting between the opposing street hood factions seated opposite each other at the table in front of the Don of San Diego.

Don of San Diego.

Kenny the Kid liked the sound of that.

He wanted it to stay that way.

The bickering between the young black street tough on Ensalvo's left, and the Hispanic punk to his right, continued over some bone of contention that had slipped Kenny's mind, the thirty-six-year-old boss realized with annoyance.

Bobby Trick sat at the opposite end of the long table from Ensalvo, watching his boss for any sign to act.

Bobby "Trick" Compsari, Kenny's *consigliere*, was Kenny's age; Kenny had brought Bobby along with him during The Kid's swift, brutal rise to power after Bolan had wiped out the Marcello faction only months ago.

Bolan! thought Kenny for the thousandth time, bristling inside.

The word on the streets was that the Executioner was somewhere in San Diego, and though Kenny did not like to gamble, the boss of San Diego was willing to wager that Mack Bolan's rumored presence in the area, and this very meeting chaired by Ensalvo, could not be a coincidence no matter which way you cut it.

Ensalvo rose abruptly and slammed a fist on the table between the black, the Hispanic and the bodyguard each street hood had brought into the room.

The bickering ceased, their attention snatched by the towering, angry boss.

"All right, all right, you slobs, you listen up and listen fuckin' good! I didn't call you two clowns together here for you to claw each other's face off." Kenny continued in an easier voice. "We're here to clear up the differences between you, to put together a smooth running machine that will pay off for all of us."

"Then you tell the spic here that the hos in my territory is my hos," the black snarled viciously, "and no wetback motherfucker from crosstown is takin' a bite out of it."

The Hispanic flared into a hot display of verbal fireworks in Spanish, and both Mexican punks started to reach for concealed weapons instinctively until they remembered their weapons had been checked at the front door when they came in thirty minutes earlier.

Ensalvo tugged his left ear, a seemingly nonchalant gesture but actually a signal to Bobby Trick.

The *consligiere* once again lived up to his name, responding to the signal by whipping up the Uzi submachine gun from where he had secretly affixed the weapon to the bottom of the table.

Bobby swung the Uzi's ugly little snout back and forth between the two-man factions facing off across the table.

That got everyone's attention real fast.

The squabbling and macho posturing between the blacks and Hispanics ceased as if flicked off by a switch, the undivided attention of the four hoods zeroing in on Kenny Ensalvo.

Kenny moved to stand behind Bobby Trick, who kept the Uzi covering the other four.

"Now maybe you boys'll be willing to listen to reason and straighten out this squabbling," Kenny suggested, gloating at the fear mingled with surprise and anger flashing across the faces of the street gang bosses.

The black relaxed back into his chair a little.

"I thought this was a parlay without heat, man."

Kenny laughed in their faces.

"Can't let you boys forget who the boss is, punk. You two fuckers agree to get along, fine, you both get a piece of what I hand out to you. You figured maybe it was some other way? You figure I got all this—" Ensalvo spread his arms in a wave that took in the exclusive residence around them, feeling himself building up a head of steam "—by being pussy enough to let some stumblebum street thugs come waltzing in here and tell me what's what? You two bums agree to work together and get the fuck out of my sight, or we work something else out here and now."

The black hardly took time to consider his reply. He tried to play it cool and pretend that Bobby Trick's Uzi was not aimed in his direction, that he wasn't scared of dying, but he was, he was.

"Uh, yeah, uh, okay, Mr. Ensalvo...didn't mean no disrespect to the family, man...uh, sir. I, uh, got the streets of Watts sewn up. I'm willing to hand over some of what I've built up for the payback your backing will bring. Sure, I'm in."

Ensalvo glared at the Hispanic.

"What about you, taco face?"

The Mexican hood bristled with rage, and both he and his bodyguard started to rise from their seats.

"I spit on you and your offer," the Mexican snarled angrily in fractured English, starting to work up some saliva to do just that.

"Bobby," Kenny said softly.

Bobby Trick triggered a noisy burst from the Uzi, which the Hispanics' flaring anger had led them to temporarily overlook.

The spray of bullets from the jerking submachine gun in Bobby's hands ripped apart the two Mexican street hoods as they began to stand. The fusillade slammed them backward over their chairs, the two bodies collapsing and streams of blood pumping wildly beneath them as they died.

Kenny looked away with distaste from the crimson slicks staining the floor of his conference room on the second floor of his house. But it could be worse, he reasoned; he'd had to dispatch a fair share of pains-in-the-ass, just like these troublesome spies, he reminded himself, which was why the floor of the meeting room was bare polished wood, unlike the carpeting Kenny favored in most of the other rooms of the house.

Ensalvo idly flicked his hand back and forth to clear some of the hazy gunsmoke that drifted lazily in the air, the bite of cordite sharp in his nostrils.

"Like I said, we work something else out," he repeated quietly.

The black hoodlum tore his eyes from the bubbling remains of what had been the two Hispanics.

"And, uh, like I said, Mr. Ensalvo, sir, I'm, uh, at your disposal."

"I know you are, punk." Kenny snickered, turning away as if the black and his bodyguard weren't there. "I'm glad you know it, too. Now maybe we can talk some business."

As he spoke, Kenny gazed out at the pitch darkness beyond the windows, feeling good.

He loved the expression of naked fear in the suckers' eyes when they realized all at once that he, Kenny Ensalvo, held the most precious power there was— the power to grant and take away human life.

It was a real good feeling that almost made Kenny forget the rumors about Mack Bolan being around.

When he rememberd Bolan again, he suddenly realized what a prime target he made at this moment, framed in the lighted window, to a sniper outside.

Kenny knew something about Mack Bolan's history. He knew Bolan had earned his handle, the Executioner, during the Vietnam War as a sniper without equal.

Kenny hurriedly sidestepped and moved to pull the drapes across the window.

He was reaching for the draw cord to close the drapes, glancing out the window into the night in the seconds before he blotted it out, when the guest house where the off-duty soldiers slept suddenly blew sky-high with a blast that set the night afire.

WHEN THE GUEST HOUSE tore apart the wet night into fury and flame, transforming pieces of the structure and bloody human remains into flying debris, Bolan blitzed into action.

His first move, Bolan knew from his extensive knowledge of organizational SOP on Mob hardsites, had to be the elimination of the headcock of this security detail.

The exploding bunkhouse and the shrill screams that needled the night commanded everyone's stunned attention for short, vital heartbeats. Those Mafia hoods who survived the immediate blast quickly roasted to death.

The gate house beyond the explosion spit out the four hoods who stared stupidly at the flames and descending debris from the blast. They brought up their weapons, tracking the fire-flickering night for they knew not what.

Bolan estimated he had but vanishing seconds before the two-man sentry patrol he'd just dodged came dashing to investigate from where he had last seen them.

The headcock, or security chief, at the front door registered an almost comical double take when the explosion from 250 yards caused his jaw to flap open. The cigarette he'd just lighted fell forgotten, sparking unnoticed ashes across his jacket while he rapidly unslung a rifle from his shoulder.

To avoid revealing his presence, the Executioner came in to take out this guy at the last possible instant, knowing how close the numbers would be shaved during the next minute now that the hit had gone hard.

The rifle wielder barely had time to register awareness of the presence of his executioner, emit the start of a gasped oath and start to pull the shotgun, still half on his shoulder, before the spectral attacker materialized before him.

Bolan sailed in, swiping the rifle off the man's shoulder and out of his grip with a sideways movement of his fist that held the Ingram.

The blow was strong enough to knock the hood momentarily off balance. Then Bolan's left hand and arm straightened out to deliver a fatal blow to the gunner's throat, crushing his Adam's apple and cutting off his air supply. He uttered a wheezy sound before his lifeless body fell to the ground.

The damp ocean air muffled echoes of the explosion that had devastated the guest house a few seconds earlier.

Hoods and activity bustled from every direction: inside the house, and down by the gate house where sentries started to advance slowly, not sure of what was going down.

The nighthitter was satisfied. For the moment.

The explosives had done their job.

Boom-Boom would've been proud, thought Bolan.

The headcock taken care of, he turned toward the oak double doors, ready to kick them open, when a minor housecock from inside unexpectedly obliged, yanking one of the doors inward with a concerned expression across his face, looking in the direction of the explosion.

Bolan blew the expression and the face right off the guy's head, sending the body hurtling back inside, leaving the door open a notch.

Bolan unhooked grenades from his belt, but before he could set the seven-second fuse, the two-man sentry team he had encountered earlier came running from around the nearest corner of the house, rushing to investigate the ferocious blast that had demolished the bunkhouse and its occupants.

The Executioner swung his Ingram in their direction and touched off a short spray of bullets that toppled the running men into somersaulting deadfalls as if tripped by ankle-high wires. Bolan held the greande in his left hand, pinned the fuse with his teeth and lobbed the grenade through the open door.

Fifteen
Cambodia ————————————————

Murphy had the point.

Fletcher watched the black man's broad back as Murphy moved through the jungle a few yards ahead of him.

Robbins brought up the rear.

Having a punk like Robbins behind him gave Fletcher an uneasy itch, but it was a hell of a lot better than worrying about Murphy. At least this way he could keep an eye on Murphy and make sure the hulking black giant didn't try anything.

Fletcher figured he was safe enough for the time being, all things considered; safe, at least from his two "buddies."

He not only had the list, but he knew exactly where their destination was located, something Murphy and Robbins did not know.

No, thought Fletcher, as the three of them trudged through thick, mucky nighttime jungle. No, they wouldn't try a double cross.

Not yet.

Murphy stopped and glared down at his right leg, then threw a glance over his shoulder at Fletcher.

"Get this fuckin' thing off me, dammit."

A wait-a-minute vine was hooked around Murphy's pant leg.

Fletcher moved forward, reached down and carefully pried the thorny creeper loose, replacing it across the rough trail.

Somebody would be coming after them.

No point making it easy to be followed.

"Watch where the hell you're going, Murphy."

"You want the point?" Murphy shot back.

Before Fletcher could say anything, Robbins whispered, "Hey, man, let's go, let's go. Gettin' close to the line now."

The punk was right, Fletcher thought.

They would be crossing into Cambodia any time now, slipping through the DMZ.

Demilitarized Zone—that was a joke.

The NVA operated freely throughout the whole area.

Fletcher was tired. So much had happened. They had been on foot for miles, trudging up and down the mountainsides, traipsing their way through the elephant grass of the little valleys.

It would all be worth it, though, when he sold the list to Linh. The major would pay dearly for this information. Enough money so Pete Fletcher could disappear to resurface back in The World with a whole new identity. South America, maybe. Perhaps the south of France. Anywhere but South Vietnam. There would be a fine house with servants. Good food, good wine. Beautiful, willing women.

Living that life would be the man who had once been Lieutenant Peter Fletcher.

If he could get out of this hellhole alive.

Fletcher would get out. He *would*.

The three men were heading west.

They came to a halt a few minutes later as the sounds of a firefight erupted in the distance.

Fighting to the north.

They listened to the gunfire for a few moments.

Robbins said softly, "Shit. Glad that ain't us."

"It just might be if we don't keep moving," Fletcher snapped.

"Still like giving the orders, don'tcha, cracker?" Murphy rumbled. "You best remember rank don't mean nothin' anymore between the three of us, if it ever did."

Murphy turned on the trail so that the muzzle of his M-16, while still aimed at the ground, was more in Fletcher's direction.

"I'm still in charge of this mission, Murphy," Fletcher began.

Murphy laughed harshly.

"Mission? This ain't a mission, Fletcher. This is three dudes running for their damn lives!

Fletcher wanted to jerk his rifle up and fire on the arrogant black, but that would only draw attention to their presence in the area. And Fletcher well knew that drawing attention to oneself was something one did not do in this jungle. Not if you wanted to stay alive.

"C'mon, guys." Robbins broke in on the confrontation, defusing it. "Hadn't we better get going?"

"Gary's right," Fletcher said. "Let's move out."

He knew he could not deal with Murphy until they reached the NVA camp, inside Cambodia.

When they were there, after the money had been paid by Major Linh and Fletcher was ready to take off and start his new life, *then* he would settle accounts with Cleon Murphy.

Until then, he knew he would need Murphy's muscle, skill with a weapon and jungle smarts.

There were other wrinkles in the plan that needed ironing out, such as how to contact Linh when they neared the base. Fletcher knew he could not trust the Viet major even a little bit.

And Robbins? He would not be of any particular use then, either....

For now, though, Robbins was helping to keep Murphy in line, so Fletcher had decided to allow the kid to live a while longer, too.

They tramped on through the jungle night.

THOSE TWO ARE FUCKIN' CRAZY, Robbins thought when they paused two hours later to take a break, hunkering down to rest at the base of a tree.

It wasn't just that one's black and one's white, he thought, reaching for and lighting a cigarette. It was much simpler than that. They're both just fuckin' crazy!

As long as Murphy could keep it under control, Gary Robbins did not really give a shit. All Robbins wanted was to get his ass out of Vietnam and get back home with enough loot to set himself up on easy street for a little while at least.

The list Fletcher carried was the key. It was going to make all of them rich.

Fletcher got to his feet.

"Break's over. We'd better push on."

Slowly, Murphy and Robbins rose to their feet.

"How close are we to the border?" Robbins asked.

"We crossed it a few minutes ago," Fletcher said. "We're in Cambodia now."

In this part of the world, boundaries did not mean much, but Robbins felt better anyway, knowing they were out of Vietnam, even though they still had plenty to worry about.

With the threat of wandering bands of Khmer Rouge rebels, Robbins figured they might actually be in more danger now than before they crossed the border.

At least they were getting closer to the NVA base.

Closer to the escape hatch out of this hell, Robbins told himself as they started off again.

There was more of a spring to Murphy's step this time as he took the point.

"Know what I'm gonna do when I get home?" Robbins asked the other two as they humped along.

He was sick of the silence that had prevailed for more than an hour between the three of them.

"If you're dumb enough to go home, you'll get your ass thrown in jail," Murphy snorted.

"I didn't mean back to my hometown. I'm not that stupid, Murph. I'm gonna buy one of them jazzy little sports cars and drive around the country. See all the places I've never seen."

"They told me when I joined the Army that I'd see the world," Murphy said. "And what have I seen? Nam."

That one syllable spit out hate and bitterness.

Fletcher, in the middle, felt the same way. He had taken advantage of the situation to feather his own nest though, he told himself, instead of spending his time bitching.

Murphy halted abruptly, his nostrils flaring.

"I smell something cooking."

Fletcher sniffed the air and picked up the scent of cooking food, masked by the ever-present odor of decaying jungle vegetation, but definitely there.

"Maybe there's a village around here," Robbins suggested. "We'd better steer clear of it."

Fletcher shook his head.

"There's no village. Not unless they built it in the last two weeks since I saw the intel maps of this area."

A possibility, he knew, but he doubted it.

More than likely the smell drifted to them from a solitary tribesman's hut.

Fletcher's stomach clenched, the aroma reminding him of how long it had been since he had eaten.

"Let's check it out."

"Good thinking," Murphy snorted derisively, already starting forward. "Do your best to keep up, cracker."

"Let's be careful!" warned tail-end-Charlie Robbins, bringing up the rear.

Murphy stayed in the lead.

The three of them humped along the winding trail faster now.

So far there had been no signs of pursuit, and Fletcher was starting to hope there wouldn't be. He had half expected Bolan to pop up right behind them for the first few hours after they made their escape from the Special Forces camp, but apparently even a hotshot like Bolan couldn't be everywhere all the time.

The lieutenant's only regret was that he hadn't had a chance to line his sights on the bastard and waste him, but it was a regret he could live with.

The smell of food became stronger and hunger grew with it inside Fletcher. He could see from Murphy's and Robbins's stepped-up pace that the delicious scents affected them the same way.

The ground sloped upward under their boots, Murphy hacking a path through the creepers and the thick tangles of leaves, Fletcher and Robbins right behind him.

The three of them halted behind a screen of brush at the edge of a clearing.

Parting the leaves slightly, Fletcher peered through the opening and saw what he had expected.

A bamboo hut with thatched roof stood in the center of the clearing.

In front of the hut was a cooking fire.

A woman was kneeling beside the fire, a naked infant cradled in one arm.

A man came from behind the hut and joined the woman at the fire.

Something was bubbling in the cooking pot suspended over the fire. There was no telling what it was, but considering some of the things the dinks ate, Fletcher decided maybe it was better not to know; but it smelled good—that was all that mattered.

In the reddish glow, Fletcher could see that the woman was pretty in a coarse way, despite her smudged face and the ragged clothes she wore.

Fletcher stole a sideways glance at Murphy and Robbins.

Judging by the look on their faces, Fletcher knew he couldn't have gotten them away from here before their appetites were sated, even if he wanted to.

Murphy did not look to Fletcher for permission. The big black stood, pushed through the brush into the clearing and grinned broadly at the startled peasant couple.

"Hey, y'all. How 'bout a little hospitality for a hungry American?"

The Cambodian peasant grabbed his wife's arm and pulled her and the child behind him as he faced Murphy. He said something in Cambodian.

Murphy gestured sharply with the M-16.

"Cut out the jabbering, gook."

Fletcher jerked his head at Robbins, indicating for Gary to follow, and the two of them joined Murphy at the edge of the clearing.

The peasant's wide, uncertain eyes took in the trio of gaunt-faced Americans. He saw Death. He spoke some more, quickly, in desperation.

Behind him, his wife's almond eyes peered over her husband's shoulder. She clutched the infant more tightly to her.

"No need to get upset, dink," Murphy drawled. "We just want you to share your food and your woman. That ain't too much to ask, is it?"

Sensing that there was no escape, the peasant grabbed at the knife tucked in his waistband, pulling it and motioning toward the intruders with a look of defiance.

Robbins and Murphy fired together.

Bullets ripped into the man, bursting him open, spinning him around face first to the ground with a soggy sound.

The young woman screamed and ran to the sprawled body that had been her husband, falling to her knees beside him and wailing.

The child began to cry.

"Guess it was too much to ask, Murph," Robbins snickered nervously.

Murphy laughed too, as if drawing strength from the sight of spilled blood in the flickering of the cooking fire.

"I ain't as hungry as I thought I was. The food can wait. I'm in the mood for something else."

He let the barrel of his rifle drop and started toward the woman.

Through her tears, she saw him coming and snatched up the fallen knife with her free hand from near her husband's body. She rose to her feet and started to back away, her face contorted with grief and rage. The woman held the blade in front of her toward Murphy, the point shaking as she tried to control shock-shattered nerves.

Murphy laughed. He lashed out with the rifle. The barrel hit the knife and knocked it spinning from her hand.

The woman whirled to run.

Murphy thrust out the barrel between her legs, tripping her.

The young mother tried to hold on to her baby, but the infant tumbled from her arms, shrieking.

Murphy kicked the woman in the side, knocking her flat on her face.

Then he stepped over to the squalling baby.

He raised his rifle and brought the butt down hard, sharply.

There was a thud.

The crying stopped.

Now there were only the sobs of the woman.

Robbins giggled, watching.

Fletcher watched, too. All he really cared about was getting what they came here for, food, so that they could be on their way again.

Murphy reached down, hauling the woman to her feet, and began ripping away at her clothes. He started laughing again and did not stop.

Robbins closed in to join him.

The woman lost consciousness, but they kept on.

Fletcher tried to calculate what time it was; how long they could spare here.

What the hell, he decided. There was time.

And as long as he was here, he might as well join in....

He set down his rifle and moved forward to help them with the woman.

Sixteen

Bolan pushed his way on through the thick, clinging vegetation, Sioung in front of him, Gunsmoke, Bloodbrother and Deadeye behind.

They were making good time; better time than Fletcher would expect them to, Bolan imagined.

This was due primarily to Sioung's presence, he knew. The wiry little Mont chieftain knew everything there was to know about this country; knew the trails and knew where to go when there wasn't a trail.

If they were going to catch up to Fletcher and his men, Bolan knew their only real chance rested with Sioung and his knowledge and guidance, wise to the ways of jungle warfare as Bolan and his men were. Bolan hoped Fletcher might get overconfident and feel he had outdistanced all possible pursuit.

All Bolan wanted was a chance.

He came to a stop as Sioung paused in front.

"Wait," the Mont said simply.

Then he faded off through the thick grass.

"You heard the man," Bolan grunted to his men. "Take five."

They crouched down on their heels, taking advantage of the moment to rest, reaching for cigarettes and canteens.

Gunsmoke cuffed back his cowboy hat to let the night sweat dry on his forehead.

"Think we'll catch up with 'em, Sarge?"

"We'd better."

Deadeye laughed, not a pleasant sound.

"Never did care for that Fletcher dude. I'm not surprised he turned out to be a fink."

"I have seen too many like him," Bloodbrother said. "Men who care nothing for anything except themselves."

Bolan kept an eye on the spot where Sioung had disappeared into the undergrowth, listening, but he did not hear Sioung's return until the little Montagnard filtered out from the darkened brush and dropped to a crouch beside him.

Bolan relaxed his grip on his M-16 as Sioung grinned at him.

"Perhaps I should make more noise next time, my friend," Sioung said. "I would hate for you to mistake me for the enemy."

"What did you find?"

"Our way is clear...for the moment. Our way must be a careful one."

"It's all jungle," Gunsmoke grunted. "What does a frontier matter?"

"Patrols will be heavier in this area," Bolan answered. "And remember, to the Cambodian army, we'll be invaders and they'll be within their rights to shoot us dead."

"Well, we'll just have to shoot back," Gunsmoke said, grinning.

"Not unless we absolutely have to," Bolan told them. "No international incidents, remember?"

Deadeye snorted.

"Neutrality! What a joke. There's nothing neutral about a bullet, man."

Bolan straightened to his feet.

"Fletcher's got enough of a lead. Let's go."

The five of them moved out, grouped as before, disregarding their weariness as they resumed slogging up and down curves in the forbidding terrain, pushing their way through the clinging, damp, dark rain forest.

To Bolan, their pace was agonizingly slow, even though he knew they were making the best speed possible.

Eventually—several hours later—they crested the rim of a small valley between two rugged, jungle-covered mountains and proceeded at a somewhat slower pace down into the night-shrouded valley.

It felt good to be walking on level ground again, even though this stretch would last for only a few klicks before the countryside began rising again.

Bolan's eyes were sectoring the area to the right when he heard the sudden warning hiss from Sioung.

The Mont sliced the air with his hand, motioning for them to get down.

Bolan and the others flopped onto their bellies, rifles up and poised for action.

Bolan elbow-crawled his way next to Sioung.

"What is it?"

"A patrol. Coming down off that hill," Sioung answered in a monotone whisper, nodding toward the direction ahead of them.

Bolan listened intently and now he, too, heard the same faint sounds that had alerted Sioung: the rattle of brush being chopped back, the clink of guns and gear, an occasional snatch of voice.

It was as if the Mont possessed some sixth sense.

The patrol wasn't trying to be particularly quiet, which could mean only one thing: it would be a fairly large, well-armed group of men.

Bolan knew his team could hardly afford a firefight. Not now. Not only was his small group outnumbered, in all probability, but also he could not spare the time.

Best to try and pass up this fight.

The tall grass they were lying in hid them for the moment but would do little good if that patrol came any closer.

WOULD THESE PATROLS never end, Lieutenant Kim asked himself as he led his men down the hill into the valley. Probably not, he decided.

Not as long as the newly arrived Major Linh was in command of his detachment.

The Cambodian army lieutenant had not even met his new commander yet, and already he did not care for this Major Linh. Kim was sure these stepped-up patrols were due solely to Linh's arrival.

The major's reputation had preceded him.

Kim glanced over his shoulder at his troops in the darkness.

Not all of them were his men, actually; this patrol was made up of a combination of Cambodian army and NVA soldiers.

Lieutenant Kim was nominally in command, but he was not sure the Viet regulars would obey him if they decided to do something contrary to his orders.

For a fleeting moment Kim wished that he was back home with his wife and baby daughter in Phnom Penh.

Such thoughts had no place in the head of a soldier, he reprimanded himself. He had his orders; he would follow them. Besides, he had heard what happened the last time some fool had opposed the wishes of this Major Linh.

It had happened only the day before, but word traveled fast in a war zone.

A certain Captain Phuong, who had been the second-in-command of the outpost formerly commanded by the major, had refused a direct order from Linh, Kim had heard.

The order had been to kill the wife and young daughter of a Montagnard chief. Phuong had refused and Linh had executed Phuong on the spot; had been about to kill the woman and child as well when the outpost came under attack.

The leader of the attack, some claimed, had been the American soldier who was beginning to be known throughout Southeast Asia as the Executioner.

Lieutenant Kim was not sure he believed all these stories of such a man; a man who, it was claimed, could penetrate any defense, overcome any odds, reach any target.

Like some ancient Montagnard god, thought Kim.

In any war, legends arose, frequently with scant, if any, basis in fact.

This extraordinary soldier known as the Executioner would be just such a legend, Kim supposed, as his patrol slogged on into the gloom of this jungle valley floor.

Or perhaps this Executioner was simply a propaganda figure, Kim thought, the tales of this Bolan's exploits deliberately circulated by the Americans and South Vietnamese to strike fear and uncertainty in the hearts of their enemies.

Kim had also heard stories of yet another American soldier, this one known as Sergeant Mercy—tales of his goodness, of how he helped the innocent victims of this war.

Lies, Kim thought.

Nothing but propaganda lies from the imperialists.

Still, of the two, Kim thought he would much rather encounter Sergeant Mercy than this so-called Executioner, assuming either one existed.

He shook his head to clear it, to rouse himself from this reverie. He was leader of this patrol, he reminded himself. He must not let his thoughts stray.

Kim slowed his progress. Up ahead in the wilderness night, he sensed something.

There! Was that a slight movement in the shadowy grass, near that clump of trees?

Kim tightened his grip on his rifle. He peered intently toward an area fifty paces or so off to their left flank, at the spot where he thought he had spotted something, or at least some movement in the gloom. He jerked his head to speak softly to one of his men beside him, his ranking noncom on this patrol.

"Do you see anything, Sergeant? Over there, near those trees?"

The soldier watched with Kim for a long moment, then shook his head. Both men, and those near enough to overhear, bent slightly lower to dodge or return fire in case the lieutenant was right.

"I see nothing, sir," the soldier answered at last.

Kim heaved a long sigh. Neither had he.

Silence and darkness reigned except for the screeching and chirping of nighttime wildlife.

Kim turned to his men.

"All of you, keep your eyes open. We will proceed very carefully along here."

He gave the signal. The patrol moved out, more slowly, cautiously, than before.

Nothing happened as they crossed the little valley.

All in my imagination, Kim decided. He had been thinking about this so-called Executioner and his thoughts had run away with him.

It did no good for an officer to be so fanciful, he told himself.

From now on, this Cambodian officer resolved to keep his feet firmly on the ground and pay closer attention to his surroundings or, he knew, he might never see his wife, his baby daughter or Phnom Penh.

It did little good to worry oneself about imaginary executioners.

FROM THE SHELTER of the trees, Bolan watched the Cambodian patrol move off through the misty moonlight.

Using evasive skills well honed during their time in Hell, Bolan's small group had crawled into cover of the trees with hardly a ripple of the grass.

At the last moment, Deadeye had snagged a thick clump with his ammo belt and jerked it a little, but other than that there had been no clue of their movement.

For a tense moment there, Bolan had been concerned that the Cambodian army lieutenant had spotted them. Then the patrol moved on.

A few feet away from Bolan, Deadeye Washington fluently cursed himself out.

"Sorry about that fuckup crawling over here, Sarge. Damn near got us all killed."

Gunsmoke chuckled.

"You mean y'all almost got a passel of Cambodians killed, Deadeye."

Bolan nodded.

"No harm done," he assured Washington.

The Cambodian patrol had started up another hill and vanished in the gloom.

Bolan pushed to his feet.

The men of his team followed his lead and got up, too.

Gunsmoke clapped Washington on the shoulder. "Don't let it get you down, man," he joked. "Can't everybody be as stealthy as the chief there."

He jerked a thumb at Bloodbrother.

Bloodbrother smiled enigmatically.

"Any time you want to play cowboys and Indians, we can reenact Custer's Last Stand, Smoke."

Harrington held out his hands, palms out.

"Hold on there, guy. Me, I'd just as soon be the red man's friend."

Bloodbrother tilted his head to one side and appeared to study Harrington's long, lanky hair.

"Would make a fine scalp," he grunted with a nod.

Bolan permitted himself a quick chuckle, knowing the men were releasing some tension with the horseplay.

Gunsmoke and Bloodbrother also drew a smile from Washington, making him forget about what could have happened, and Bolan knew this was part of their purpose as well.

"Let's get moving," he told his men. "It would have been worse if we'd had to fight, but we lost time anyway dodging that fight."

Time was the one thing they could not afford to lose.

They picked up their pace through the dark, heading west, tracking three rotten American soldiers, a cannibal named Linh and their own fate into the belly of the monster.

Deeper into "neutral" Cambodia, which could well be neutralized before this night was over...in violent death and spilled blood.

Seventeen _____

From outside the bamboo hut Tuan Duc heard the grumbling and snorting noises of the oxen stirring in their pens, the crackle of the cooking fires and the chittering of insects in the surrounding jungle.

Inside the hut, the principal sound was his wife's harsh, heavy breathing.

Tuan Duc sat cross-legged on the dirt floor, holding Bach Yen's hand.

She lay beside him on a rough pallet, the swelling of her stomach testifying to the fact that very soon this young couple were going to become parents.

The woman's eyes were closed.

Tuan smiled down at her, thinking that she was more beautiful now than ever before.

Her pains had begun earlier in the day, while the two of them were working the fields with the others of this refugee camp.

Tuan had insisted they return to the camp village and the relative comfort of their tent, though Bach Yen said she could wait until nightfall.

Soon he would have a fine son to help him, Tuan thought proudly.

He was a farmer; all of those in this small semi-permanent camp of fifteen families were farmers.

They knew little of what happened in Hanoi or Saigon or Phnom Penh, nothing of what transpired in Washington or Peking or Moscow.

But, as in all wars, Tuan Duc knew firsthand that those who suffered most were the simple people, the civilians like him and his very small family of two, about to become three.

Tuan Duc wished the war would go away. He was tired of terror and bloodshed and devastation; tired sick of having to hide when the thieves and soldiers and scavengers came pillaging.

He had other things to worry about now.

His wife released her breath, exhaling with relief as one of the pains passed.

Tuan squeezed her hand, smiling as she opened her eyes to look up at him.

"You should go soon," she told him. "Send the old woman in."

"Our child...will be here soon?"

She nodded.

"Yes. Soon."

Tuan took a deep breath. Bach Yen was right; it was time to summon the old woman who would assist with the birth, but for some reason he could not bring himself to leave her side just yet. He would stay a few moments longer....

"Ours will be a fine baby," he said gently, leaning over to stroke her cheek. "Healthy and strong. We will have many grandchildren."

A fine dream...but probably only a dream, Tuan Duc thought to himself.

There was hardly enough food to go around most of the time, and violence could break out at any time.

Children born in this place, at this time, had a slim chance of reaching adulthood.

Tuan Duc willed himself not to think of such things.

Bach Yen whispered an endearment to him, then they sat quietly for several minutes, awaiting the next pain that would grip her, when he would leave to fetch the old woman to help.

Tuan knew little about the birthing of babies, but his wife assured him that all was going as it should.

It would not be much longer now.

They began talking of aimless things, but then the woman broke off abruptly, her hand tightening on her husband's, pain contorting her lovely face once again.

And a heavy blast rocked the hut, tremoring the earth beneath them!

Tuan jerked upright.

Bach Yen screamed in sudden fear.

Through the opening of their hut, they saw the night light up.

The hellish lights of throbbing violence, shouts of fear and rage mingling with sounds of pain, assailed their ears.

Tuan Duc looked out upon a scene of utter carnage.

Men, women and children ran wildly about throughout the night-darkened camp, frantically searching for some kind of cover, for protection.

Khmer Rouge!

They came swarming out of the hilly ridges around the village, shooting, shouting, killing.

They called themselves rebels, guerrillas, but Tuan Duc knew they were nothing but blackhearted scavengers, bloodthirsty marauders who would slaughter anyone unlucky enough to cross their path.

Their business was raping, looting and bringing death to those who wanted only to be left alone to live their own lives. These Khmer Rouge pillagers were armed with whatever weapons they could steal or "liberate" from their victims: American M-16s, Soviet carbines, French MATs, even rocket launchers, which they were now using to turn the camp that was Tuan Duc's home into a billowing inferno with incendiary rounds.

As Tuan watched in shock and horror, a friend of his, a man he had worked with in the fields for years, was blown apart by machine-gun fire several feet away.

Another villager came running by the primitive dwelling, then had his legs cut out from under him by bullets, more slugs ripped into him as he fell dead almost at Tuan's feet.

Tuan knew he had to move, had to do something, but he was momentarily mesmerized by the gruesome horror of this sudden attack seemingly out of nowhere.

A young girl staggered past, body in flames.

An older woman leaped upon the burning child, bearing her to the ground and trying to beat out the flames.

A Khmer Rouge monster laughingly pulped them both with a blast of automatic riflefire.

The camp headman ran from his tent, shouting, trying to rally his people into some sort of resistance.

Two Khmer Rouge plunderers leaped on the headman with swinging brush axes, gleefully hacking the screaming man into quivering chunks of flesh.

Close by, the headman's wife and daughter were already being pulled to the ground by groups of men.

Fingers clutched at Tuan's arm.

He spun in terror, only to stop himself when he saw that it was his wife clinging to him.

Somehow she had gotten to her feet and, in spite of her condition, had come to join him.

Their eyes touched briefly, sharing the hell they were witnessing.

As a nearby tent went up with a whoosh of flame, accompanied by the agonized screams of its occupants, Tuan Duc knew what he had to do.

He scooped his wife into his arms, his small but wiry frame hoisting her weight without scarcely bending. He ran outside and around to the rear of their dwelling.

Bach Yen wrapped her arms tightly around her husband's neck, burying her face against his chest, whimpering her fear and pain.

Their hut was on the edge of the camp, jungle close behind it, for which Tuan was thankful.

As the slaughter continued in the insane night behind them, Tuan Duc ran for the thick undergrowth, carrying his beloved wife in his arms.

If I can only hide her there, he thought, perhaps she will be safe!

He knew the hope was a small one, but it was all they had.

He forced his way into the tangle of vines, fronds and branches, thorns pulling at both of them. Tuan Duc found a spot at the base of a balsa tree and lowered his Bach Yen to the grass there.

She did not want to release him. He had to pry her grip loose from his neck.

"Do not leave me," she sobbed brokenly. "Stay here with me! We can hide—"

Tuan stood over her, chest heaving, tight with emotion.

"My child will not have a coward for a father," he told his wife fiercely. "This camp is our home. I must help defend it. I must fight!"

"No, my darling—*please!*"

He knelt beside her and stroked her hair.

"I will be back," he told her. "You have our child. Our fine, healthy child. . . ."

He stood and left her then, running toward the direction of the fighting in the camp, not looking back.

Bach Yen could see him through breaks in the foliage. She saw him hurry to the side of their tent and pick up the hoe that was leaning there.

Tuan Duc worked in the fields with that hoe. Now he would use it to try to defend his home.

A big Khmer Rouge killer in ragged pants and tunic appeared nearby, a machine gun spewing death in his hands.

The flesh-heating projectiles riddled a tumbling group of women and children huddling near the edge of the camp.

The bandit laughed as blood and flesh sprayed the air.

Face twisted in hatred, Tuan Duc raised his hoe and ran toward the killer with a howl.

The bandit swung around, triggering another, almost careless burst.

Bullets caught Tuan in the right shoulder and sent his arm spinning away from his body, the severed limb trailing bright red streamers.

Tuan Duc cried out and staggered, staring in wide-eyed shock at the quivering ruin of his shoulder.

With a grin, the Khmer Rouge bandit squeezed his trigger once more, this burst starting at Tuan Duc's groin and tracking up his torso, stitching the farmer with crimson blossoms that ripped the life away from Tuan Duc.

Lying hidden undetected in the jungle nearby, Bach Yen saw her husband fall, almost cut into halves by the savage's gunfire.

She jerked her head away from the terrible sight, sobs racking her, racked as well by the pain of impending childbirth.

The time had come!

Regardless of what else was happening, her baby was about to come into the world.

Only now it would come into the world without a father.

Bach Yen wept from the bottom of her soul, clenching her fists against the pain and the hate, and bore down with everything she had....

SOUNDS OF GUNFIRE and explosions reached Bolan and his men from the night, the noise coming from somewhere close, only a few hundred yards to their right through the wall of nighttime jungle.

The five of them halted tensely in the dark, listening briefly to the fierce sounds.

There had been no more delays since the near-miss with the Cambodian border patrol several hours earlier but they had been slowed by the darkness.

Bolan's mind was full of Fletcher and the need to catch up with the fleeing renegade, but they could not ignore the clamor of what sounded like a minor-scale battle.

"Sounds like somebody's gettin' into it," Gunsmoke noted.

Bolan turned to Sioung.

"What's over that way?"

"A small refugee camp of farmers," the Mont answered. "There would be no reason for the military to attack it."

"The Khmer Rouge don't need reasons," Bolan growled.

He had seen the horrifying results of raids by the deadly Cambodian rebels on other deep penetration missions across this frontier.

"Looks like we're gonna play Lone Ranger again, eh?" Gunsmoke said.

"Let's take a look," Bolan said.

His eyes were fixed on the flickering glare of fire, now faintly visible through the jungle.

"Come on, Tonto," Gunsmoke said jauntily to Bloodbrother.

"Someday, Gunsmoke, someday..." was the Blackfoot's kidding reply.

Bloodbrother let his voice trail off as they pushed off their course through the jungle.

Bolan moved to take the lead now; he and his team advancing lightly on their feet, slowing down only when they were about to reach the clearing where the camp was situated.

The gunfire and shouting were very loud now and Bolan could identify several of the weapons from their sounds.

He was able to identify the screams, too.

The ugly sounds of cannibals at work.

Bolan's team came tearing out of the jungle, instantly taking in the situation.

There was plenty of light to see by, several of the tents in the camp ablaze.

Bolan was firing his rifle a split second later, blowing away one Khmer Rouge punk and before that killer had spun to the ground in a loose-limbed deadfall, the Executioner shifted his stance and pumped more rounds into another of these rebels.

Gunsmoke, Bloodbrother, Deadeye and Sioung boiled out of the jungle behind Bolan, spreading out to launch their own offensive.

There had been a dozen or more rebels in the force attacking the village and they had expected to find nothing but easy pickings.

Instead, in the middle of what had been a successful foray, these cannibal suddenly found themselves facing five very competent warriors.

The Executioner went to work, zigzagging forward in a combat crouch, moving, searching out targets fast as he could.

It was easy to spot the Khmer Rouge, to pick them out from the villagers.

They were the ones doing the killing.

Bolan felt the hot breath of a bullet zip past his ear and he spun to see two rebels firing at him with automatic weapons—one man standing, the other cannibal kneeling nearby on one knee.

Bolan triggered a burst that caught the standing guy and knocked him backward to the ground, the raider's hands clenching his weapon tighter in death, the rifle yammering wildly as its dead owner sprawled in the dirt.

Bolan tracked over to the other punk and fired again, paying no attention to the slugs sizzling past him, his M-16's bullets stitching across the rebel's body, flinging the guy away in a deadfall.

The Executioner kept moving deeper toward the center of the camp.

Another of the Khmer Rouge killers dashed running from behind a burning tent. He carried a brush ax and an old .45 automatic, and as he spotted the American, he jerked the pistol up and fired almost point-blank at Bolan's back. But some isntinct had warned Bolan and he flung himself to the side in a diving roll, returning to his combat crouch several feet away with his M-16 blazing death.

One of the slugs zipped the rebel's hand, shattering it, sending the .45 pistol spinning away into the night. The man screamed in pain before launching himself bodily at Bolan, viciously swinging the ax in his uninjured hand.

Bolan ducked and let the blade of the ax slice through the air where he had been one heartbeat before, then he stepped in closer and brought the butt of his rifle slamming up into the man's jaw.

The guy's bone disintegrated with a grinding crunch, blood spraying from his mouth. A second blow pulped the side of the creep's head and he fell.

Bolan did not waste time looking to see how his companions were doing. He had been with them long enough to know they were right at home in this kind of fight, striking quick and deadly.

GUNSMOKE HARRINGTON'S twin six-shooters leaped from their holsters into his hands as he burst from the jungle line. The lights dancing in his eyes were more than just reflections of the battle fires. He split off from Bolan's right, rounding a line of tents. He heard a woman's scream, one of many screams in this night.

Two Khmer Rouge cannibals had a refugee woman cornered, Harrington saw as he skidded to a stop.

She was backed against the side of a tree, hands held out in front of her imploringly.

The gesture meant nothing to the two men advancing on her, lust evident in their eyes and aggressive movements. They closed in on her, both men armed with assault rifles.

Gunsmoke returned his pistols to their side leather and just stood there a second or two with his feet spread, arms hanging loosely at his sides.

One of the Khmer Rouge attackers reached out with a filthy hand and tangled his fingers in the woman's dress. He snarled threateningly at the terrified female, taking pleasure in bracing himself to rip off her garment.

"Wouldn't do that if I was you," Gunsmoke drawled in soft, mocking tones from close by, speaking to the two men loud enough.

Neither bandit understood English, but they knew a challenge when they heard one. They spun, rifles tracking into firing position, their latest victim forgotten for the time being until they could blast apart this stupid, grinning American in the funny hat....

Gunsmoke's revolvers opened up with bucking, roaring death, their reports rolling through the night.

Neither Khmer Rouge bandit had time to get off a shot, the slugs zapping into them, sending them staggering backward in frantic death dances, rifles fallen from nerveless fingers.

Gunsmoke executed the road agent spin with the pistols and let them drop back into their holsters. He lifted his right hand, touching it to the brim of his hat.

"There you go, little lady," he said, smiling to the still-cowering Cambodian woman.

She broke and ran, disappearing into the violent night.

Gunsmoke gave a little shrug and turned back to the battle.

Several yards away, Tom Loudelk looped his left arm around the neck of one of the rebels, using his right to drive his combat knife between the man's ribs, into his heart.

The bandit sagged lifelessly.

Bloodbrother flung the corpse away, already moving on into the thick of the fight with long strides.

Another of the Khmer Rouge savages spotted him and tried to turn around in time to bring his weapon up, but before he could, one of the refugees threw himself into the fray, ax in hand, and drove the rebel down to the ground in a welter of arms and legs and blood.

The American Indian moved past them, searching for another target.

The battle came to him.

Sensing movement behind, Bloodbrother faded to one side.

A machete in the hand of a Khmer Rouge butcher slashed down at him, missing by a fraction of an inch.

Bloodbrother was facing a man larger than the usual Cambodian, almost as tall as Loudelk; his face was ugly, jagged with scars. He handled the heavy machete like a toy knife, making the sharp point dance in the air in front before him.

Bloodbrother's rifle was slung at his shoulder; he could have unlimbered it and blown the rebel away, but he permitted himself a smile instead and raised the bloodstained Gerber Mark II combat knife already in his hand.

The invitation was plain.

With a yell of hate, the bandit charged forward, slashing outward with the machete at Bloodbrother's body.

Loudelk twisted aside, lashing out with his own blade to slice across the bandit's upper arm, drawing first blood.

The bandit howled, leaping back, narrowly avoiding the native American's follow-up slash, the one that would have slit his throat if it had connected.

Plainly, caution and anger were warring within the Cambodian. Anger won and plowed him forward again.

Bloodbrother caught a machete slash with the hilt of his knife, the clang ringing out above the other sounds of fighting and killing, deflecting the larger blade; then Loudelk drove his knee hard into the man's unprotected groin.

The bandit yelped and staggered, clutching blindly at himself in agony, leaving him no chance to ward off Bloodbrother's follow-through.

Loudelk grabbed the man's shirt and jerked him forward. Then the Indian brought his knife up to meet the opponent, the razor-honed blade piercing the flesh of the rebel's throat.

Bloodbrother felt the knife grind against the man's spinal column, then his bunched muscles drove it on through, the blade point breaking through the skin to protrude from the back of the dead man's neck, the hilt resting against his throat. With a grunt and a wrench, Loudelk tore the blade loose and pushed the corpse away from him.

It accordioned to the dirt, blood fountaining from the gaping wounds.

Deadeye Washington was close enough to see Bloodbrother dispose of the machete-wielding Khmer Rouge punk, but he did not waste time admiring the Indian's effectiveness.

Deadeye had his own hands full.

A heavyweight landed upon his broad back, arms snaked around his neck, cutting off Washington's air supply, causing little stars to dance before his eyes.

Deadeye grabbed up and behind and found a handful of lank, dirty hair, then bent over and tugged.

The bandit who had jumped him went flipping through the air with a cry and landed heavily on his back. Before he could do anything else, Deadeye lunged forward and launched a kick.

His booted foot crashed into the man's head, impacting against the temple, smashing bone splinters into the brain.

Deadeye stepped over the body when something made him turn around and peer across the open area toward the center of the refugee camp.

The ability to feel eyes watching him had been born in him back home as he grew up in the streets.

Vietnam had honed that ability until it was as good as a sixth sense.

He spotted the bandit, close to ten yards away, lining sights on him with a captured M-14.

Washington didn't have to think. The butt of his own M-16 snapped home against the stock; aiming was an instinctive thing.

He saw the muzzle-flash of the other man's rifle even as he squeezed the trigger. The M-16 kicked against his shoulder. He heard the flat *whap* of compressed air as the bandit's round winged past his ear.

The bandit flopped groundward.

Deadeye started looking for another target.

He heard Bolan call his name. Snapping his head around, he saw Bolan wave for him to head for the east edge of the battle-filled camp. Deadeye started in that direction at a run.

Some of the Khmer Rouge marauders had clustered together after becoming aware of the unexpected counterassault.

Bolan wanted to flank them and get them in a cross fire, and he and Deadeye had the best shot at doing that.

The tide of battle was beginning to turn, the arrival of Bolan and his men the deciding factor.

The villagers saw this, and seeing it, they reacted. They started to fight back in earnest.

Several of them cornered one of the Khmers, a swaggering killer moments before, and now they were holding him down, releasing all their pent-up fear and rage in a berserk flood of violence. With their hoes and axes, they were chopping the rebel to pieces.

Sioung saw Bolan and Washington racing past the burning tents and into the jungle and knew what they were trying to do. He could do nothing to help them, though, because he was already occupied.

He leaped forward and struck with his own ax as another of the rebels started to blast into the pack of kill-crazy refugees.

The ax slammed into the back of the bandit's head and dropped him.

Sioung kicked the man's machine gun away, then leaned over to finish him off with another swift chop. As he straightened, he saw that the group of refugees were backing away from their grisly handiwork, horror etched on their faces—horror at what they had been driven to, though the bandit had well deserved it and they knew that, too.

It was good that these men had not lost the will to fight when they had to, Sioung reflected, and it was good that they still retained enough humanity to recognize the tragedy of what they had been forced to do and what they had become.

BOLAN AND WASHINGTON moved close together now, pushing through the fringes of jungle around the refugee camp.

Stray bullets clipped through the trees overhead.

Deadeye suddenly stumbled and yelped, "Holy shit!"

He would have fallen if it had not been for Bolan's strong right hand gripping his arm and hauling him upright.

Bolan whirled, M-16 up and ready to fire, to confront whatever had surprised Deadeye and thrown him off stride.

Bolan was unprepared for what he saw.

Lying on the floor of the jungle, knees drawn up and legs spread wide, was a very pregnant young Cambodian woman staring up at them, eyes wide with fright and other emotions.

"Damn, I nearly stepped on her, Sarge!" Deadeye exclaimed.

Bolan dropped to one knee beside the young woman, resting the butt of his rifle on the ground.

She cringed away from him.

They had to look terrifying to her, Bolan thought. There was no telling what she had been through already this night, but she was about ready to have her baby, there was no mistaking that.

A frightening time for a woman who was barely more than a child herself under any circumstance.

And to be having her baby practically in the middle of a savage battle...

"You'll have to cover us, Deadeye," Bolan snapped decisively. "You should be able to get them in a fire with Gunsmoke from here."

"What about you?"

Bolan smiled down at the woman as reassuringly as he could and rested a gentle hand on her shoulder.

"I'm going to be a little busy," he told Deadeye.

He heard Washington shifting positions behind him. He knelt beside the woman, but he did not turn to observe, not even when Washington's M-16 began snarling sizzlers into the night once again.

Bolan spoke to the woman in soft tones, trying to get her to relax. That was the most important thing, he knew, that she be relaxed.

The irony of it was not lost on him.

He had a slight knowledge of her language. He kept repeating soothing phrases, his hand still on the woman's shoulder. He could feel her tension gradually easing.

She knew now that the grim-visaged Americans weren't going to slaughter her, and the impending birth of her baby was becoming uppermost in her mind again.

A spasm shook her.

Bolan could tell that she was in the advanced stages of labor.

The baby was close, real close.

There had been nothing in his training to prepare him for delivering a baby during a firefight—or at any other time, for that matter!

It was a natural process, though, and if you approached it using common sense...or so he tried to tell himself.

The woman let out a short, throaty scream, her breathing harsh and rapid now, her contractions more intense, almost on top of one another.

Bolan moved between her open thighs and crouched there, still trying to speak calmly, soothingly to the young woman.

Deadeye muttered a curse and ducked as projectiles chewed up leaves and branches barely a foot over his head.

Bolan stayed where he was.

The woman screamed again, the sound practically lost amidst the cacophony of fighting and killing so close by.

Deadeye rammed home a fresh magazine into his M-16 and opened fire again on Khmer Rouge bandits. He could see the muzzle-flashes from Gunsmoke's pistols across the village.

"That's it," Bolan said quietly to the woman, lapsing into English. "That's real good. Just keep doing what you're doing."

A grenade went off in the village, the blast uprooting a small tree.

The woman strained, digging her fingers into the soft loam of the jungle floor.

Bolan leaned forward intently, helping, struggling to see in the shadows. He saw something....

The baby's head.

Hands that could field-strip virtually dozens of weapons, that could wield a knife with silent and deadly efficiency, that could exert sufficient strength to choke the life out of an enemy...Bolan reached down with those hands and grasped the baby's head with the utmost care and tenderness, easing a new life into the world.

The weaponfire continued to bark harshly and chatter and roar behind him, people shrieking, dying.

"Come on!" Bolan whispered to the woman.

And then the baby was out and Bolan was holding it aloft and swatting its butt to start it crying and breathing, its thin little wail of life also buried beneath the sounds of war.

Bolan heard it, though, and felt the feeble kicking of newborn muscles, and emotion surged through him and made his chest feel like it was going to burst.

He gently cleared the newborn's nose and mouth, then massaged the mother's abdomen. At his slow tug on the umbilical cord, the placenta separated, and he used a clip from his ammo webbing to clamp the little guy's belly button. Then he placed the baby in the mother's arms, where she hugged it to suckle hungrily at her breast, the newborn's crying subsiding to almost soundless gurgles.

Bolan was somewhat surprised to find himself grinning from ear to ear.

"Congratulations, Sarge." Deadeye chuckled close by.

Bolan looked up to see his buddy peering over his shoulder, and he became aware that the noises of battle were gone.

Except for the crackling of fires, silence reigned.

"The rebels?" Bolan asked.

"Two or three of 'em took off. The rest are dead."

The mother cuddled her newborn son closely.

Bolan could see his tiny mouth move as he sucked.

Life goes on, he thought. You can't stop it.

The reality of the situation was depressingly bleak, though, he realized anew in the next few moments—the little refugee camp devastated, at least half of its population killed in the attack, including this baby's father.

Sioung passed along the latter fact after talking with the survivors.

By the time the five men of Bolan's team moved out, though, the mother and her child were being cared for in one of the tents still left standing.

At least they would have a *chance* for survival.

And with the weapons taken from the dead outlaws, the camp itself might be better prepared if another bandit raid befell them.

Bolan could never have turned his back on these people in need and not helped, no way, but as he and his men pushed off again to the west and he set a grueling pace, a bitter truth gnawed at him.

This delay could well have bought Fletcher and his crew time enough to reach Major Linh....

Eighteen _____

The NVA sentry snapped to attention as the new base commander strode down the hall of the small command building.

"Captain Trang is waiting to see you, sir," the regular said.

Major Linh passed to open his office door.

"Very well. I wish to see the captain, as well."

The major entered the office and tossed his cap onto the desk as he walked behind it.

The young captain who was waiting for him sprang to his feet and saluted the instant Linh entered.

Linh returned an offhand, perfunctory salute and seated himself behind the desk. He glanced across some of the papers spread out on the desk, up-to-the-minute intel report covering area activities, ignoring the junior officer for some moments. Finally, Linh glanced up.

"Sit down, Captain."

Trang relaxed somewhat and sat, a touch of nervousness in his attitude. He carried a file folder, from which he removed two sheets of paper, extending them across the desk to Linh.

"I wanted to hand these reports to you personally, Major. I believe they merit your immediate attention."

Linh took the intel reports.

"I will be the judge of their importance."

"Of course, sir."

Linh let his eyes scan the closely spaced typing on the sheets.

"These are decoded from one of our agents in the area of the American Special Forces camp they call 105-A?"

"Yes, sir."

Linh allowed a smile to tug briefly at his lips.

"Excellent."

The information contained in the decoded report was surprising—and very intriguing.

Linh read of the capture of Lieutenant Fletcher and his men by an American sergeant named Mack Bolan. The details of Fletcher's subsequent escape were also contained in the report, as well as speculation that Fletcher had stolen a vital, top-secret list of American planted spies and agents in North Vietnam.

Linh had long suspected the existence of such a list. He felt gratified to have that suspicion confirmed and was even more gratified to read that the Americans suspected Fletcher was on his way here, to this very NVA base, to sell that list.

Linh had already beefed up security around the base and increased the number of patrols in the area. He would have his men on the lookout for Fletcher, too.

The last tidbit of information contained in the report was the most intriguing of all.

A small force had been sent out after Fletcher to attempt to recapture him and retrieve the top-secret list.

Leading that force was Sergeant Mack Bolan.

Linh would have laughed aloud had it not been for the presence of Captain Trang.

This could not have worked out better if he had planned it. It would be a vital coup, the major instantly realized, if he could get his hands on the list Fletcher supposedly had stolen—and Linh was sure Fletcher had the list or the Americans would not have reacted so promptly in trying to capture Fletcher and the two men reportedly traveling with him, by sending the Executioner after them.

This is my chance, thought Linh, for revenge on the human demon, Bolan.

The memory of what had happened that very morning burned bitterly in Linh's mind. He had dealt with that cowardly dog, Phuong. Phuong would never disobey another order. But the real culprit, the one who had brought down such shame on Linh's head by rescuing the Montagnard's woman and squalling brat, was *Bolan*.

Linh replaced the reports on the desk and looked across at Trang.

"This is...very interesting, Captain."

"I did well to bring it to your attention?"

This man is too desperate for approval, Linh thought. He would have Trang replaced. For the moment, though...

"Yes, Captain, you did well. Now, I have some orders for you to carry out. These reports only make them more important."

"Yes, sir."

"I want the sentries doubled at all entrances to the compound and along the perimeter. In addition, patrols around the perimeter will also be doubled."

Trang frowned.

"These duties have already been doubled, sir, according to your earlier orders."

Linh held his temper, though it took effort.

"Then double them again, Captain."

Trang nodded obediently.

"As you wish, Major."

"In addition," Linh continued, "our reconnaissance patrols will be increased in number and they will be especially watchful for this man, Fletcher. The report does not say when Fletcher escaped, but he could reach this area at any time. As soon as he and his men are captured, they are to be brought to me. Immediately, and unharmed, do you understand?"

"Yes, sir."

Linh returned to a perusal of the reports then, dismissing Trang from his mind. He looked up a few moments later to find the captain still standing there.

"Yes, Trang, what is it?"

"Sir—" Trang looked as if he wished he was somewhere, anywhere, else "—the, uh, men have already complained about the double duty. If their duty is increased even more—"

Trang broke off and gulped his fear when he found himself staring down the unwavering barrel of Major Linh's drawn side arm.

"Tell them," Linh instructed icily, "that the first one who complains about his orders or shirks his duties will be shot down like the unworthy dog he is. And that includes you, Captain. Now do you understand?"

Trang jerked a nod.

"Of course, sir...a-all will be as you say."

"I thought it would be."

Linh reholstered his pistol.

Trang scurried out of the office.

Even the unpleasant scene with Trang could not spoil the excitment Major Linh felt.

He had given no orders concerning Bolan because he knew the capabilities of the men under his command. They were adequate cannon fodder, but faced with a man of Bolan's talents, Linh realized his troops were clearly inferior. His patrols would not encounter Bolan unless Bolan wished such a confrontation to take place and if that occurred, thought Linh, Bolan and his men would probably wipe out the patrol.

No, Linh told himself, Bolan will come *here* in pursuit of Fletcher.

He would come to *Linh*; the Executioner was confident of his arrogant American daring.

Linh knew enough about Bolan to realize the Executioner had, what was the decadent American expression for it, ah yes—*balls*.

That was it.

Bolan had the balls to walk into the jaws of death.

And Major Linh intended to gladly accommodate him.

FOR A CHANGE, things at Three-Niner-Bayou were quiet.

The camp had settled down following the after-dusk VC attack and its inhabitants had primarily concerned themselves with getting things back to normal, the damage done by the mortars being repaired as much as possible, the injured having been taken care of, the dead taken care of too, "tagged and bagged" for transport to Saigon the following morning.

Security was tight.

The MASH facilities were full, most of the wounded servicemen occupying its beds resting quietly. But a few were in such pain that even the drugs they had been given could but dull it slightly, their occasional moans vivid punctuation to the hushed voices of the doctors and nurses who moved among the beds, regularly checking on their charges.

"Dust-off" evac choppers would arrive in the morning; for now, it was up to the front-line medics and nurses to keep the shattered young men alive.

Doc Brantzen studied the chart of one soldier, then replaced it at the foot of the bed.

This boy was one of the lucky ones. He had sustained a nasty flesh wound in his thigh but barring infection or complications, he would recover. And he would do his recovering Stateside.

The war was over for him. He'd managed a million-dollar wound, as the grunts called it— enough to get him back home, but in a few months he'd be like new, back drinking beer on the block, working a normal job, looking for a woman if he didn't have one waiting for him already.

Sometimes Jim Brantzen wondered if this war would ever end.

A few beds away, Shawnee leaned over and adjusted a pillow for a soldier who tossed in fitful sleep.

Shawnee was tired. The night had been long and hard and so had the day before it and she was starting to feel it. She wished she could go somewhere and lie down and forget about war. It would be far more pleasant, she thought, to think about Mack Bolan.

Then a realization came to her.

She could not think of Bolan without thinking about war.

The two were hopelessly entwined in her mind, and she prayed it would not always be that way.

For Mack's sake.

That big, beautiful man deserved something better than war for a way of life.

At the moment, she did not know if Bolan was alive or dead.

The tautness of her nerves made her jump slightly when a hand touched her shoulder lightly. She looked around at Dr. Jim Brantzen's concerned face.

"Why don't you take a break, lady?" he suggested. "I can handle things here for a while."

Shawnee shook her head.

"I'm fine, Jim. Just a little tired. And worried about Mack."

Brantzen nodded.

"If you feel anything like I do, 'little' has nothing to do with it, but you need everything you've got here, Shawnee. Mack will have to take care of himself."

"I know, Jim. Sometimes, though...he tries to take care of everybody else, too."

The two of them walked down the long aisle between beds, stopping every so often to check on one of the men.

There were still several hours to go on their shift.

At the end of the ward was a small alcove that contained a coffeepot and some folding chairs.

Brantzen drew them each a cup, and doctor and nurse sipped their steaming brew wordlessly for a long minute or two, though each knew this could only be a quick break.

"Heard anything about Chopper?" Shawnee asked.

Brantzen shook his head.

"Not yet, I'm sorry to say."

The double doors into the ward swung open and Colonel Winters stepped through. He spotted Shawnee and Brantzen and joined them.

"Got another cup of that battery acid?"

"I think we can dig one up for you." Brantzen nodded a tired hello.

He poured another cup.

"Colonel, is there any word about Mack?" Shawnee asked.

"Nothing for sure," Winters growled. "We haven't heard anything specifically about the mission, but we did receive some intel concerning a firefight involving the Khmer Rouge and a Cambodian refugee camp. That camp is right along the track our men should've been passing through at the time of this reported battle."

"Then Mack was tussled up in it," said Brantzen with certainty, handing the cup to Winters.

"Thanks, Doc. What makes you say that? We don't know for sure the team was involved."

Shawnee laughed shortly.

"Begging your pardon, Colonel, but when did Mack ever pass up a fight when he thought he could do someone some good?"

Winters inclined his head in acknowledgment.

"You do have a point there. Damn, I just wish we knew more about what was going on over there."

The three sipped their coffee in moody silence for a few moments.

Shawnee could see that Colonel Winters was worried deep inside. The colonel tried not to show it, but Shawnee had noticed it before in the colonel whenever Bolan or his team went out. Though she knew none of the details, she knew the Executioner's mission this night had to be of the gravest importance for the colonel to send out his best men the night of a Vietcong attack, when the jungle would be thick with VC.

"The hardest part is knowing that Mack and his men are out there, needing help, with us back here unable to help him." Shawnee looked at Winters squarely. "I don't know what this mission is about, sir, but it must be terribly urgent."

"It is, Shawnee. And vital. Damn, I wish I *could* do something."

"Can't you, sir?" she asked her CO without batting an eye. "Are you *sure* there's nothing you—we—can do to help those men of ours out there?"

Winters finished his coffee and stood up.

"I'd better get back to work. And, uh, we shouldn't be overly concerned about Mack. He's got good men with him, including Sioung for an extra edge."

"He's not indestructible, Colonel. He's just a man."

Brantzen cleared his throat.

"I agree with you that there should be something we could do, Shawnee, but—"

The doors burst open before anybody could say anything else.

One of the guys from the radio shack ran up to them and threw on the brakes when he saw Colonel Winters. He paused to salute.

"At ease, son," Winters growled. "You look like you've got some news."

"Yessir." The young man tried to catch his breath. "Dust-offs coming, sir." He addressed Brantzen. "Wounded from a patrol ambush south of here."

"How many?" Brantzen asked.

"I don't know for sure, but a lot, I think."

"Thanks." Brantzen turned briskly to Shawnee. "Let's get ready."

"And I'll get out of your way," Winters said, and to the nurse the colonel added, "and I'll think over some of the things we talked about."

He went out after the radioman.

Shawnee and Jim Brantzen exchanged looks, then turned back to the ward.

Bolan is out there somewhere in this night, doing his job, Shawnee thought.

Another long, deadly night.

Nineteen ─────────────────

"Damn fuckin' jungle!" Murphy snarled.

He pried his foot loose from an entangling swarm of vines that made every gained kilometer tougher going than the last.

"Keep your voices down," Fletcher whispered. "We're getting close to that Commie base we're looking for. I'd just as soon make an appearance when *we're* ready instead of getting ourselves hauled in by a patrol that might be trigger-happy."

Murphy nodded truculently.

"Makes sense, cracker, but you're still too damn free with this giving orders shit, for somebody who ain't in command anymore."

Fletcher reined in an angry retort that almost sprang to his lips. An argument here would be worse than pointless, he told himself. It could very well be dangerous. Too dangerous.

He had a sneaking suspicion that Major Linh just might be expecting them. He knew the NVA had agents all over the place, and it was likely there was at least one with access to Three-Niner-Bayou who would pass on the report of Fletcher's escape during that VC attack those long hours ago.

From what Fletcher knew about Linh, the Viet major was smart. Linh would be well aware that he was the most likely customer for a stolen top-secret spy list.

From behind Fletcher, Robbins grumbled.

"I'm gettin' awful tired, Pete. Sure as hell hope you know where you're going."

Fletcher noticed that for the first time, Robbins had fallen in with Murphy's habit of disregarding Fletcher's rank.

"I know where we're going," Fletcher assured them. "You guys just let me do the thinking."

"Why sure, cracker." Murphy sniggered. "Just like we let you do all the planning up to now, all the planning that landed us in this deep shit. We coulda done years in a stockade, asshole."

"We're not in a stockade now, are we?"

"Gettin' out was just pure dumb luck," Murphy shot back, "and you damn well know it."

Robbins chimed in.

"Yeah, just dumb luck, Petey."

Fletcher experienced a renewed urge to mow down these two right here and now, but he forced that down, too.

Let them have their fun, he told himself once again. The thought had served to pacify him several times during this all-night trek. Later, yeah. Later. Then these two shitheads would find out who was in charge!

Murphy moved on.

Fletcher and Robbins stayed close behind.

The claustrophobic, smothering closeness of jungle and shadows was deep, nearly impenetrable.

Fletcher regretted in retrospect the time they had spent back at the hut of the Cambodian tribesman, taking their pleasure with the wife before Murphy killed her.

Fletcher had hoped to reach the NVA base before daybreak.

He was more worried about the patrols than he let on to Murphy or Robbins. If they encountered a recon patrol from Linh's base, the dinks might easily shoot first and then look to see whom they had blasted.

Now that Pete Fletcher was this close to his goal, so close to the life he had always been destined to lead, he was not about to let anything like that screw it up. He hoped.

It was 0400 hours.

This close to the base, surely he could make it the rest of the way by himself. The only reason he had brought the other two along in the first place was to have their backup in case of trouble, he told himself.

Now, it was beginning to look as if Murphy and Robbins might have already become expendable.

Fletcher fingered the selector switch of his M-16. One flick and he could take out Murphy with a quick burst. Then, he was confident, he could spin around and waste an unsuspecting Robbins before that friggin' hayseed could make a move to defend himself.

Trouble was, Fletcher reasoned further, that would bring down a patrol on his head for sure.

He was so deep in thought that he almost did not notice Murphy had stopped.

Fletcher came to a halt.

Robbins moved up beside him.

Murphy turned to face them.

"What's up now?" Fletcher asked peevishly.

A stray beam of moonlight penetrated dense foliage, providing enough illumination to see the mean look on Murphy's face.

"Been doing some thinking, cracker. This Major Linh, he won't care about much of anything right now except getting his dink hands on that list, wouldn't you say?"

Pete Fletcher felt a cold finger track its way up his spine.

"He'll want the list, don't worry about that."

"I'm not worried about it. What I'm trying to figure is, why do I need you?"

The muzzle of Murphy's M-16 was aimed in Fletcher's general direction.

Fletcher swallowed, his throat parched dry. At this range, it would not take much aiming. I've waited too long, he realized with a creeping sense of panic.

"You need me, Murphy, to deal with Major Linh. I've had experience with his kind before—"

"Piss on your experience," Murphy sneered. "If I've got the list and Linh wants it, that's all I need to know."

Fletcher wondered if he could dive to the side and get his rifle up into firing position fast enough.

The snout of Robbins's weapon pressed against the base of his spine.

"Forget it, Petey." Robbins snickered. "I got the drop on him, Murph. He won't pull nothin'."

"Real good, kid. You got a good hate for this lieutenant, too, huh?"

"Damn right. You want me to waste him, Murph?"

Fletcher knew he was close, too damn close to death all of a sudden, without warning, on this smelly jungle trail. It can't end like this! his mind screamed. There had to be a way out. There had to be!

Murphy held out a big hand.

"Gimme that piece of paper."

Fletcher inhaled a deep breath, acutely conscious of the rifle barrel prodding his spine.

"I won't give it to you," he answered in a voice he willed to be steady.

"Then I'll just take it off your body." Murphy shrugged almost absently.

"Lemme kill him, Murph." Robbins giggled, awaiting the other man to give him the order.

"We're a team, huh, kid?" Murphy chuckled.

"You bet, guy. Just you and me."

"Just me, sucker."

Murphy's rifle belched flame.

The bullets caught Robbins across the bridge of his nose, spraying brains out the back of his head, the impact hurling Robbins around.

Fletcher felt a hot splash of blood from the bursting wound.

Shock at the unexpected act kept Fletcher frozen for a split second more and by the time he started to make a break, Murphy had him in his sights again.

"Just stand still, cracker. I can still do to you what I did to him." He gestured with the barrel of his rifle. "Back away."

Fletcher was glad to put some distance between himself and Gary Robbins's body.

"Sure, Murph, sure…uh, just take it easy, huh?"

Murphy thought that was funny.

"Right, easy. Now, boy, you gonna hand over that piece of paper or not? I'm not too crazy about poking around a dead body to find it, but I will if I have to."

Fletcher knew Murphy meant every word. He stalled, anyway.

"Why'd you shoot Robbins? He was on your side."

"I don't need him on my side," the black snarled. "Don't need anybody now, especially not a stupid punk like him." The muzzle of his rifle lifted significantly. "The list, cracker."

"I'll have to set my rifle down."

"Do it then, just be real careful about it."

Moving slowly, Fletcher placed his M-16 on the ground. Then he reached inside his boot and worked free the folded sheet of onionskin. He held it out to Murphy.

"Here. Go on, take it, damn you."

Murphy stepped closer, somewhat tense himself now, wary of a trick.

Fletcher thought about dropping the list, then jumping Murphy when the man's eyes followed it, but Murphy was quick, too damn quick to play those kinds of games with, so Fletcher let him snatch the list out of his hand.

"Guess I'm boss now, huh, cracker," Murphy sneered, grinning hugely. He stooped, shoved the paper into the side of his boot and started to straighten.

Fletcher dived into Murphy's knees in a rolling block.

The bigger man's rifle spit almost in his ear, the muzzle-flash searing Fletcher's cheek.

Murphy staggered and lost his balance, started to fall, dropping the rifle.

Fletcher drove his fist up into Murphy's groin with every ounce of his strength.

The blow elicited a howl of pain from Murphy.

Fletcher wasn't worried anymore about attracting the attention of a patrol. Murphy was going to kill him unless he killed Murphy first. All Fletcher cared about right now was survival.

He surged to his feet, catching the larger man in the stomach with his shoulder and bowling Murphy out of his way. He started to lunge for his rifle.

Murphy flailed out and latched onto his ankle.

Fletcher fell heavily.

Then Murphy was on Fletcher's back, battering him around the head and shoulders with vicious punches.

Fletcher got his hands and knees under him and managed to heave himself into a roll, throwing

Murphy off to the side. He lashed out with a foot and felt the satisfying jar of his boot against flesh and bone. Murphy grunted in pain.

Fletcher stormed up again, looking around for his rifle, realizing with a surge of fright that he was turned around and did not know where either of the weapons was. Before Fletcher could orient himself, Murphy crashed into him with a flying tackle of his own, both men slamming again to the ground, the breath going out of Fletcher with a whoosh.

Murphy landed on top, his greater weight pinning Fletcher down. Murphy's left hand found Fletcher's throat and bore down, pinning Fletcher to the ground. His right fist rocketed around, smashing once, then again and again into Fletcher's face.

A harsh, commanding voice spoke in Vietnamese.

Figures materialized out of the shadows of night, closing in on Murphy and Pete Fletcher.

An NVA patrol!

Murphy was roughly pulled off Fletcher by two of the NVA soldiers, who then covered both men with rifles as the rest of the patrol closed in and did likewise, warily.

The leader of the patrol stepped over to Fletcher, barking a command at him.

Fletcher gathered his strength, hauling himself to his feet, still shaky; but at least, he told himself, he was alive. That was more than he had expected a couple of seconds ago at the hands of Cleon Murphy.

The leader of the patrol switched to English.

"Hands on top of your heads, dogs! You come with us!"

Fletcher forced a smile and tried to look and sound more confident than he felt.

"Of course we're coming with you. We want to see Major Linh immediately!"

The NVA regular looked at Fletcher with no emotion except hateful contempt, and motioned curtly for the Americans to start walking.

Murphy fell in step alongside Fletcher, both of them closely surrounded by North Viet soldiers who prodded them roughly with their rifles.

Fletcher hurt all over. His head still had not stopped spinning from the fight with Murphy, but he forced himself to put one foot in front of the other and march forward as he and Murphy were shoved down the jungle trail, the NVA patrol ignoring Robbins's sprawled corpse as if it did not exist.

"You really got these dinks eatin' out of your hand, don'tcha, Lieutenant cracker?" Murphy rumbled bitterly.

"It'll be all right," Fletcher assured him, hardly recognizing his own voice.

Fletcher did not know if he was trying to convince Murphy or himself.

MACK BOLAN REACHED BACK with a hand to indicate for Gunsmoke to stop, as Sioung had just motioned to Bolan in the inky predawn gloom.

Gunsmoke repeated the gesture, bringing the other three to a halt.

No words were exchanged. Bolan crouched beside Sioung. The two of them studied the dark human shape sprawled on the padded-down ground of the winding trail. Then, while his men covered him, Bolan crept forward and knelt beside the heap of what, until not too long ago, had been a man.

Moonlight filtering through the tree fronds told the identity of the dead man.

Corporal Gary Robbins, soldier-gone-bad.

The punk who had wanted out of Nam so bad.

He was out of Vietnam, all right, thought Bolan.

He had died in Cambodia.

Bolan felt the body. Still warm. That had to mean Fletcher and Murphy were up ahead, somewhere close.

There might still be time.

Sioung knelt, closely studying the dark ground around Robbins's corpse.

"Many men came through here," the Mont stated.

"How long ago?" Bolan asked.

"Not long. Five minutes, perhaps ten."

Bolan nodded.

A patrol must have stumbled across Fletcher and his men, and Robbins had twitched wrong.

They were close to the NVA base now. Damn close.

The NVA, or Cambodian army patrol would take Fletcher and Murphy in.

Linh could have them by now.

Bolan growled "Come on" to his men.

The five of them resumed making their way through the clinging jungle.

Ten minutes later, they found Major Linh's base.

Bolan and Sioung scrambled up trees to get a better look at this NVA staging area and Bolan immediately started calculating possible strategies.

A high barbed-wire fence enclosed the rectangular compound, machine-gun platforms mounted at each corner of the perimeter, NVA regulars manning each machine gun.

Sioung motioned silently to Bolan, pointing out the location of several forward observer posts.

Bolan felt fairly confident that he and his men could get past these sentries, but that still left the problem of getting inside the compound.

The killground, cleared around the sprawling base, was not brightly lit, and there was not enough illumination from lights atop poles evenly spaced along the perimeter, to wholly prevent a covert penetration of the base under normal circumstances, thought Bolan. But he was certain that Linh had beefed up security down there; the NVA base looked waiting and ready for trouble, almost as if inviting it.

The grounds to the sides would be either mined, rigged with punji pits, or both.

Four guards were posted at the front gate, a sandbagged machine-gun pit nearby with an M-60 facing the entrance.

The base seemed fairly awake, more so than usual, considering the predawn hour.

Major Linh was most definitely expecting company.

Bolan motioned to Sioung, then started slipping carefully back down to the ground from his treetop perch. When he dropped onto the soft loam at the base of the tree, Gunsmoke was at his side an instant later.

"Bloodbrother says he heard something," Gunsmoke whispered. "Coming up behind us."

"Everybody down," Bolan whispered.

He hit the ground at the base of a thick bush and waited as his men similarly sought cover.

A moment later, he heard what had attracted Bloodbrother's attention: someone moving through the jungle night toward them, several people, and whoever they were, they were not making much effort to be quiet.

A returning patrol, Bolan thought.

Had to be. Anxious to get back to camp, to get some chow and some sleep, none too worried about running into trouble this close to home.

As Bolan waited for them to advance closer, a plan formulated itself in his head. Dangerous, sure, but what wasn't?

Sioung was only a few feet away.

Bolan relayed to the Mont what he wanted done, in tones so low they would not be audible any farther.

Sioung passed on the orders to the others.

Bolan saw the point man of the enemy patrol push his way through the clinging foliage.

The man strode past him, less than five feet away.

Bolan held his position, waiting for the proper moment to strike.

When the time came, there would be no margin for error whatsoever, not this close to that base.

It was a six-man patrol.

The Executioner waited.

A heartbeat more until the members of the patrol were situated right.

Bolan went in for the kill, coming to his feet in a smooth, powerful surge. His arm whipped around and the knife he gripped in his fingers flew through the heavy night air.

The blade caught the NVA point man just to the left center of his back. The enemy trooper had time only for a muted grunt of pain before pitching forward onto his face.

Before the first man hit the ground, Bolan was on the next one in line, his left hand gripping the barrel of the man's rifle, pushing it aside, while his right lashed out for the throat, the rock-hard side of Bolan's clenched fist hacking at the man's Adam's apple to cut off the outcry that had begun.

The man gasped for air.

Bolan punched him in the stomach, then drove a shoulder into him and rode him to the ground, locking his fingers around the man's throat and squeezing, applying kill pressure.

The NVAer thrashed around some but was disoriented, his blows ineffectual. The Viet went limp and Bolan smelled the stench of the dead man's sphincters releasing.

A few paces away, Sioung went for the throat of his man, coming up close behind him, too close for the Viet to bring his weapon into play. Sioung knife slit the soldier's throat with one smooth stroke, blood splattering over the Mont guerrilla fighter's hand and arm. He ignored it.

Gunsmoke grabbed the rifle his target was carrying and twisted it up, slamming the barrel into the man's mouth to keep him quiet. Harrington unleathered one of his six-guns and brought it across the man's head with a heavy thud, hearing the crunch as skullbone caved in.

The enemy trooper slumped to the ground, blood leaking from his ears.

Gunsmoke hammered him again with the pistol barrel, to make sure.

Bloodbrother hit his man with all the power in his rangy frame.

The soldier dropped, and Bloodbrother was on top of him as soon as he touched the ground.

Loudelk's knife flashed up, then down, then rapidly up and down once again.

The hapless NVA patrol's rearguard was Deadeye's responsibility.

Washington knocked the guy's rifle aside and tackled him, the impact as they landed driving the air from the man's lungs.

Deadeye wrapped thick, powerful fingers around the enemy's throat to quickly, silently strangle the life out of the downed man, the muscles in Washington's shoulders and broad back flexing, rolling under his camou fatigues until the NVA man stopped wriggling and kicking his feet against the jungle floor.

It was done. This part, anyway.

Bolan gathered his men around him and saw that they were all okay.

There had been no sounds except a few thuds and grunts, no shooting or outcry from the dead men. The skirmish had gone undetected. Had they been discovered, the jungle would already have been alive with reinforcements from the nearby base.

Bolan knelt by each corpse in turn.

Three of the dead enemies' uniforms had escaped the blood-letting—the ones disposed of by Gunsmoke, Deadeye and Bolan himself.

The infiltrators would only need two uniforms.

"Get a couple of these men stripped," Bolan said to his team.

He moved back to where he could see the NVA encampment and further considered the various angles of his stratetgy while the ghoulish stripping of dead men went on behind him.

Chances were, he considered, Pete Fletcher and Cleon Murphy were already in Linh's hands. Whether or not Linh already had the list was another question, but even if Linh did have that list, Bolan intended to see to it that the major got no chance to make any use of it.

They probably had a snowball's chance in Saigon, but that was the name of this Executioner's game when the stakes were this high.

He eased back to his men, who had finished retrieving the uniforms from two of the dead soldiers.

"All right, Gunsmoke, you and Sioung have just joined the North Vietnamese Army."

Gunsmoke held up one of the uniform jackets and looked upon it with doubtful distaste.

"You sure about that, Sarge? Without even knowin' what other little critters might be living in here?"

"They won't mind sharing." Bolan grinned dryly. "The two of you get dressed. Hurry."

It did not take long for Gunsmoke and Sioung to don the NVA garb, putting the uniforms on over their own clothes so they could hurriedly tear them off when the time came, the two of them the only ones close enough to the size of the dead men to carry off the masquerade Bolan had in mind.

He knew that all other factors aside, his size and that of Bloodbrother and Deadeye made it impossible for them to pretend to be Vietnamese, even at night in dim lighting, not to mention their racial persuasions.

They wouldn't have gotten within fifty feet of the base that way, but he, Deadeye and Bloodbrother *could* pass as more prisoners, especially with Sioung and Gunsmoke behind them wearing NVA uniforms, prodding them along with rifles. Role camouflage, it was called, and infiltrator Bolan was a master of it.

"Gunsmoke, you're in charge of the hardware," Bolan said, briskly, handing his side arm and rifle to Harrington.

Bloodbrother and Deadeye did likewise.

Gunsmoke took the pistols first, tucking them behind his NVA uniform belt, scratching unenthusiastically at his belly as he did so.

"Told you these getups had other occupants," the Texan groused.

He took their M-16s, too, and slung them over his and Sioung's shoulders, taking on the appearance of a walking arsenal, but they had to get their weapons into the camp somehow.

Besides, thought Bolan, if Gunsmoke and Sioung were pretending to be authentic NVA regulars, they would not have left captured weapons behind; they would have brought the gear in along with their prisoners, just as they were doing now.

"When—if—we make it inside," Bolan said, "we'll head for their command hut. That's where Linh will have Fletcher and the list. Let's go."

He, Bloodbrother and Deadeye placed their hands on their heads and moved out, not walking too boldly.

Close behind them came Sioung and Gunsmoke, their rifles trained on the backs of the three in front of them.

Sioung issued harsh, guttural commands in Vietnamese from time to time.

The scene looked right, Bolan knew.

It could get them onto the base.

Once in, though, there was no knowing what would happen...except that this Cambodian hell would explode apart one damn way or another.

The fuse had been lit miles away, in Special Forces camp Three-Niner-Bayou.

It had sputtered and hissed all during the long hot night trek of pursuit; during the near-confrontation with the first patrol; during a firefight with the Communist bandits at a Cambodian refugee camp when Bolan had taken lives and helped to bring a new one into the world; and now...now the fuse was burning down to the very end, closer and closer to igniting the grand slam that would bloodily climax this desperate mission.

Yeah, it was that close.

Heartbeats away.

Hell was about to explode.

Twenty

Lieutenant Peter Fletcher was worried.

There had been no conversation on their way into the NVA base and the silence from the sentry patrol who led Fletcher and Murphy to Linh's headquarters hut had a grim feeling to it.

Murphy turned hate-filled glances on the lieutenant from time to time, and it was clear to Fletcher that the black thought they were in deep trouble.

Fletcher was afraid he might be right.

When they reached the NVA compound and Fletcher saw the unusually heavy security around the base perimeter, he was even more convinced that Linh had been expecting him to show, which meant the NVA commander probably knew all about the list, as well.

The night patrol and its prisoners were ushered through the entrance.

As the gates swung shut behind them, the patrol leader issued a curt command and gestured sharply at a nearby structure, and Fletcher knew this was where the major would be awaiting their arrival.

They marched toward the HQ hut, Murphy raking Fletcher with another burning glare.

"If we ever get out of here alive, cracker, you and me still got a score to settle."

Fletcher let his anger boil over.

"That's fine with me, boy. I haven't forgotten that you tried to kill me back there."

Murphy stopped in his tracks, then made a lunge toward Fletcher, big hands clenched into fists.

Their captors quickly put a stop to the impending fight, savagely poking both Americans in the back, threatening with their rifles.

Fletcher and Murphy broke off from each other grudgingly, and their guards continued to prod them toward the HQ structure.

"Next time I'll do a better job of wasting you," Murphy muttered under his breath.

There won't be a next time, Fletcher thought. Once Linh had the list, he would be grateful enough to the man who had supplied it to do Fletcher a favor...like removing a troublesome pest. Or so Fletcher told himself.

He wasn't sure why the NVA troopers were being so rough with them, but he supposed that you could not expect common foot soldiers to understand.

To these dinks, he and Murphy were just two more American prisoners, thought Fletcher. Major Linh would know better.

The command building was built on a shallow platform, protection against the inundating floods of the monsoon season.

Fletcher and Murphy climbed the three steps to the narrow porch that ran the length of the front.

Inside the structure were several rooms opening off a central hallway, the whole place lit by crudely wired electric lights.

Fletcher heard the *chuffing* of a generator coming from somewhere nearby.

There were several sentries stationed inside the small building. They kept their weapons trained on the American prisoners, who were shoved down the hall by two soldiers while the rest of the patrol waited outside.

Fletcher hoped Murphy had sense enough not to try anything, not with more than half a dozen rifles covering them.

The patrol leader who had captured them stepped around the Americans and opened a door. He entered what Fletcher saw was an office, respectfully addressing a man seated behind a desk.

The seated man had a narrow, pinched face, his dark, reptilian eyes unmistakably cruel as he looked out at the Americans.

Linh.

Had to be.

"Bring them in," Linh commanded in English.

The patrol leader turned, snapping an order at his men, who in turn prodded Fletcher and Murphy into the office.

Linh spoke to the patrol leader in Vietnamese.

The soldier nodded and withdrew from the office, taking his men with him, leaving the two Americans face-to-face with Linh and another Viet officer, a captain, who covered them with a Chi-com K-50.

Linh studied the Americans. He smiled thinly.

"Lieutenant Peter Fletcher, Corporal Cleon Murphy," he said in controlled tones. He indicated the NVA officer covering them with the machine gun. "Captain Trang and I have been expecting you."

Fletcher smiled, putting in as much charm as he could muster.

"That's right, Major. We're here and we're glad, I don't mind telling you."

Linh fired a cigarette, letting the smoke curl wispily toward the ceiling before he spoke again.

If he's trying to make us nervous, he's succeeding, thought Fletcher. The lieutenant worked hard not to let this show.

"I was informed," Linh resumed, "that one of your companions met a most unfortunate end."

Fletcher fired a glare at Murphy.

"Uh, yeah...very unfortunate. He trusted someone he shouldn't have."

"A failing quite common among you Americans, I have found." The smile slid off Linh's face. It had never reached his eyes, anyway. "The list," he demanded sharply. "I will have it now."

Fletcher exerted all his willpower not to look at Murphy. He didn't wish Linh to know just yet that Murphy had the list. Nobody is going to squeeze me out, Fletcher told himself. Not at this stage of the game.

"I won't insult you by pretending not to know what you're talking about, Major," Fletcher said smoothly, "but I would like to know just how much you feel the list is worth."

"You intend to *sell* the list to me, Lieutenant?"

Linh looked intently at Fletcher as he asked the question in a mocking tone that was barely disguised.

"Uh, that's the idea," Fletcher said, sensing it was all going wrong, that he had made the biggest mistake of his life.

Linh slapped one hand down on the desk sharply, the report resounding like a pistol shot.

"I think you are a bigger fool than I had supposed, stupid American. The list! Turn it over to me at once."

Murphy shifted uncomfortably.

"Uh, look here, Petey," the black man growled in a strange voice Fletcher had not heard him use before. "Uh, maybe we, uh, better do what the major here says...?"

Fletcher wanted to scream at the moron to shut up. You just had to know how to handle these dinks, Fletcher reassured himself. Even the supposedly clever ones like this sonfabitching slope across the desk from them.

"There's no need for threats, Major," Fletcher said quickly. "I'm sure we can work something out, make some sort of deal."

Linh laughed, an arrogant sound of genuine amusement. He barked a command at Captain Trang.

Trang straightened alertly, training his rifle on Fletcher and Murphy.

Linh stood up from his seat behind the desk and leaned forward, resting his fingertips on the desktop.

"There will be no deals made here, American. I want that list. Give it to me, or my man will shoot you down and we will take it from the body of whichever one of you has it."

THE SENTRIES AT THE GATE were not quite as alert as Bolan had expected them to be.

His little group marched bold as brass up to the entrance: Bolan, Bloodbrother, and Deadeye in front as prisoners, Gunsmoke and Sioung following closely behind in NVA uniform, according to plan.

The guards at the gate spotted them coming, but there was nothing threatening about the appearance of the newcomers and the M-60 machine gunners nearby paid only cursory attention.

Bolan, Bloodbrother and Deadeye had their hands on their heads, Gunsmoke and Sioung strutting along behind them as if extremely proud of themselves for capturing three Americans behind enemy lines.

Too lazy to raise their weapons when there was no officer around, the gate lookouts watched as what they took to be two comrades-in-arms marched the prisoners up to the gate.

Sioung barked at the sentries rapidly in Vietnamese.

Bolan caught enough of the exchange to know that Sioung's attitude was an arrogant one; he claimed that he and his companion had captured these Americans by themselves.

The gate guards laughed and one of them said it appeared that these were more prisoners like the ones brought in a few minutes earlier, no doubt captured from the same American patrol. He indicated a structure across the way with a flagpole in front of it, which Bolan knew had to be Linh's HQ.

He felt a surge of anticipation.

The sentry could only be referring to Fletcher and Murphy, and the NVA sentry spoke as if they had been brought in very recently.

Sioung demanded that they open the gates.

The guards complied, swinging the two-by-four-and-barbed-wire gate open, standing aside so the little group could pass through.

There were two more guards just inside the gate, Bolan saw immediately, in addition to the four outside. Facing the gate but a good fifteen yards away was the central machine-gun nest.

There were a lot of shadows around the wall despite the lighting from atop the poles.

Bolan exploded into action before the gates could swing shut.

His hands came off the top of his head and shot out to grab the throat of one of the inside sentries, the paralyzing grip cutting off any sounds of warning from the man as Bolan's thumbs dug in to grind against the pressure points in the guy's neck.

The soldier ceased his brief flailings and went limp.

Bloodbrother was doing the same thing to the other inside guard, squeezing the man into lifelessness.

Deadeye had brought up the rear in this short line of imitation prisoners.

When Bolan and Bloodbrother went into action, Washington stopped and reached out to either side of him, grabbing the two sentries on each side of the gate. He jerked the startled NVA troopers toward him, stepped back and slammed their heads together.

Their skulls crushed with thin, crackling sounds like breaking eggshells.

Gunsmoke and Sioung both flared into action as well, Gunsmoke pivoting to their right, Sioung to their left.

Gunsmoke's combat knife appeared in his hand with eye-numbing speed, flashing out, the blade burying itself in one guard's middle.

The guy slumped, dead meat.

Gunsmoke caught him before he could fall to the ground making noise.

It was left to Sioung to take one of the guards alive.

The Mont bowled into the man in a sudden, savage lunge, the guerrilla fighter using all the strength in his wiry little body. The two of them tumbled to the ground outside the fenced-in perimeter, the partially open gate helping to shield them from inside.

Sioung grabbed the man's rifle and twisted it to one side as they toppled, tearing the weapon out of the man's hands.

The sentry opened his mouth to raise an outcry.

The point of Sioung's knife pricked lightly into the soft flesh of the guy's throat, stopping him from making a sound.

The man looked up at the Mont with wide, terror-filled eyes.

Bolan, still gripping the throat of his victim, shifted the guard's corpse around, leaning it against the wall. He snagged the man's tunic on a nail sticking out from one of the poles supporting the barbed-wire fence, to hold the body up.

Bloodbrother did the same with his guard.

The ruse would hardly fool anyone for long, especially with sunrise so near, but for the moment it looked for all the world as if the two sentries were still standing guard there in the shadows.

Bolan hoped the deception would be successful enough to buy the time he and his men needed. He stepped rapidly over to where Sioung was holding the surviving sentry.

The man lay extremely still, the tip of the Montagnard's blade having already drawn blood, a thin dark red snake winding its way down the side of the Viet soldier's throat.

"Ask him where Fletcher and Murphy have been taken," Bolan said.

Sioung repeated the question in Vietnamese.

The soldier tried to shake his head, but the knife stopped him. He rattled out a stream of beseeching jabber.

Sioung ignored the pleading, repeating the query one more time, pressing harder on the knife, causing blood to trickle a little faster.

The man talked then, fast, whispering, too frightened to lie.

Sioung kept the knife where it was and looked around at Bolan.

"They are in Major Linh's command hut, as you supposed."

Bolan nodded.

Sioung removed the knife from the guard's throat and the man took one deep breath before Sioung plunged the blade into his body again.

The guard arched up off the ground for a second like a pulled-back bow, then relaxed.

Sioung withdrew the blade, wiping it clean **on** the dead man's tunic, and stood up.

"I no want to cut this dog's throat," he whispered to Bolan. "Would have splashed blood all over Sioung's uniform."

"Close the gates," Bolan said.

They assumed their poses again, less than thirty seconds having elapsed, the three in front carrying themselves like prisoners, Gunsmoke and Sioung swinging the gate shut behind them.

The machine gunners at the M-60 had noticed nothing in the darkness save the gate opening and closing.

The Americans' route would take them within a few yards of the machine-gun nest. To detour farther away from it would look too suspicious.

Bolan knew he and his unit had to pass it by without being spotted as impostors. He had little doubt they could take out the NVAers manning the M-60, but not without drawing a whole lot of attention to themselves, to put it mildly.

They had been able to get away with disposing of the gate guards only because of the shadows near the wall, the sheer audacity of the maneuver, their silence in killing and plain dumb luck. And penetration specialist Bolan knew that in a situation like this, the only thing you could do with good luck was embrace it because it never lasted very long.

They would just have to take their chances with the M-60 gunners when the withdrawal came.

The three phony prisoners dragged their feet, as if they wanted to go anywhere but the command hut. Real prisoners would have a pretty good idea of the torment awaiting them in such a situation and Bolan knew this had to look good.

As they passed the machine-gun pit, one of the gunners stood and called out to them.

Sioung took it in stride, the Mont "NVA trooper" growling back an answer about taking more of the American imperialist running dogs to be questioned by Major Linh.

That must have satisfied the gunner, because he laughed approvingly and sat back down behind the sandbagged fortification.

Bolan knew they couldn't see his face in the gloom. He allowed himself a grin.

"Imperialist running dogs?" he echoed in a whispered chuckle when they were out of earshot of the M-60 crew.

"When dealing with idiots, one must not appear too intelligent," Siouing replied.

"Looks like we've made it," Gunsmoke noted.

Deadeye snorted.

"Right. All we've got to do now is get inside that HQ building, find the guys we're after, get the list away from 'em, waste Linh and get back out alive."

"Just trying to be optimistic, guys," Gunsmoke replied lightly.

His men were nervous, Bolan knew. Any one in his right mind would be. It was live-or-die, put-it-all-on-the-line time.

"We'll head for Linh's office as soon as we get inside," Bolan told them. "They haven't had time to finish interrogating Fletcher and Murphy already if they were just brought in like that sentry said. That's where we'll find the list."

Quick nods from the others signified their understanding.

This would have to be a lightning-strike hit. If they could get into Linh's office, retrieve that list and terminate Linh, Fletcher and Murphy fast enough, then they might be able to make it back to the gates, and once through and into the jungle again, Bolan knew they would have a chance.

"GODDAMN YOU, FLETCHER," Murphy spit, "I'm not about to let you get me killed."

The black soldier turned to Linh.

"I've got the list," he told the Viet major standing behind the desk, "and you can damn well have it if it'll buy me a pass outa here."

Murphy started to bend over. Fletcher knew what the black was going to do. Murphy was reaching for his boot where he'd stashed the sheet of onionskin after taking it from Fletcher. Murphy was going to give Linh the list!

Fletcher grabbed Murphy's arm.

"Dammit, you black sonafabitch, this isn't fair!" Then he snarled at Linh. "We almost got killed getting you this list, Major. We deserve something!"

Linh said nothing, glaring across the desk at them.

Murphy looked down at Fletcher's restraining hand on his arm, and what little control the black had left snapped. He swung a fist at Fletcher.

Fletcher saw the punch coming and tried to duck, but the long night and everything else he had been through during the past twenty-four hours slowed down his reflexes.

Murphy's fist caught Fletcher on the side of the head, knocking him loose.

Fletcher staggered off balance and fell to one knee, his senses swirling, feeling as if the walls of Major Linh's little office were closing in on him.

Linh watched impassively, as did the machine-gun-toting Captain Trang. A glint of amusement danced in Linh's eyes.

Murphy's punch, though grazing, packed enough power to spin the world crazily in front of Fletcher's eyes. He had not recovered fully when he looked up to see Murphy coming at him, wild-eyed, crazed.

Murphy kicked, his boot toe catching Fletcher in the side, driving Fletcher to the floor.

Fletcher banged hard against the floor, clutching at his side, moaning. It felt to him as if Murphy's kick had broken his ribs. From the corner of his eye, he saw another kick coming, Murphy seemingly having forgotten the desperate situation they were in. It appeared as if all the out-of-control, raging black man cared about then now was stomping Fletcher to death.

Fletcher tried to ward off the blows but he was not fast enough or strong enough.

Murphy kept pummeling him.

When he finally stopped, Fletcher was stretched out on the floor, moaning weakly, his face a bloody mask.

Murphy stood over him for a long moment, breathing heavily, blood-smeared fists still clenched. Then, slowly, he remembered where he was. He turned to face the cold, arrogant eyes of Major Linh.

"I assume then," Linh snapped at Murphy, "that you are the one who has the list."

"Damn straight I've got it," Murphy snarled. "Tell your boy Trang not to get trigger-happy and I'll give it to you."

Linh's nod was almost indiscernible. The Viet said nothing.

Murphy reached down and extricated the folded piece of paper from his boot. He straightened and unfolded it.

Fletcher found the strength to crawl onto his knees. He watched as Murphy withdrew the list. He saw the death of his dreams.

"No, damn you—"

"Give it to me," Linh demanded.

Murphy extended the piece of folded paper across the desk.

"You don't want to deal with a no-account asshole like the lieutenant here, anyway." Murphy delivered a contemptuous sneer in Fletcher's direc-

"Now you and me, Major, we can settle this between us, can't we?"

Linh snatched the list from Murphy's fingers, allowing his eyes to quickly scan what was typed there. He looked up and smiled, a death-mask grimace.

"Indeed we can."

He nodded to Trang.

Trang triggered his SMG, unleashing a noisy three-round burst that stiched Murphy in the center of his back, ripping him apart, the K-50's recoil riding up slightly so the final slug pulped Murphy's head, dropping him to the floor.

Then Trang tracked toward Fletcher.

Fletcher widened his mouth to shout but the sound was lost in another short burst that rattled the walls of the small command structure.

The villa in the south of France. The sports car. The willing women. All of Lieutenant Pete Fletcher's dreams, along with his life, blew away as the bullets pitched him backward, chest and stomach a splattering ruin. Fletcher shuddered and died, sightless eyes staring at the ceiling, blood bubbling.

Linh resumed his seat behind the desk, spreading out the folded piece of onionskin paper on his desktop, smoothing it with his hands, trying to flatten out the creases. He waved offhandedly to Trang, indicating, but without looking at, the messy bodies of the two Americans.

"Get some men, Captain. Clean that up."

"Yes, Major."

Trang stepped over the corpses, exiting the office, closing the door after him.

Linh experienced an exhilarating feeling of exultation.

Foolish Americans. Idiots. To bring him such a treasure as this top-secret spy list on a silver platter, then expect him to spare their lives! They had actually expected to be *paid* for their treachery!

Well, thought Linh, they have been paid.

Paid in death.

The only fitting remittance for such traitors.

He concentrated his attention on the prize he held in his hands.

And on the next step in what could be the ultimate coup in getting himself out of this stinking jungle command, up through the ranks of command to Hanoi.

Mack Bolan.

Linh had the list, but he wanted more. He wanted Bolan's head on a stick for all to see, to witness Linh's greatness.

He knew Bolan would come for the list, and when he did Linh would be ready and Mack Bolan would be as dead as the two Americans on the office floor.

Linh wondered where the Executioner was at this moment.

Twenty-One _____

Time was running out, but fast, when they heard the sounds of machine-gun fire from within the HQ building where the gate guard had told Sioung they would find Fletcher, Murphy and Major Linh.

Bolan and his death squad had made the inky gloom at the base of the command structure without being discovered.

The NVA jungle base continued to snooze around them.

The beefed-up security precautions had all been intended to repel an attack from the outside. The attention of the men stationed along the perimeter remained on the jungle night outside.

Bolan was reminded of Special Forces Camp 105-A, Three-Niner-Bayou, and how it had not been that many hours since he and these three men had left behind there an identical situation, an identical setting.

The warrior reflected briefly on how the existence of the universal soldier in war is much the same no matter what the side.

Philosophies, styles of life, societies; they all differed, yes, just as good differs from evil, but it all came down to the same thing for the guy sent to fight in the rain and mud, no matter which army you were in.

There was always the waiting, the watching, for those unannounced flash points of kill or be killed, that could strike any time.

Like right now.

Gunsmoke and Sioung still wore their appropriated NVA uniforms.

The five had made their way more or less secretively after rounding a corner behind the M-60 machine-gun pit.

Bolan figured that he and his men could lapse into the role-playing of guards and prisoners again if necessary, if they were spotted and/or questioned between the gate and where Fletcher and Murphy had supposedly been taken for interrogation by Linh.

The Executioner's small penetration team hugged deeper shadows of buildings and equipment throughout the short trip to the frame structure, which looked as hastily thrown together as the rest of this NVA base.

A North Viet army half-ton truck sat in front of the HQ, and Bolan could see several rows of armored troop carriers parked across the way.

Bolan and his men fanned out along the base of the HQ hut the instant gunfire, from somewhere inside, ripped apart the cloak of night, the small penetration unit no longer concerned with any attempt at maintaining the illusion of prisoners and NVA guards—not this close to the payback.

The gunfire came in short clusters.

Then nothing.

"Cowboy time," Harrington grunted with some show of enthusiasm.

"Wonder what it's about?" Washington whispered.

Then came called questions in Vietnamese from various points around the compound but apparently, Bolan decided, random shooting within these precincts was not all that unusual, for there was no real response.

He motioned for the four men with him to stay in place for an additional handful of seconds. But everything inside of him urged Bolan to push straight on into this building to see what had happened, to get his hands on the top-secret list. Still, he felt it would do no good to go racing inside, only to be bottled up by some NVA troop who finally worked up enough interest to investigate.

A few seconds passed and it became obvious that there would be no real response, no one coming to this structure to see what the shooting had been about.

Bolan motioned his men to follow him.

"Let us find out what it's about."

He and Sioung, Harrington, Washington and Loudelk edged around to the nearest door into the structure, not the main doorway facing the compound, in front of which the half-ton sat parked for daytime duty.

Bolan instead guided his men through a side entrance, which led them to a corridor that ran down the middle of the HQ building.

Closed doors lined the corridor along either wall, the hallway dimly lighted.

Bolan filed in first, his retrieved M-16 up and ready. When he glanced around the corner where the doorway from outside gave way to the corridor, he could see the hallway was clear. He motioned the other four men in after him.

Washington, bringing up the rear, eased the screen door shut soundlessly after them.

The noisy jungle night of chattering, screeching wildlife did not diminish once they were inside the structure; in fact the sounds were magnified by the small building's tin roof and it seemed stickier, hotter inside.

Bolan's camou fatigues were plastered to his body with sweat from the humidity, and the men with him were in the same shape, he knew.

Sioung, Gunsmoke, Deadeye and Bloodbrother remained crouched in the dimness of the short passageway connecting the outside doorway to the corridor, the three infiltrators waiting for Bolan, each holding their own weapons again, watching him closely for any signal to follow his lead while eyeing their surroundings.

Bolan strained to listen from where he crouched and in a few seconds he could discern a low, nearly inaudible exchange of voices speaking Vietnamese, the conversation practically lost beneath the quiltwork of natural night sounds from outside.

An NVA officer emerged into the corridor from one of the doorway, leaving the door open behind him.

Bolan continued to spy from around the corner, undetected by the officer—not Linh; this guy was a captain. The man was followed into the hall by three NVA regulars to whom he had obviously been giving instructions in the minute-and-a-half since the sounds of gunfire.

No one had entered or left the command structure yet, which meant that if Fletcher and Murphy had been brought here, no matter what happened to them, the list of US and ARVN spies in the north was still inside this building.

The Viet captain led the regulars, all of whom toted SKS carbines by shoulder straps, in the direction away from where Bolan and his men watched, waiting.

The Viets strode briskly to the next door down the hallway, one of the regulars hurrying forward to open the door for his officer.

"Take 'em," Bolan growled to his men.

There was only one way this figured in the short time since those shots had been fired.

The NVA captain had been present with Linh when the shooting took place. Linh dispatched the officer across the hall to fetch assistance in clearing away what Bolan imagined would be the human refuse of what had been Fletcher and Murphy.

Good riddance.

And Linh had the list!

The NVA officer spotted the infiltrators' movements when he turned to enter the door held open by the NVA soldier.

Bolan instinctively knew that entrance led to the office with Linh and the list.

The captain started to exclaim something to the regulars, who realized something was wrong and also started to turn.

Bolan let fly his combat knife, flung by the blade after quick aim.

The officer never finished what he started to say. He turned to fully face Bolan and the men who materialized with the Executioner fifteen feet down the corridor.

The captain caught the knife with a surprised gasp that made his face turn color when the blade buried itself to the hilt in his heart, then the hemorrhaging began and the officer died.

The three NVA soldiers had a couple more seconds to live, enough time to try to spread out as best they could within the confines of the corridor, unlimbering their rifles.

Washington and Bloodbrother threw their knives simultaneously, neutralizing soldiers two and three, while Washington stayed behind covering their backtrack.

The fourth NVA regular turned in the opposite direction to flee toward a door located at the far end of the corridor. But before he could do any more than start into his first step to escape and alarm the base, Sioung executed an agile running leap to tackle the soldier in a sprawl that ended with Sioung atop the man's back.

The Mont guerrilla wrapped a length of knotted rope around the soldier's throat, twisting it behind his head. Sioung jerked the man's neck sharply, efficiently snapping the spine with a brittle crack like the overloud pop of a knuckle.

The soldier's body arched stiffly, froze in that position, then slowly collapsed to lie limp.

Sioung unwound the length of rope, pocketing it, swinging his rifle back into firing position again just as Bolan took long strides that put him at the open doorway toward which the men had been heading. Gunsmoke and Deadeye closed in from a couple paces behind him.

Bolan pile-drove himself into the office with a forward roll. The lightning-fast maneuver brought him in well below the pistolfire that erupted at a point considerably higher than Bolan's entrance the instant his blurred figure became visible.

He landed in the middle of a sparsely furnished office before Linh could track his pistol down on target.

Bolan had the NVA major in the sights of his M-16 but he held his fire on this cannibal.

Not yet.

Linh was turning to take another shot at Bolan, but froze when he saw the Executioner had the drop on him. Then the Viet major glanced at the doorway as Sioung, Gunsmoke, Bloodbrother and Deadeye filed in with their rifles.

Bolan saw a look of resignation cross the cannibal's narrow, cruel face and the Executioner could almost see the wheels turning inside Linh's head, his snake eyes evaluating his options, finally making the only choice he could.

Linh dropped his pistol and raised his hands, sullen, waiting.

"You know what I came for, Major," Bolan told him. "Drop the list on the floor between us. Then step back."

As Linh appeared to consider this demand, Sioung, Gunsmoke and Bloodbrother stepped all the way into the room.

Washington eased the door shut after them, except for a few inches through which he spied upon the corridor, his right index finger, like that of the other infiltrators, curled around the trigger of his M-16.

Gunsmoke and Bloodbrother moved to opposite sides of the venetian-blind-draped office window, parting it somewhat to observe the night outside.

"All clear out here, Sarge," Gunsmoke reported.

"So far," Bloodbrother added.

Sioung took a position near Bolan, also training his M-16 on Linh, who stood with his back to the wall behind his desk.

No one in the room paid any attention to the two corpses sprawled atop each other in the middle of the floor, but one glance when he first stepped in had told Bolan all he needed to know about Pete Fletcher and Cleon Murphy.

The two soldiers-gone-rotten were both quite dead in puddles of their own life forces, which was all Bolan needed to know about those two.

He concerned himself with the living.

Bolan's principal concern right now was the possibility that Linh could have hidden the list somewhere in this office in the two minutes or less since the gunfire that had killed Fletcher and Murphy.

Bolan and his men might have a few more seconds remaining to themselves, a minute at most, before the dead sentries propped at the front gate were discovered, which did not leave sufficient time to thoroughly search the room.

The NVA major was astute enough not to yield his ace in the hole simply because he was requested to.

"What list do you mean?" he asked Bolan, a reptilian smirk crossing his features as he spoke perfect Oxford English. He kept his hands raised, eyeballing Bolan steadily. "Are you...with these men?" Linh indicated Fletcher and Murphy almost casually. "They were captured, brought to me, but they had no list."

Bluff time, Bolan thought, not bluffing at all.

Making sure Sioung had his rifle aimed squarely at Linh, the Executioner took a step toward the major.

Linh could not go anywhere, his back remaining pressed against the wall.

Bolan raised his M-16, pushing forward slightly. The snout of the rifle touched Linh's mouth. Bolan applied a bit of pressure. The muzzle of the M-16 parted Linh's lips and teeth and entered his mouth.

The major's eyes became easier to read than before, reptilian glimmers registering the taste of gunmetal when the end of the M-16's muzzle touched the back of his throat.

"The list, Major," Bolan iced softly. "Right now. Or you're minus a head."

Gunsmoke glanced across from where he stood at the window, chuckling at Linh's predicament.

"I'd hand it over, Major. I don't think the sarge is joshing."

Linh blinked once, twice, and nodded.

Bolan stepped back, removing the rifle barrel from the Viet officer's mouth.

"Yes, I have your list," Linh said evenly. "If I give it to you...you will spare me?"

"The list, Major."

Linh sighed resignedly, though he appeared mighty relieved not to have the M-16 rammed down his throat any longer. He delicately, carefully reached into a pocket of his tunic, producing a folded piece of onionskin typing paper. He gave a slight underhanded toss and the piece of paper flipped across the few feet to land where Bolan stood. Then the major raised his hands again and stood, waiting.

Bolan bent to reach for the folded onionskin with his left hand, gripping his weapon, still covering Linh with his right.

He had to chance a quick look at the piece of paper to make certain it was the same list that Colonel Winters had sent them after. Then he could deal with Linh.

Bolan remembered Linh eluding him at the other base the morning before. Linh was full of tricks, the Executioner was only too well aware. It would be just like this snake to hand over a blank sheet of paper.

Bolan picked up the paper. He unfolded it with the thumb and fingers of his left hand, regretting the split seconds he would need to divert his eyes from this NVA cannibal. But there was no other way to ensure that this was *the* list, and besides, Bolan figured, Sioung had Linh covered. He glanced down at the onionskin. He glimpsed a list of typed Viet names.

And in that instant, Sioung shouted something and triggered a single shot that reverberated in the confines of the tiny office, slamming Bolan's eardrums like a fist.

Bolan looked up.

Linh was gone.

A sliding panel snapped shut in the wall behind where Linh had stood, a ragged chunk of wood missing from where Sioung's bullet had gouged the sliding panel.

Gunsmoke and Bloodbrother both whirled where they stood lookout at the window, Washington jerking around from the door.

"Sonofabitch, that is one slippery gook," Gunsmoke growled with emotion.

"That major's got more secret getaways than a rat," rasped Washington, returning his attention to the corridor beyond the almost-closed door.

Bolan rushed over to the sliding panel in the wall, knowing he was too late.

He'd lost Linh again.

He clawed at the wall where an almost invisible break indicated the edge of the panel, but his attempts were futile in the brief seconds he worked to reopen it. Then he gave up trying to pursue the Viet because it did not matter anymore.

He turned toward the others while reaching for a cigarette lighter on Linh's desk. He thumbed the lighter, very hurriedly feeding the highly flammable onionskin into the little flame that hungrily consumed the list. He shredded the charred remainders into a glass ashtray on the desk.

"He move too fast," Sioung growled contritely, head bowed in humiliation. "I fire one round because more bring soldiers. Should have killed Major Linh when Sioung first come in here, for what he do to Ti Bahn and Tran Le."

"I should have let you," Bolan growled. "Don't blame yourself, Sioung. Right now, we've got to get out of here before—"

He was interrupted by the rising bray of a klaxon alarm siren that filled the night from outside, very close by.

"If I'm not mistaken," Gunsmoke drawled, turning from the window to join the others in exiting the office, "there's our cue to giddy-the-hell-up outa this armpit."

Washington stepped out into the corridor first, covering both ends of the hallway, crisply tracking his M-16 right and left as Bolan, Sioung, Bloodbrother and Harrington rapidly filed out behind him.

"That half-ton out front," Bolan said. "Quick!"

He hurried down the short hallway and outside, the four men coming along fast behind him.

They emerged from the HQ structure to find the base stirring to life in response to the loud, abrasive ululating of the klaxon. Lights came to life here and there as voices, querying in Vietnamese, carried from various points around the perimeter. Other, authoritative voices barked orders in response.

Bolan and his men raced to the truck.

None of the hubbub of the awakening base appeared to be directed at their vicinity yet. The blaring alarm sure had the base responding, but to what, the Viet troops were not quite certain, though Bolan knew this would alter drastically within the next handful of seconds. He rounded the front of the vehicle and leaped into the cab for a quick look.

"The keys are in it," he told the others, positioning himself behind the wheel. "Climb aboard!"

Sioung and Gunsmoke joined Bolan in the cab. He cranked the canvas-top heap to life, popping the clutch and grinding gears away from there.

Deadeye caught footing on the running board by the cab door, slipping a huge arm into a webbing restraint for support. Loudelk tumbled over the back gate into the bed of the half-ton as the truck, surged forward, Bolan wheeling the NVA vehicle around sharply, setting off a smokescreen of red dust, aiming the truck in the direction of the front gate.

Washington held on with his left arm, while with his right he gripped his M-16, propped against his right hip.

The truck picked up speed, Bolan hammering the gas pedal almost through the floor. The half-ton rumbled along, closer toward the gate where the dead sentries had been propped such a short time ago.

Bolan kept his senses attuned to the big picture out there beyond the truck's windshield, to the night coming alive on this jungle base as NVA and some

Cambodian regulars spewed from the barracks and along the perimeter to take note of the roaring half-ton and its escape route.

Sporadic gunfire commenced peppering the night from different angles, dull spanging noises telling Bolan their truck was taking hits.

The troopers at the M-60 worked fast, tracking the tripod-mounted machine gun around to fire on the half-ton as it came barreling past.

Three NVA regulars appeared to the right of the vehicle's final run toward the gate, crouching to rake the speeding truck with near-miss riflefire.

Sentries near the front gate discovered the propped-up corpses there and held their ground in the face of the oncoming half-ton, opening fire before common sense prevailed and they dodged to either side when they saw their frantic rounds go wild. The half-ton showed absolutely no indication of slowing down, increasing its speed if anything.

Deadeye opened fire at the regulars, shooting at them from the right.

Two of those unfortunate guys caught it across the chest, stitched into oblivion, while the third Viet kid soldier flattened himself to the ground, a stream of projectiles zapping a jagged line in the wall behind him, sending this one frantically scrambling for cover.

From the open rear of the truck, Bloodbrother Loudelk speedballed a hand grenade into the machine-gun nest before the gunners there could swing the M-60 around to strafe the half-ton as it whammed past.

The grenade blew the machine gun of those manning it out of existence, tossing unhinged bodies and equipment across the sandbags.

Steering with one hand, Bolan straightarm-aimed his .45 automatic out of the side window of the cab, picking off two of the three new gate defenders before they could open fire on the vehicle as it whizzed by; then the half-ton plowed its way through the closed gate, crashing out.

Gunsmoke Harrington emitted an earsplitting rebel yell. Sioung did not know what it was but he too let out a throaty war whoop.

With these two human banshees wailing beside him, and Washington and Bloodbrother hammering at their backtrail, toppling enemy troopers everywhere, Bolan steadied the half-ton rig with both fists and they made it through clear.

The truck rocked without lights along the bumpy road that led into the jungle, away from the base.

More gunfire erupted from behind and projectiles whistled past the cab of the bouncing, noisy ride. Then the truck roared beyond effective range, driver Bolan coaxing all the speed he could from the revving engine, noting for the first time that the truck's fuel gauge showed less than a quarter tank full.

A rocket launcher bellowed after them from the base, sending up a plume of flame as the grenade detonated perilously close to their left. A geyser of earth from the roadside fountained high into the air, raining clumps of dirt and vegetation into the cab while momentarily tilting the truck toward its right side.

The vehicle leaned into a careening wobble for several hundred feet, which Bolan fought, stabilizing the half-ton's balance, slapping all four tires back onto the rough dirt road.

Another boom came from behind; another impacting mortar exploded like some giant match striking off to their right, this time off target enough so as not to affect the racing, rough-riding half-ton.

Bolan steered them around a drop where the road dipped out of sight beyond the lights of the base. He practically stood on the gas pedal, zipping them the hell away from there.

Deadeye maintained a firm hold on the truck's cab, balancing his mighty bulk on the running board.

The road became rougher, more and more pockmarked with potholes that threatened to take out the half-ton before their fuel supply ran out.

Bolan knew from their earlier push in that the road would get worse and taper off into nothing with another few kilometers. Sioung had led them parallel to this road on their advance and had mentioned the road and what became of it when Bolan's group had earlier paused to study their maps.

It wasn't much of a chance, but it was the only hope they had.

He tooled the truck along, even though he knew that at this very instant, Major Linh would be mobilizing all the available manpower, firepower and vehicles he could spare back at that base to give chase one more time.

It would be almost like the day before when Bolan and his men had rescued Sioung's wife and daughter, except then, Bolan reminded himself, all of the major's available transportation had been destroyed and Bolan had nine men with him then, not four like now.

He had not intended hitting Linh's base at all. Originally, he had pushed his small unit like hell with the hope of catching up with Fletcher, Murphy and Robbins in time, before those jerks could reach the NVA base.

So much for that.

This probably is not what Colonel Winters and the CIA guy, Tuttle, meant by avoiding an obviously U.S.-related incident, Bolan thought wryly. Thus far, actually, what had gone down back there could *not* be tied in to the U.S., no matter what Linh charged.

Gunsmoke glanced at Sioung.

"What d'ya figure our chances are of making it home?" he asked the Mont.

"We have chance," Sioung replied matter-of-factly. "The night is our friend, as is the terrain."

Bolan stared ahead, out through the windshield of the half-ton as he drove, trying to read the night. He switched on the headlights. He had little choice, considering the condition of the road, the treacherous terrain, the speed at which he pushed their vehicle along. The twin beams of the headlights pierced the blackness ahead of them like ghostly fingers pointing the way.

"I'd say the odds on whether or not we make it," Bolan told Gunsmoke, "depend on what we find waiting for us between here and there."

Sioung nodded.

"It is as you say, Sergeant Mercy."

"Reckon that is so," Gunsmoke grunted. "Let's just hope we don't run into anything between here and there."

"Yeah," Bolan grunted, with no optimism whatsoever. "Let's."

MAJOR LINH SCOWLED as he watched the half-ton's rear brake lights disappear around the steep grading turn where the road dipped and curved. Bolan again, Linh inwardly cursed the driver of the stolen vehicle.

The major whirled on his nearest noncoms, who ordered their men to cease firing mortars after the truck.

These troops regrouping to await their orders were so different from the ragtag morons he had been assigned to command at the interrogation post of his last duty station, thought Linh.

He had rushed to sound the alarm immediately upon making his escape from Bolan and that Mont creature, Sioung. Linh's faith in always having an escape route handy was again reconfirmed. He realized how lucky he had been, having been caught under the gun for those brief seconds when Bolan and the Mont had actually trained their rifles on him, and to have escaped.

Linh felt certain his good luck would be very bad luck for Mack Bolan.

He briefly recalled lying facedown in the paddy field the morning before, alongside the dead body of Sergeant Thi, thinking *next time, Bolan, next time.*

Huey helicopters had lifted off the Executioner and his unit, leaving behind death, and Linh to face the truth of his own cowardice under fire.

Linh's insides cramped into knots of anger and determination, reminding himself of the one vital difference between yesterday morning and right now. His determination grew into confidence and he smiled a self-satisfied smile to himself, and at a captain who came running over to report the situation, which Linh could plainly see for himself.

Linh waved aside the beginnings of the report.

"Never mind, Captain, never mind. There's no time to lose. Mobilize every available man immediately! I will accompany you in giving chase."

"Yes, Major!"

The officer saluted.

Linh returned the salute and watched the man hurry away. The major also took in the scene of reorganization in the wake of the second attack he had suffered in twenty-four hours from the man he knew he now must kill at any cost.

If Hanoi did learn of these twin indignities suffered by him at the hands of the Executioner, something Linh had already taken steps to avoid, and if the high command further learned that he had not taken revenge on Bolan, then Linh knew that he could just as well kiss goodbye any hope of ever being transferred out of this front-line duty he so detested, and Bolan would have escaped with destroying not only that list, but also Major Linh's future as an officer.

Linh's very existence would well be endangered if Bolan and his damnable team were allowed to escape this time. Which, of course, will not happen, the major assured himself. He thought again of what Bolan did not know and continued smiling as he turned and strode hastily toward the base communications shack.

This was the "next time" he had hoped for yesterday morning. And *this* time he had the Executioner in a trap that even a warrior of Mack Bolan's caliber could not hope to fight free of: an NVA battalion of eight hundred men, based only four klicks to the north of the route Linh knew would be traveled by Bolan and his withdrawing unit.

Colonel Ngu's battalion had covertly infiltrated the area only the week before, and Linh was willing to bet that U.S. intelligence did not even have word of the presence of such enemy troop strength in this area almost exactly midway between Linh's base and the Cambodian-Viet border. Which meant that Bolan would not be aware of a troop mass of such proportions so close by, either.

Linh's smile grew even wider. Bolan will think he has an even chance of outdistancing the force I send in pursuit. He stepped inside the communications shack, feeling very satisfied indeed.

Twice he had been humiliated by Bolan. And yet, he considered, twice *he* had humiliated *Bolan*, as well.

The Executioner had had the drop on a mortal enemy and certainly each time Bolan had intended to kill him. Both times Linh had accomplished what few men ever lived to consider; he had survived being caught in Executioner Bolan's sights.

Yes, he and Bolan would meet again, Linh assured himself, and Linh knew it would be with himself standing over Bolan's fresh corpse. Then Linh's rise to the top would be unstoppable, as if the defeats at Bolan's hands had never happened.

He had to contact Colonel Ngu. He would request that Ngu blanket the area with near full strength along any possible escape routes that might be taken by the Bolan group. Then Linh intended to pursue Bolan with a full complement of his own troops.

And Mack Bolan and those with him would be caught in a cross fire from which no one, not even Bolan, could ever hope to escape. Ngu would damn well want a piece of this action and would blanket the area ahead with everything he had.

Yes, Bolan, we shall meet one final time, thought Major Linh. Though you do not know it, I already control your fate.

There would be *no* escape from Cambodia for the Executioner, alive or dead.

Twenty-Two _____

Colonel Ngu stood, studying the people he would have to kill.

He would have preferred delegating this distasteful job to someone else, some underling of lower rank to whom the slaughter of civilians might seem more in line with his duty.

But he reminded himself that colonel or not it was his duty to see to the odious task at hand, his duty and no one else's.

The peasants of these parts—these unwashed hill people with their strange dialects and childish superstitions—had to be made aware of the truth that *this* NVA colonel was not a man to trifle with; if missteps in conduct were taken, retribution would be decidedly swift and final.

There might have been NVA commanders in Ngu's position who did not feel the same way, but if there were, Colonel Ngu had never met any.

Coupled with the distrust and superiority inherent in any North Vietnamese toward these barbarians—which made eradicating the countryside of these vermin a not altogether unpleasant task—was a very practical strategic application of the pacification of any area where unstinging obedience from the locals was necessary, as Ngu found it to be here.

Human examples always had to be made, it seemed, in order to force the rest to follow like the sheep they were so the military could get its work done. And this was precisely what was about to occur just outside the NVA base camp commanded by Ngu.

The new base, located only a handful of klicks inside the border of Cambodia, was situated on high ground, carved from dense jungle foliage that had to be trimmed back daily.

The base was a supply dump and staging area for military strikes across the border at U.S. and ARVN forces before pulling back to the safety of "neutral" Cambodia.

Ngu had always found it amusing how people— invariably the defeated, to Ngu's way of thinking— always managed to think they could bring some sort of morality, some sense of right and wrong, to such an utterly amoral proposition as war.

The imbecile Americans, thought Ngu. They send thousands upon thousands of their men halfway around the world, invest millions, no, he corrected himself, more likely billions, in a fray where they had no business intervening in the first place.

Then, after this significant investment of time, money, effort and sacrificed human life, the idiots determine an imaginary line across which they will not cross—for "honor's sake," they tell themselves—though the Americans knew very well that staging areas and supply dumps like Ngu's operated up and down the length of the border separating Vietnam and Cambodia.

Ngu often wondered when, or if, the United States would wake up to reality and either fight their war to win it or pack up and return to their plush existence back in America.

He had long suspected, and had so advised his superiors, that the present ideal situation could hardly be expected to last.

Ngu predicted that before the Americans gave up and pulled out of Southeast Asia, the time would come, probably in the not too distant future, when U.S. forces would finally decide to forgo "playing fair" and proceed to bomb Laos and Cambodia back into the stone age, most likely with a pronounced vengeance to make up for all they had endured.

Ngu hoped he would not be around, or at least would be safe well below ground in his commander bunker of this newly constructed base, when that happened.

To Colonel Ngu, soldiering was his life, as it had been his father's and his grandfather's before him. There were few options open to a young man in the strapped economy of the north other than to become a laborer, a farmer or a soldier, and for a man of ambition the latter held the only hope for advancement to prestige and power. So Ngu had become a soldier, one who prided himself on always giving his best when handed a mission. Which was why he now stood before this cluster of Cambodian villagers who had been herded together here in the night, only steps outside the front gate.

Ten men from the village, and their families.

Sentries stood close by at their posts, and Ngu had the two noncommissioned officers who had brought the villagers here. But the looks on these peasants' faces clearly said they had every hope of returning to their homes, of being released after this detention and interrogation.

Ngu would have preferred not to deal with this at all, true, but as man in charge of this base, he had no intention of suffering the kinds of problems that had so plagued his neighbor of sorts, Major Linh, in these Cambodian highlands. Ngu was glad he had not been assigned to work with Linh.

The high command in Hanoi obviously intended some sort of major offensive in the near future, though no such orders had as yet filtered down to the field commanders, but to Ngu the buildup in this area could have no other possible explanation.

As yet, Ngu's military record was clean. And he intended to keep it that way. In his estimation, Linh's principal error of judgment had been in failing to maintain a strict hold over the local inhabitants of whatever region he was ordered to secure.

Colonel Ngu commenced evenly pacing from one end to the other of the tightly bunched circle of perhaps thirty-five people before him. He strutted in his best officious, military stride, hands clasped behind him, knowing these savages were unarmed and of no danger to him. Still, he had ordered his soldiers to remain nearby. One did not take unnecessary chances, and he felt secure, watching the automatic rifles trained on this cluster who thought they were going home.

"You all know why you were brought here and interrogated," Ngu began, addressing the peasants in their dialect, not looking at them as he paced back and forth. But he was all too aware of their looks of growing uneasiness and apprehension. "I have received intelligence that the countryside around your village is rife with tunnels, some dating back to the days of the French. I want you to tell me the locations of these tunnels, so they cannot be used against us. You have been told this by my officers, and you have refused to cooperate."

One middle-aged man, apparently elected to speak for the group, stepped forward hesitantly.

"Begging your pardon, my colonel, but all of us here—" he indicated the families gathered behind him "—are farmers, Colonel, not criminals. As we have already informed your officers who interrogated us, we *cannot* help you, we are most sorry to say. None of us has ever discovered or been told of these tunnels of which you speak."

Ngu paused and this time he did turn his gaze on the group, specifically at the farmer who had come forward to address him.

"And I am most sorry to say that I do not believe you," Ngu snapped. "I don't believe any of you. We know there are resistance groups in these highlands working for the Americans and South Vietnamese in attempts to disrupt our work here."

"But my colonel, such groups live and fight in the jungle," the man responded respectfully. "The few villages in the area, such as our own, are too closely watched, as you are undoubtedly aware.''

"I am only aware," Ngu retorted icily, "that you mountain creatures know more about this than you are willing to tell. I intend to learn what I wish to learn from you people, no matter what it takes, do you understand?"

"But—" the man began.

"I see you do not understand. Very well."

He unholstered the pistol at his hip.

An audible gasp went up from the cluster of civilians like a single indrawn breath, and they shrank back several paces en masse, the naked fear of these men, women and children was almost a palpable thing.

Exactly as Colonel Ngu intended.

"Colonel, I—I—thought we were to be freed, to return to our homes." The peasant spoke worriedly, easing back a few paces to rejoin his family, eyes widening at the sight of the pistol in Ngu's fist.

"You will all be allowed to return to your home, after one of you steps forward to tell me what you know about the location of tunnels in this region." Ngu solemnly stared at the man who had been addressing him. "You."

The man hugged his wife and the adolescent son who stood beside her, kissing the woman on her forehead. Then the man stepped forward again to squarely confront Ngu. The peasant gulped audibly.

"I swear to you, my colonel, we have told you everything we know."

"That is your final statement, then?"

The man blinked.

"My...final...Wh-what do you mean?"

"You may go."

The man blinked again uncomprehendingly.

"Go? You mean...leave?" He looked back to indicate his family. "And my wife and son?"

"They will have their turn."

The villagers almost fell apart, exchanging looks of dread.

"Their...turn?" the peasant echoed. "My colonel, I do not understand—"

Ngu raised his pistol.

The villager fell back with a sudden new fright.

Moans emanated from the peasants behind him.

Ngu did not aim his pistol at the man. He used the side arm to point down the road into the dark, away from where the group had been gathered.

"I said you may leave us," Ngu repeated, his voice grown stern, harsh. "Now. Run. Run for your life if you will not talk."

Some of the peasants began frantically pleading for the man's life, their babble silenced by the rifles staring down at them, pointed by the soldiers behind Ngu.

The peasant fell onto his knees in front of Ngu, panicking, falling apart completely, kneeling in the dirt at Ngu's feet, grabbing the commandant's legs imploringly.

"Please, Colonel...please! We know nothing, I *swear* this to you—"

Ngu kneed the peasant away disdainfully as if shaking animal feces from his boot.

"Get up and run, damn your eyes, or I'll kill you on the spot!"

The peasant's eyes circled with some newfound reserve of strength, or perhaps madness, thought Ngu, who watched the farmer throw a frantic look back at his wife and child. Then he turned and took off, legs pumping with all they had in the direction indicated by the colonel.

Ngu lifted his arm, sighting along it, drawing a careful bead on the man's receding back.

Ngu took no particular pleasure in this, but he knew this must register maximum effect on these people or it would mean nothing.

He carefully squeezed off a round that pitched the fleeing man forward onto his face, in the dust where his body remained, twitching briefly, then not moving.

The peasant's wife moaned her shock and sorrow, collapsing to the ground, wailing sobs to the earth.

The young boy crouched beside his mother, not knowing how to react, in shock also as he looked up with wide, uncomprehending eyes that for some reason strangely troubled the man who had killed his father. Then Ngu broke eye contact with the child and glared at the other villagers.

The ragtag group of peasants stared back with stunned, empty expressions, not unlike the child's, glassy-eyed at the inhumanity of what they had witnessed, as Ngu fully intended them to be.

Hardly a pleasant job, but *his* job.

He returned the stares, his domineering glare threatening for more violence, and they collectively inched back several paces again, until they had nowhere to go.

Ngu again held his pistol down at his side.

"Who will be next?" he demanded. "This shall continue until one of you steps forward and tells me what I wish to know."

No one spoke.

Ngu chose another man at random, gesturing with his pistol for this villager to step forward.

"You. You will do. Come forward."

The man's family began whimpering.

The villager held back until Ngu thought he might need assistance from some of his men to drag this one out for him to kill.

He was about to call for assistance when one of his men stepped up to him, respectfully interrupting the "interrogation."

"Your presence is urgently requested in the communications shed, sir."

Ngu masked his irritation as he holstered his pistol.

"Very well. See that these people remain here until I return."

The junior officer nodded. The peasant woman's weeping continued to fill the air. The officer glanced at the corpse of the fallen peasant. "Shall I have the body moved, sir?"

"No," Ngu said as he turned to take his leave. "The body stays where they can see it."

Irked by the interruption, Ngu crossed the compound to where an NVA trooper waited with a communications hookup to Major Linh's base.

After speaking a very short time with the somewhat disturbed Linh, Colonel Ngu's irritation turned to interest, then anticipation.

"Do not worry, Major," Ngu assured Linh after hearing what he had to say, "even with a Mont guide, these men you speak of cannot move fast enough or far enough to elude the net I will spread."

"The man Bolan must be stopped at all costs, Colonel."

Linh's voice sounded breathless across the static on the line.

"Yes, yes." Ngu, his interest piqued, found himself already losing patience with the man on the other end. "I said not to worry, Major. I will dispatch nearly five hundred men immediately to blanket the entire area the man Bolan and his team must pass through. You will be closing in from the rear. The Bolan team shall be stopped."

"I go now, then, Colonel," Linh replied. "We shall drink a toast over their dead bodies!"

"Before the sun rises," Ngu confirmed.

He broke the connection and left the communications area briskly, intending to spare only another minute at most, to see if any of those peasants had confessed during his absence to any knowledge of the network of tunnels. Then he would turn the interrogation over to his second in command.

The colonel welcomed the respite this adventure would offer from the often stifling, stale desk duties that were his lot as commander. Tonight would bring something different, and he hurried to the base command shed to implement the immediate search-and-destroy operation that he would lead.

He would take his best men, his best officers, the best his infantry detachment had to offer, North Viet infantry, every bit as wise in the ways of jungle warfare as Linh had cautioned Ngu this Mack Bolan was supposed to be.

And, Ngu reminded himself, it would be a fine opportunity to impress Linh, and the high rankers in Hanoi, with Ngu's superior command of this situation when this Bolan and his team were found and killed. Colonel Ngu had no doubt that such could be the only outcome of the next few hours.

Bolan led a five-man team, according to Linh. The combined forces of Ngu and Linh, closing in on those five from every direction, a tightening circle, would number close to six hundred trained NVA forces.

Ngu did not allow his confidence in the outcome to dampen the quickening of his pulse when he thought of being out there on an operation with his men again, where a commander should be. He could almost smell the exhilaratingly sweet odor of burnt cordite and spilled blood already.

Bolan's blood.

At odds of six hundred to five, in terrain controlled by the NVA, there was no way possible for the Executioner to survive this night.

Twenty-Three _____

The NVA half-ton sputtered, wheezed, jolted and finally ran out of gasoline, as Bolan had been expecting it to for the past three klicks.

He fought the steering wheel, managing to guide the truck into a sideways turn before the vehicle came to a complete halt, blocking the narrow road that by this time had dribbled away into not much more than a slightly widened trail.

Bolan climbed down from the driver's side of the cab. Gunsmoke and Sioung unloaded from the right side of the truck, Washington clambering down from the rear of the tarp flap where he had joined Bloodbrother after the truck had put enough distance between itself and Major Linh's base.

The men of Bolan's team regrouped at the side of the truck. Gunsmoke and Sioung shed their NVA uniforms. Washington looked at Bolan with approval at the way Bolan had managed to park the truck.

"Good work, Sarge. That oughta stall 'em out for a little while. The jungle's too thick along here for them to pull around. They'll have a hell of a time pushing this baby out of the way."

Bolan tossed the truck's keys as far as he could into the jungle underbrush, then he moved quickly to unlatch the hood of the truck. He tugged loose the distributor cap and got rid of this with another long, overhand pitch in the direction opposite to which he had thrown the keys.

Sioung knelt and placed his ear to the ground for several seconds.

Gunsmoke observed this and grinned at Bloodbrother, indicating what the Mont was doing.

"I thought you folks were good at stuff like that, Loudelk, and here you let Sioung think of it."

Guess I've been hangin' out with peckerhead cowboys for too long," Loudelk growled laconically.

Sioung stood.

"Vehicles," he reported to Bolan. "Many. Perhaps one, no more than two kilometers from here. Coming this way."

"My bet is troop carriers," Deadeye grunted.

"Linh will be after us full force," Harrington said with a nod, "closing in every damn second. And us without wheels!"

"That refugee camp we helped out is less than a klick from here," Bolan said. "Let's put ourselves well to the other side of it in case they do catch up with us. I don't want anything going down around a lot of civilians. They've paid enough as it is."

The five men took off down the trail, heading east, Bolan and Sioung running point, followed by Deadeye and Bloodbrother.

Harrington took his turn as tail-end-Charlie through the dark, which Bolan knew would be yielding to the dawn within the hour, the eastern sky having already taken on the pale promise of the coming day. Then the jungle became thick again, the fronds of the trees meeting overhead along this stretch, and gloom reclaimed the world of the winding trail.

"Hope those people from the refugee camp have left the area," Bloodbrother said. The group jogged briskly along the roadway, which had gotten rougher and narrower every step of the way, the terrain inclining steeply into the harsh frontier separating Cambodia from South Vietnam.

"They will have gone," Sioung stated. "It is said that this area has caves and tunnels, many extending miles."

"I've heard stories about such tunnels," Bolan added as they continued moving. "Some of them are close to thirty years old, aren't they?"

The Mont nodded.

"They are maintained. They are the only hope of escape and refuge for civilians in time of danger in these hills."

"Across the border," Washington pointed out, "most of the tunnels have been dug by the VC to get away from us."

"Not tunnels and caves of this area," Sioung insisted. "NVA and Cambodian troops are the enemy of these people. I know of only a small number of such tunnels, but know no details about those in this area. The refugees from the camp will know and will have gone through them."

A short time later, Sioung again held up a cautionary hand, signaling the group to stop.

The five men fanned out.

Bolan inched toward Sioung.

The Mont guerrilla was standing on a ridge that dropped to a steady incline into a sort of wide gully that offered a clearing for the pitched tents of the refugee camp.

As Bolan stared at the devastated settlement, he briefly recalled the bloody three-sided firefight between the refugees, the Khmer Rouge bandits and Bolan's men that had raged only a few hours before.

Bolan and the four men paused, swatting at bugs and mosquitoes, giving a quick scope-out to the area below.

The refugees were gone, as Sioung had predicted, along with their tents, belongings and, apparently, their dead. But the warrior knew there was a good chance those slain in the earlier fighting had been given a mass burial before the survivors pulled out lock, stock and barrel, leaving behind only the ruins of tents burned to the ground.

Other than this, there was little to indicate that there had been a camp here at all: some scattered tin cans, a torn-apart child's rag doll and spent cartridge casings everywhere, littering the former campsite like a brass carpet in the moonlight.

Bloodbrother said softly, "Let us beware of booby traps the bandits or military have placed down there after the refugees left. There is the smell of death about this place, and not just of those already dead."

"I sense it." Bolan nodded. His eyes scanned everything to be seen down there in the vaguely moonlit clearing and along the opposite ridge. "But we don't have much choice. All right, everyone, move out; don't bunch and keep low."

Bolan struck off, taking the lead this time, his men zigzagging in a line behind him. He led the way down the incline. Boots had trouble grabbing the slippery loam, at the same time too often trying to snag and trip over vines coiling treacherously across the trail at ankle level.

Bolan reached the flattened clearing first and hit a combat crouch, tracking his weapon across the remains of the refugee camp, seeing and sensing nothing except the night and what little they had been able to make out from the ridge.

The others joined him.

"Nothing to slow us down here," Deadeye said scowling.

"Nothing to slow down Linh and his yahoos, either," Gunsmoke agreed. "Say, do you boys hear what I hear?"

For the first time, Bolan picked up faint engine sounds, heavy-duty vehicles grumbling toward them from out beyond the veil of night, well behind the ridge from the direction in which they had come.

Then a telltale clattering split the night ahead of them as an approaching chopper zoomed into an all-encompassing rumble, all within a matter of seconds.

"Hit the dirt," Bolan snarled to his men.

They fell flat, trying to make themselves into indiscernible clumps on the ground.

An NVA helicopter skimmed by overhead at practically treetop level, buzzing eastward in the direction of the advancing force commanded by Major Linh. They had obviously spent little time dealing with the obstacle of the truck abandoned such a short time ago by Bolan and his men.

The chopper's flight lights vanished beyond the western ridge, taking the noise of the enemy whirlybird along with it.

"Enemy gunship," Gunsmoke growled. "Coming from the east?"

The Americans and Sioung commenced very cautiously picking themselves up, remaining low, ready to dart for cover or fire on an aircraft with their M-16s.

"Think they spotted us?" Deadeye asked.

Bloodbrother snorted.

"We damn sure better fade out of here fast."

Bolan looked eastward, beyond the opposite ridge silhouetted in the moonlight. He thought he heard vehicles from that direction too, but it could have been the night, this echoey terrain playing tricks.

"Bloodbrother, cop a gander at that opposite ridge over there. Gunsmoke, tag along. And keep an eye out for bouncing Bettys."

Loudelk and Harrington split for the direction indicated by their team leader, moving fast but careful to avoid the bushes and small trees where the anti-personnel devices would most likely be placed if anyone had decided to leave some behind.

The two men were fully aware of the damage these bouncing Bettys—waist-high explosive charges—

could inflict if detonated when you unknowingly nudged one when you thought you were only elbowing aside an errant branch or stepping through a clump of weeds.

Bouncing Bettys weren't always fatal, but they did almost always manage to blow apart the genital area and from grim experience Harrington and Loudelk knew that a lot of people taken out by the little fuckers wished they had been killed.

Bolan signaled Sioung and Washington to return with him back up the ridge behind them. They zig-zagged in a swift withdrawal from the clearing, covering one another as they regained the ridge, bellying down below it so as not to show themselves to anyone who might be able to eyeball them from below the other side.

From this point, the rugged wilderness undulated downhill along their backtrail. Except for a winding column of troop-truck headlights wending its way to a tip about a half klick to their rear, the murk of jungle was an endless black void stretching to infinity to the west.

The snaking dozen or so headlights appeared as a string of sparkling diamonds strewn haphazardly across black velvet.

Bolan had enough respect for a man of Linh's rank and experience to know there probably had been more trucks in that pursuit convoy when they started from Linh's base in chase of Bolan's band.

The Executioner was certain that troop carriers would have been stopping at intervals to unload NVA and some Cambodian soldiers in a sweep of the countryside, though Linh would be doing that only to cover his bets; he would know Bolan would have no intention of dallying inside this neutral country with his mission objective accomplished.

Linh would be spreading his troops out in a net after Bolan, but the NVA cannibal was traveling real heavy, plenty of firepower to get the job done, knowing he was closing in.

"Where is NVA chopper?" Sioung asked.

There was no sign of the enemy helicopter that had just flown over them, no visible flight or landing lights.

"They'll have set down at the head of the column," Bolan guessed. "We passed a few spots wide enough for an LZ."

Washington cursed soulfully.

"Sure are a lot of the bastards down there, Sarge. Maybe we're suckers for hangin' around."

"Let's find out what we're heading into first," Bolan counseled. "Here come Gunsmoke and Bloodbrother."

Harrington and Loudelk had someone in tow, Loudelk gripping his rifle with one hand while he reached back clasping the hand of a figure that became clearer as the two men and their "company" joined Bolan, Washington and Sioung.

For some reason Bolan was not all that surprised to see who joined them: the young woman whose baby he had delivered a few short hours ago during the refugee camp fight, and the swaddled infant the Cambodian woman clutched to her breast.

Bolan turned to the grim expressions worn by Bloodbrother and Gunsmoke.

"Bad news, Sarge," Gunsmoke reported. "Real bad."

Loudelk peered over the ridge, toward the string of diamonds on black velvet that was Major Linh's pursuing force.

"Maybe five times as many trucks coming in from the east," he told Bolan, "no more than a couple hundred yards the other side of that ridge. You remember how the land there dips down again, then starts climbing to the east?"

Bolan nodded. "I remember. Are the troop trucks to the east unloading yet?"

"Unloading, and the force is spreading out as they advance," Bloodbrother said. "If this was daylight, they'd be able to see us already from that higher ground. They're tightening a noose around us."

Deadeye studied the rim of gray beginning to inch its way above the eastern horizon.

"Be daylight in another fifteen minutes."

Bolan looked from the east, where those troops were closing in, advancing closer by the second, back to the string of headlights, Linh's column less than a half klick away to the west.

"This," he said quietly to Sioung, "is what we Americans call being stuck between a rock and a hard place."

Harrington grunted.

"With no damn place to run to at all. Goldawgit, I shoulda never left Nacogdoches."

MAJOR LINH EXPERIENCED a sinking feeling in the pit of his stomach when Colonel Ngu's helicopter touched down in the center of this deeply rutted stretch of trail.

The convoy had rumbled along the pockmarked route with as much speed as the driver of his jeep and those of the troop carriers following the jeep could coax from their vehicles, considering the nearly impassable terrain.

Linh knew they would not be able to drive at all after more than another half kilometer, at most. He would have to order those men still with him to debark, spread out and start advancing eastward in search of the Bolan group.

Linh's first response was anger when Ngu's chopper set down.

The major's pursuit had not made as good time as he would have liked. He had ordered periodic stops over the last two kilometers for a troop carrier at each point to disgorge its men in case the Executioner's team intended some sort of flanking maneuver.

Linh doubted this, but he took precautions nonetheless. Then there had been the half-ton in which Bolan and his unit had made their escape, reminding Linh too much of yesterday morning at another base where Bolan had bested him.

The half-ton left blocking the road, two klicks back, had not slowed Linh's force for long. He had ordered the damnable delay blown to bits and his column had rolled across its smoking rubble.

After he had traveled a few more kilometers, he felt that he had to be practically on top of Bolan's little group, with no help from Colonel Ngu, wherever he was.

But suddenly Linh knew where the colonel was, when Ngu alighted from the landed chopper and swaggered briskly forward toward Linh's vehicle. Linh's initial anger at what had appeared to be another delay became a sinking feeling when he realized that it was now too late for solo glory.

The major strode to meet Ngu, who stood sizing up the troop-carrier convoy stalled behind Linh.

"These are all the men you've brought?"

"One hundred men, Colonel." The collar of Linh's tunic suddenly felt too tight, constricting. He wanted to kill Ngu. "I have deployed the rest of my men along the way as we went, in the event—"

"An error," Ngu snapped. "I flew over the Bolan group on our approach only moments ago. I ordered my pilot to continue on in as if we had not seen them. They're in the flat clearing where I'm told a refugee camp was located."

"You should have strafed them—"

"I know what I should have done." Ngu bristled. "Have you forgotten who is in command here, Major?"

"Uh, no...of course not, Colonel."

"I have five hundred men closing in from directly due east of here," Ngu continued. "I have heard of the man, Bolan...of his capabilities. He could have shot us down, with some luck. Why take the risk when we have infantry for this sort of thing? I came to direct and observe, not to be killed. Order your men out of those trucks immediately, Major. Have them spread out and advance toward the ridge due east of here, closing the end flanks of their advance to connect with my troops coming this way.''

Linh saluted Ngu, almost enthusiastically.

''But of course, Colonel, without a moment's delay!''

Linh felt his ill disposition toward Ngu evaporate, fanned into nothing by the manner in which events had fallen together.

He would have to share the glory with Ngu. Perhaps not ideal, Linh thought, but the end result would be the same: Mack Bolan and his group trapped in that clearing one-half kilometer ahead, with nowhere to run from a tightening noose of six hundred or more of the best fighting men two NVA commanders could muster.

Linh would have preferred waiting another twenty minutes, perhaps less, until the clearing where Bolan and his men were trapped, or at least the fringes of jungle on the ridges, would be flooded with the light of the new day. The sky to the east was already changing from pale gray to crimson, he noted.

He rejoined Ngu at the head of the column, remembering at this moment, for some reason, that he had had time to catch only a short catnap, during the brief helicopter flight to his new command, during the past twenty-four hours.

In some ways it felt to Linh as if a very long time had passed since one sunrise ago, yesterday morning, when Bolan's team had raided his previous outpost and made off with those Mont hostages.

A mere twenty-four hours.

And here Linh was with the chance he had wanted so badly, fate handing him a rematch, as it were, a second chance to prove himself. He no longer felt any animosity toward Colonel Ngu because, yes, Ngu was handing him his golden opportunity.

Six hundred to one.

A tightening circle. A tightening *noose*, yes.

A rising sun.

And nowhere to run.

Linh had never felt surer of anything.

Within the next thirty minutes, surely less, Mack Bolan, the Executioner, would be caught inside that tightening noose. And Major Linh intended to fire the coup de grace himself, the killing shot, into a mortal enemy's temple, which would explode bloodily, beautiful, matching the bloody sunrise.

Then, and only then, Linh would have his revenge.

Bolan would cease to exist, and Major Linh would be vindicated. He could almost taste it now, thick upon his tongue.

All that remained was the killing.

Twenty-Four _____

"Her name is Bach Yen," Bloodbrother told Bolan. "She wants to thank you for delivering her child."

The Executioner and his men, and Bach Yen and her infant, remained crouched beneath the ridge overlooking Linh's convoy, less than a kilometer downhill from this ridge where Bolan and the others had positioned themselves.

Bolan turned to the woman and bowed slightly in the Asian fashion, saying in her own tongue, "I was honored to do what I could."

Bach Yen clutched her newborn child to her bosom with her right arm. She grasped Bloodbrother's big hand with her left, as she had when Loudelk and Gunsmoke first appeared with her a few seconds ago.

The young woman looked no older than fifteen or sixteen, obviously frightened, obviously in shock by all that had happened to her this past night.

Bolan knew that this woman, like the men and children of this part of the world, would have a toughness, both physical and of the spirit, seldom encountered in more "civilized" societies. It was not uncommon for a pregnant woman in these parts to be working the field, perhaps pushing a plow behind a water buffalo, stop, lie down and have her child and two hours later be back working that same plow behind that same water buffalo in that field.

Existence on the cutting edge of survival breeds that kind of human being, that way of life.

Bach Yen had nonetheless been through, had seen, too much horror this night. The young womanchild clasped her infant and Bloodbrother as if she would rather die than release hold of either.

She commenced chattering in her own language when she thought Bolan spoke her tongue, rattling off an urgent stream of whispers nonstop, until Bolan lifted an open-palmed hand to show her that he knew only a few phrases.

He addressed his questions to Loudelk, who spoke her language fluently.

"She says there's a network of tunnels hidden by the foliage on the incline leading up to that ridge across the clearing," Loudelk translated. "That's the way the rest of the refugee survivors from this camp got away after the battle here."

"Ask Bach Yen why she remained behind after the others left," Bolan said to Loudelk, though he continued looking at the young mother so she would know he was conversing with her through Bloodbrother as translator.

Loudelk translated, unleashing another urgent jabber in Bach Yen's language. Then he turned back to Bolan.

"She says she thought we would return. That we might need help. She wants to help us for the assistance we have given her. She says she owes us her life and that of her child—a debt she must repay.''

Gunsmoke had not taken his eyes from the headlight column of Linh's pursuit caravan, which remained stationery down there on the lower ground.

"A tunnel," he echoed. "That there sounds like just the miracle the old doc ordered, buckaroos.''

"Does the military know about these tunnels?" Bolan asked for Bloodbrother to translate.

Loudelk did translate and Bach Yen replied, her hand still clasping Loudelk's, while Bloodbrother hefted his M-16 in its firing position from his other hand. The Indian translated her reply into English.

"She says a Captain Trang sent a unit to comb the scene here after the refugees had time to get away. The soldiers were looking for dropped valuables, food, information. They made a thorough search of the area but they did not find her. She was hiding in the opening of the tunnel. She says her people didn't construct the tunnel. They found it. It travels for more than a kilometer to the southeast of here. The mouth of the tunnel is well hidden by brush and undergrowth.''

"That'd put us well to the other side of those troops closing around on us from the east," Deadeye pointed out. "We could come out behind their lines and keep heading east until we reach our base.''

"We shall need a diversion," Sioung said. "They know we are very close or they would not so deploy their troops, is it not so, Sergeant Mercy?"

Bolan centered his gaze once again on that stationery string of headlights, estimating, gauging, formulating a strategy even as he replied to the Mont's question.

"It is so, Sioung. And I think we could have ourselves one hell of a diversion. Bloodbrother, Gunsmoke...would you say those troops closing in from the east are close to the same distance away from us as Linh's troops down there?"

"Give or take," Gunsmoke said. "What y'all got in mind, Sarge?"

Loudelk grunted his understanding before Bolan could respond.

"He's thinking we could turn those dogs of war on one another, right, Sarge?"

"It just could work," Deadeye said.

"We'll make it work," Bolan told them. "There's a reason those troop carriers of Linh's have stalled out down there."

Sioung picked up the thought.

"They are unloading. They advance on us by foot."

"They think they've got us trapped and they don't want those heavy trucks to slow them down in this terrain, or get damaged in the shooting," Bolan agreed. "Which means we've got to run this scam on them right now. Deadeye, you and Gunsmoke track back over to that ridge across the clearing. We'll give you two minutes from when you leave. You know what to do?"

Loudelk nodded, but Gunsmoke looked down with some dismay at his holstered six-shooters.

"Could be a mite too much range for these babies of mine, Sarge, but I reckon the noise is the thing, eh? I always was good at makin' noise."

"Hold your fire after sixty seconds," Bolan instructed, then, to Bloodbrother, "ask Bach Yen how we find the opening of this tunnel."

Loudelk translated.

Bach Yen replied, not letting go of the big native American's grip.

The Blackfoot Indian turned to Bolan.

"There's a cluster of rock and boulders next to three balsa trees, midway up the ridge, about ten yards north of this point across from us."

"We'll meet there, then," Bolan said. He synchronized watches with Bloodbrother. "Good luck, guys."

"Same back at'cha," Harrington drawled as they swung around to leave.

Bloodbrother, Bach Yen and her infant still in tow, faded with Harrington eastward beneath a horizon acquiring the red of the coming dawn, though gloom's dark mantle still claimed the land.

"Sioung," Bolan said, "take one of the flanks. You know what we're going to do?"

"Yes, Sergeant Mercy. I await your signal. I only pray this diversion holds our enemy back and will not prove our undoing. They shall return heavy fire."

"But hopefully not at us," Bolan grunted.

Sioung scampered off several yards away into the darkness.

Washington bellied over to an approximate midpoint between Bolan's and Sioung's positions, assuming the same pose as the other two just beneath and behind the ridge.

Each man spread out, with weapon aimed down in the general vicinity of their back trail, where the headlights of the troop carrier convoy began winking out one by one, engine sounds vanishing, too.

The muggy, oppressive predawn blackness seemed to take on a strange quiet. It was as if the insects, birds and bats of night, and the waking monkeys, tigers and wildlife of the new day together sensed the coming storm of warring humans, about to shatter the tranquillity of their domain.

Bolan eyed closely the luminous dials on his wristwatch and when it was a second short of two minutes since parting from the others, he peered across to see Washington readying himself for the pull of his M-16.

Sioung, nearby, watched Bolan for the signal, which Bolan gave.

The warrior curled his finger across his weapon's trigger and opened fire at the same instant that three other automatic rifles commenced breaking the silence into a million sharding fragments.

Bolan, Deadeye and Sioung rained a nonstop automatic salvo downhill in the direction of Linh's force, though no targets could be discerned below there in the dark.

Bloodbrother and Gunsmoke began unloading in the same manner upon the advancing NVA footforce spread out somewhere across the higher ground to the east.

The small reports of Gunsmoke's six-shooters punctuated the nonstop din, but sounded like auto-fire just the same, the Texan firing and reloading with such rapidity.

Then return fire began slamming in at the twin-directional salvo from Bolan's men. Mortar teams unleashed hammering rounds that really blew up the night as hundreds of NVA troopers from east and west and to either quadrant connected with the advancing foot soldiers.

Rockets and machine-gun fire pounded the area, and in most cases overshot the twin ridges as the two NVA forces peppered Bolan's group with everything they had from less than a half kilometer in every direction.

The return thunder was too fierce for even shouted words to be heard. Projectiles whistled and ricocheted everywhere.

The firing of Bolan's men from below cover of both ridges ceased on schedule, though this could barely be noticed amid the bursts of flame and shooting that split the darkness asunder around the ridge-encircled clearing where the refugee camp had been.

Bolan scrambled back down the incline of the ridge toward the settlement. Sioung and Washington flanked the warrior, and the three men dashed across the clearing while the earth shuddered beneath their feet under the full fury of the two enemy forces advancing in a pincer movement to annihilate the small American unit.

The NVA troopers were concentrating maximum firepower where they figured they still saw the foreigners' muzzle-flashes.

But in fact, Bolan's strategy had worked perfectly: most of the rounds from both groups were overshooting the ridged clearing where Bolan and his men hunkered down. Each NVA force mistook the firing from the other NVA faction as enemy fire, the mountainous terrain accommodating this deception staged by the Executioner and his team.

When Bolan, Deadeye and Sioung were halfway across the clearing, the shrill whistle of a rocket zeroed in, too deafening to be ignored.

"Incoming!"

Bolan yelled the warning to the others.

The three of them leaped away in different directions, bellying to the earth, hugging it as the ground shook harder beneath them, the rocket impacting with a dirt-and-rock-tossing blast only meters away.

Then the three fighting men were up and zipping across the rest of the clearing to the point on the eastern ridge, indicated by Bach Yen, where they met Gunsmoke and Bloodbrother and, of course, the Cambodian woman and her baby.

Bach Yen still held on to Bloodbrother's hand.

The three of them were crouched low, close to the mouth of a tunnel visible only because Gunsmoke Harrington held back the undergrowth covering it, the Texan hurriedly motioning them in.

No one wasted any time, Bolan leading the way, his white-hot M-16 pointing ahead of them into the dank darkness of the subterranean passageway, which was large enough to accommodate the small group as they hurried along in a crouch-walk.

Behind Bolan, Bloodbrother guided the woman in and followed her, while Deadeye, Sioung and Harrington brought up the rear.

Harrington, the last in, paused to quickly reconceal the tunnel entrance before hurrying to join the others. And outside, a world of thunder, destruction and gunfire continued unabated, as both sides fully opened up on each other with rocket and mortar fire, indistinguishable from the blood-red sunrise.

Bolan led his rushing group deep into Mother Earth, which trembled around them as blasts rocked the surface.

The Executioner's thoughts were racing as he urged his group farther, faster, toward escape.

Or doom.

Only the next few minutes and the opposite end of this tunnel would tell.

If those surface explosions did not cause the tunnel to collapse upon them before they could reach the other end.

MAJOR LINH AND COLONEL NGU scrambled for cover behind the major's lead vehicle of the convoy, when the first gunfire opened up on them.

Soldiers from the trucks also sought safety behind the heavy troop-carrier vehicles. One hundred or so NVA regulars pulled their rifles and startled eyes around to the point on high ground where the winking pinpoints of rifle-flashes were spotted. The troopers returned fire.

Within seconds, mortars and portable rocket launchers had begun blazing return fire.

The incoming fusillade, from a quarter-kilometer or so away from where Linh's troop trucks had been unloading, had intensified, angry projectiles riddling the night around Linh and Ngu.

Explosions pounded their eardrums, impacting mortar and rocket blasts turning the darkness into surreal day though the sun had another few minutes before it peeked above the reddened eastern horizon of Cambodian mountainside.

"Tell your men to cease fire!" Ngu shouted into Linh's ear. "Immediately, do you hear me...? The fools! Our forces are firing on one another! Stop them! Stop them!"

Linh nodded, not fully comprehending what Ngu could mean. He crawl-rushed over to his nearest officer, relaying the order for his men to cease firing, while from the corner of his eye he saw Ngu grab a field radio, raising his own force to the east.

It took a whole minute, which seemed to Linh like forever, death raining in from that higher ground, his soldiers toppling, explosions chewing up the earth.

An incoming mortar zapped one of his troop carriers, which mushroomed into a secondary explosion as the gasoline tank exploded. Shrapnel razored the air with flying chunks of red-hot metal and bloody human parts.

At last, some of the shooting and hellfire tapered off, and before long the riflefire ceased altogether, replaced by the pitiful moanings of the wounded and the crackling flames of the demolished troop carrier.

Linh struggled to his feet and hurried over to the colonel.

"H-how...could they have done it?"

Ngu clenched a fist, pounding the hood of the command vehicle.

The beginnings of this day seeped across the countryside, revealing, through the unfolding dawn, the ridge to higher ground ahead of them.

No more automatic riflefire originated from that ridge, as it did to the fuse for this two- or three-minute, vicious exchange of heavy fire with the NVA faction on opposite high ground east of the refugee camp.

"You have obviously not fully digested the dossier of this man, the Executioner," Ngu snapped. "In combat, the man is almost superhuman, capable of anything. As am *I*!" Ngu spun and stalked off toward his waiting helicopter, which had escaped damage. Ngu barked over his shoulder at Linh. "Come, if you wish to accompany me as I personally slay this Bolan once and for all."

Linh hurried to keep up, climbing into the chopper with Ngu, discovering that he and Ngu were the sole passengers aboard except for the pilot, who lifted them off as soon as Ngu and Linh were aboard.

Linh's nerves were frayed. He thought once again of himself lying facedown next to the dead Sergeant Thi yesterday morning in that paddy field, taking fire from Bolan. The major decided that his thirst for vengeance against Bolan had dulled his acute aversion to being on the front line when the bullets flew.

Yet Linh knew he must accompany Ngu on this flight.

Linh could hardly refuse to accompany the colonel; how bad that would look on his record, and Ngu would tell everyone what a coward Linh was under fire. Linh could never allow that. And there was the fact that Ngu appeared so utterly confident. Linh found some comfort in this.

Ngu seemed like a card player about to play a sure hand, and Linh decided that was good enough for him. He still wanted to see Bolan dead more than anything else in the world.

Their chopper banked to the east at high speed.

"What is your plan, Colonel?" Linh asked above the noise of the throbbing rotor.

"This area is honeycombed with tunnels," Ngu replied crisply. "You were aware of that?"

"Aware, yes, but I have only this night assumed command, as you know. My predecessor told me he has been unable to locate—"

"Spare me your excuses," Ngu snarled. "What is needed is the proper method of obtaining information. I only this night learned, from villagers I interrogated, the exact location of one of these tunnels, only one-and-a-half kilometers east of here."

"You suspect this tunnel could afford Bolan and his men with an escape?" Linh asked, thinking that perhaps he had the colonel, now.

Ngu silenced him with a withering glare.

"We could hardly have expected Bolan to know about the tunnel. Also, the villagers I interrogated claimed never to have actually used the tunnel, that it's been there as long as any could remember, and insisted that they knew not where it led. They had reason to tell the truth. But it matters not, Major, for I know the exact spot where that tunnel *ends*, you see. We will be waiting there, hovering above the opening, when Bolan and his people emerge. This helicopter is armed with 40 mm cannons and machine guns mounted on turrets.''

Ngu stood, steadying himself as he started toward the pilot.

''I will give our pilot exact directions to where the tunnel ends,'' he shouted to Linh, ''and I will radio both our forces to move quickly east to join us. They will arrive in minutes, but will be too late in any event. Bolan and those with him have only postponed the instant of their deaths, nothing more.''

Ngu moved on forward to speak to the pilot, giving Linh a chilly, humorless smile in parting that made Linh most grateful the colonel was on his side, more or less, as the copter sped low and fast toward the rising sun.

We both want the Executioner dead, Linh thought.

And it's about to happen!

BOLAN HEARD TREMORS of the NVA chopper's rumble outside the mouth of the tunnel, waiting for them. His small group had some twenty feet or so remaining to stoop-run before they gained the exit, where bright daylight shafted through the foliage and underbrush disguising the end of the tunnel.

The warrior estimated they were slightly more than one and a half klicks from where they had entered the passageway, when the surface would had still been only half-gloom.

Bolan raised a cautionary arm, motioning to the others to stop. He could tell those with him heard the chopper sounds, too. He hurried closer to the opening.

Bloodbrother moved up after him, the Blackfoot Indian crouching close, finally letting go of Bach Yen's hand, easing the Cambodian woman and her newborn infant farther back.

Gunsmoke, Deadeye and Sioung squeezed around Bach Yen and her child to join Bolan.

"Damn things just hangin' up there," Gunsmoke twanged, though no one had as yet stuck his head out for a look.

"You figure it's one of ours, Sarge?" asked Deadeye, little hope in his voice.

Bolan moved forward a few more paces to part the vines and tangled growth that concealed the tunnel opening. He peered out, upward toward the sound.

Hot, brassy sunlight poured down from above the eastern horizon. The rays reflected off the clearly visible North Vietnam army markings on the helicopter hovering menacingly a little more than treetop level above the rocky ground where the mouth of the tunnel was hidden. The foliage at the end of the tunnel rustled violently in the backwash of the chopper's rotors.

Bolan ducked back inside the earth.

The others read his expression.

"They cannot know the *exact* location of this tunnel," Sioung said, "or they will have blown it closed already, to trap and suffocate us while they covered the clearing behind."

"They're waiting for us, all right," Deadeye agreed, and his eyes traveled uncertainly to Bach Yen where the teenage mother and her infant crouched beyond earshot, barely visible where they waited well back from the indirect daylight seeping in from outside the tunnel. "You don't think the little lady led us into a trap, do you, guys?"

Loudelk bristled visibly.

"You're crazy, man! She led herself into a trap right along with us, if that's the case."

Gunsmoke motioned the two to cool it.

"Much as it pains me to say it, Deadeye, the Injun's right. Reckon the rest of those NVA boys oughta be closing in on our tails from above and below ground even as we speak. What now, Sarge?" he asked Bolan.

"We fight, what else?" the warrior replied sharply. "That chopper is waiting for us but they don't know exactly where we'll pop out and they don't know how hard. Hit it with everything."

There was no more time for conversation, Bolan knew. They had to do it and do it now.

He catapulted from the mouth of that tunnel, his men on his heels, their M-16s abruptly opening automatic fire on that low-hovering chopper.

The NVA pilot responded promptly, pulling at his stick, the enemy warbird starting to rise.

"We've got to get him on the first try," Bolan told his team.

"Or those cannons'll pulverize us," Gunsmoke said, his six-guns blazing.

The chopper glinted in the morning light, gaining altitude briskly, the sounds of projectiles spitting through its metal and Plexiglas up there audible to those firing from the ground.

Then the chopper wobbled dramatically, even as it continued to gain some altitude.

Bolan knew someone's bullets from below had taken out the pilot.

The chopper dipped slightly and the new day's sunbeams allowed Bolan to momentarily register a familiar face up there; a heartbeat glimpse of a very terrified Major Linh peering down at them. Bolan also saw another figure aboard the chopper, scrambling to toss aside the bullet-riddled body of the pilot, this second officer taking the controls.

Then the helicopter gained more altitude, pulling back but not too far.

"Hold your fire," Bolan ordered. "He's out of range. Get the woman, Bloodbrother—we're making a run for it."

"We're not gonna make this one," Deadeye groused, but he joined the others in a full-tilt charge toward lower ground where crevices in the sloping mountainside would offer some cover.

Bolan knew they had to get away from those NVA troops who at this moment would be closing in on them from behind. As he led his people down toward the only cover he could see, he glanced back and spotted the first dozen or so NVA regulars topping the hill, hurrying to intercept them.

The chopper came out of its steady hover for a fast swoop in toward the group led by Bolan. He knew that within the next instant the officer piloting the deathbird would start unloading with the cannons and miniguns and Washington would be right. It would be all over.

At that moment, a big Huey gunship sailed into view from the treetops to the east, its eggbeater rumble melding with that of the NVA whirlybird.

The pilot in the enemy copter eyeballed this new threat, commencing immediate evasive action, banking around as fast as he could to confront the Huey.

Bolan and the others looked skyward as this new wrinkle unfolded.

And Bolan had another quick glimpse of Linh way up there, eyes rounded plates of fright dominating a mortified face even at this distance.

Then the Huey began unleashing heavy-duty firepower, its turret-mounted machine guns blazing away at the NVA chopper. Then the hot, red ball of the rising sun was matched in its intensity when the NVA aircraft disintegrated in a blossoming fireball as bright as it was loud. And that was the finish of two cannibals named Major Linh and Colonel Ngu.

Bolan and those with him on the ground dived behind rocks and boulders to escape the fiery debris, echoes of the explosion eaten up by the increasing decibel level of the Huey descending to set down lightly on level ground within thirty feet of Bolan and his group.

Bolan saw Pol Blancanales at the Huey's controls.

Boom-Boom Hoffower lived up to his name, manning the M-60 mounted at the open side door, riddling the hillside, knocking down NVA regulars who couldn't gain cover fast enough.

Flower Child Andromede stood in the doorway, his M-16 also hammering out cover fire, yelling for Bolan's group to hurry the hell up.

Which they did with a breathless charge for the Huey.

Bolan reached the chopper first, turning to plant his feet wide apart on the ground, pulling up his M-16 for cover fire as the others ran to the gunship behind him.

Bloodbrother and Bach Yen, holding hands again, leaped into the Huey's side door first, the Cambodian woman never losing pace nor hold of her tiny infant.

Sioung and Deadeye piled onto the chopper's deck just as the first half dozen NVA and Cambodian regulars dribbled into daylight from the mouth of the tunnel through which they had been chasing the Executioner's team.

Bolan banged off a final goodbye burst, the M-16 riding his steady grip, a tight figure-eight of lead drilling apart those enemy troops, punching five or six of them back into the mouth of the tunnel like a giant's invisible fist.

Flower Child extended an arm.

"Let's beat it, daddy-o!"

Bolan grabbed the arm. Flower Child pulled the Executioner aboard as Pol worked the controls and lifted off, Boom-Boom strafing their backwash, toppling more cannibals before the deadly gunship lifted them out of range.

The Huey banked gracefully eastward, toward South Vietnam.

Getting them away from there.

Bolan collapsed into a sitting position on the seat running along the inside of the Huey. He looked around, seeing everyone had made it; no one had caught any bullets this trip. Luck had somehow decided to shine on the cause of right, after all.

When they landed, he would find out how this Huey, with these hellground buddies of his, had managed to show up like the cavalry to the rescue. But right now he felt like a prizefighter at the end of a long, brutal bout. He felt drained and yet somehow strangely renewed, satisfied, like the expressions of those with him aboard this noisy, zipping gunship.

Bolan closed his eyes and sighed, letting the aches drain away from him.

They would be back at the Special Forces camp within half an hour and at this moment, it was all this tired hellgrounder needed to know.

Mission accomplished.

With a passion.

They were heading home.

Thank God.

Twenty-Five

_____

Except for the gunship's steady drone as it sailed eastward, all was silent aboard the Huey.

The mesmerizing throb of the whirling blades and fatigue of the all-night jungle trek, in pursuit of Fletcher and company, combined to lull Bolan's senses.

As he sat on the Huey's bench, he let his tired muscles and battle-weary mind, which had of necessity been wound snare-drum tight throughout the physical and emotional exertion, and indeed, during the fighting and closeness of death, relax now.

The Executioner drifted off into the sort of half-sleep one might experience on a long train or bus ride. But he retained an awareness of where he was, of the M-16 straddling his lap, of those with him aboard the Huey on this flight out of the narrowest escape Bolan had ever experienced. And yet this state of slumber brought a dream so real, so vivid, Bolan could taste, feel and touch it, even though he knew it was a dream.

A subconscious desire for the dream not to end imbued it with a bittersweetness painful to the man who knew it was part dream, part remembrance of an event that actually took place.

THE THREE OF THEM had gone off to rural, rustic Vermont for some fishing: Mack, home on leave before returning for his second tour of duty in Nam, fourteen-year-old Johnny, who "just this once" had been given permission to play hooky, and Sam Bolan, father.

The three Bolan men had spent that day along the banks of a stream, fishing poles in the water, lazing away the warm summer day. They chatted idly about this and that, none of it very important, but all of it the stuff of day-to-day life and, for that reason alone, very important to a warrior home from the war.

At night the fall air carried a nip to it but the Bolans fought off the chill by heaping more timber on the campfire after the day's catch had been devoured.

They talked some more, late into the night, with a loving father-and-sons bonding that made conversing an easygoing pleasure.

Especially, yeah, for a soldier home from war.

"Can I have another beer, pop?" Johnny asked close to midnight.

"Sure, Johnny," Sam chuckled gruffly. "You can have another, but that'll be three, boy. You tell your ma I let you drink all them suds and we'll both never hear the end of it."

Mack sipped his own beer and winked at his dad across the campfire.

"We might have trouble getting the kid home—" he chucked a teasing elbow into Johnny's ribs "—if this guy knows he can get all the beer he wants out here in the wilds."

Johnny, sitting next to Mack on a log, popped the top of another brew.

"Aw, cut it out, guys. This is a real special occasion, isn't it?"

"It is that," Mack replied.

"I'll drink to that," Johnny said, grinning as he hoisted his can of beer, just a bit tipsy.

"And let's drink to ma and Cindy," Sam Bolan said, raising his can of beer. "Cindy had her school play and she wouldn't cut out on that for anything, and of course your ma—" Sam chuckled lovingly "—heck, I reckon she gets her fill of me the other fifty-one weeks of the year. Said a fishing trip was no place for a woman, and who knows, maybe she's right, but tell the truth, I think ma just wanted the three of us to have some guy-time together."

"Those women of ours have sure set some impossibly high standards for any lady in my life to live up to," Mack told his dad and his brother. "We've got the best in ma and Cindy."

"The best," Johnny agreed.

Some of Sam's ever-present gruffness softened a tad.

"I'm sure glad you boys realize that about those two. A man's nothing without a good woman to share his life with, the bad times and the good, the struggles and all the rest of it. Always remember that, boys. Family, that's what it's all about.

"Everything can change on you. Your life can turn upside down, you can lose it all, but if you've got family, that's everything you'll ever need. It's what makes us different from all the other forms of life on this planet, and the women, God bless 'em, are the strength that holds it together and makes any of it mean anything.

"Whatever you boys do in your lives, wherever you go, you remember what your father said: You're what you are because of *family* and, sons, that's worth fighting for. Don't *ever* forget that. I guess you could say it's worth dying for...."

BOLAN AWAKENED FROM THE DREAM with a sense of unease, vaguely familiar, achingly dissettling.

He looked up to see Pol setting the Huey gunship down on the helipad of Special Forces Camp Three-Niner-Bayou, and for one instant Bolan realized why the aching aftertaste of that dream had felt familiar.

It was the same strange, pronounced premonition he had experienced the last time he'd seen his family, when his plane had been lifting off from the Pittsfield airport to start him back on his journey to this tour of duty in Hell.

He had looked back to see ma, pop, Cindy and Johnny waving goodbye and had somehow had the awful thought that he would never see them again. The premonition was almost palpable now because it had remained glued to his subconscious despite all else while he was over here, even if the letters from home did assure him everything there was all right.

The Huey touched down and Pol cut the engines, the rotors and engine winding down their rumble. Everywhere Bolan looked inside the chopper, he saw happy faces.

Sioung debarked to find his wife and child, Ti Bahn and Tran Le.

Bloodbrother helped Bach Yen and her infant from the warbird, then accompanied the Cambodian refugees toward the emergency room for a medical examination.

Bolan, Pol, Flower Child, Deadeye and Gunsmoke grouped wearily alongside the Huey as maintenance crews came forward to take over the chopper.

Yeah, lots of smiles, and relief going around.

"Deadeye, Smoke, you guys have earned yourselves a day off at least." Bolan grinned at those two hellgrounders. "Fall out."

"I hear that," Washington said with a sigh. "Thanks, Sarge."

Harrington nodded weary agreement.

"Thanks to you too, buddies," he told the three sniper-team members who had flown in to their rescue. "If no one minds, this cowboy'll get the lowdown on how your yahoos managed to show up, *after* I catch about forty hours of shuteye! Later, pards."

Harrington and Washington ambled off toward their hooch.

Flower Child tutted kiddingly to Bolan as they watched the fighting team disperse.

"That's gratitude for you. Don't suppose you fellas were able to get your hands on any Cambodian weed while you were over there? Naw, don't imagine you had time, all the partying you were up to."

"How did you home in on us?" Bolan asked Pol.

"Just followed the shooting," Blancanales said. "We had the location of Linh's base. Once we got into the area, you weren't all that hard to find, Sarge, least that NVA chopper wasn't. They don't have that many aircraft, y'know, and your show was the hottest thing happening for miles around."

"Hope you won't get it in a sling for penetrating across that border," Bolan grunted. "Does Colonel Winters know you went in to pull us out?"

"The colonel ordered us to go," Boom-Boom told Bolan happily, "not that we weren't straining at the bit already, but here's the one you should thank." He looked over Bolan's shoulder. "Shawnee and Doc Jim and the colonel sat down over coffee last night and I guess that nurse pal of ours worked on the colonel's conscience something fierce, something about you and your men being more important than some bullshit neutrality no one was honoring or some such.

"Anyway, after the rap she laid on him, old Howlin' Harlan must've done some heavy soul-searching. Finally, he came and got us and told us to do it. He was grumbling something about it being a hell of an Army when a nurse has to goose a colonel into what he should've done all along."

Bolan turned as Shawnee joined them from the ER structure fifty yards from the helipad.

The lady came into him at a run, her black hair catching the morning sunlight. She and Bolan connected with one hell of a hugging embrace.

"Oh, Mack, we're so glad you made it!"

"I am, too, with a welcome like this." Bolan chuckled appreciatively. They hugged tightly once again before breaking off. "I hear we owe you some mighty big thanks, lady."

"We're the ones who owe you, Mack," she told him. "The one thing I had to promise Colonel Winters, though, was that I get you over to him as soon as you landed."

"Which was a couple moments ago," Bolan said, feeling the tension of the mission melting from him like ice off a hot tin roof. "Bad form to keep a colonel waiting. Thanks, men," he told Pol, Boom-Boom and Flower Child, "and I do mean for everything." Shifting his gaze from their happy nods and smiles, he turned to Shawnee's suddenly more somber expression. "Walk me over to the colonel's bunker?" he asked.

"Of course."

They headed away from the chopper, across the bustling compound of Camp 105-A, which did not look as if it had sustained a full-force VC attack the night before.

"You seem to have something on your mind that won't wait," Bolan said when he and Shawnee were by themselves and halfway to where they were going. "Fontenelli?"

The lady broke into a faint smile.

"No, I'm happy to say that we got word from Saigon during the night, Mack. Chopper's going to make it. And Gadgets and Zitter are getting healthier and more obnoxious with their nurses by the minute. They'll be back on active duty in no time."

Bolan stopped to turn and face this fine, incredible woman, eye to eye.

"What is it then, Shawnee?"

"Well...I guess I'm a little worried about what the colonel wants to see you about. He hasn't told anyone, only that it's very urgent. And then there's...us."

"Do you want to talk about us now?"

"No, not now. You have to see Colonel Winters and I should be getting back to the ER and...well, I guess that's really what it is all about right now, isn't it? Duty. Responsibilities."

He nodded.

"And it's going to stay that way until this war is over or we're sent home. There isn't time for two people falling in love or anything else in this hell-ground, Shawnee, except for trying to stay alive and help others and do the best you can. Is that what you wanted to tell me?"

She gave him a small, pretty laugh.

"I knew you'd understand, you incredible man. What happened between us on the roof of your hooch last night before the attack...it was...special, precious, one-of-a-kind, and it will always be in my heart and my memory, just like you will be, Mack. But...but in other ways, maybe it would be best if...if we just made like it never happened, you know?

Who knows what the future could—will bring for us when we're out of here, but... Oh, shit, Mack, help me, will you? I never thought I'd find a man like you, guy, and it's tearing me up to say these things after we shared something so wonderful.''

He touched both her arms gently with his hands and planted a light, chaste kiss on her forehead.

''I'll help, Shawnee,'' he said, smiling. ''You're right. This is a place for loving friends, not friendly lovers.''

''Thanks, Mack...for understanding.'' She sniffed away what might have been the beginning of too much emotion, and when she looked up at him again, those steady, tough, beautiful eyes of hers were sharp as ever. ''Right now, soldier, I've delayed you long enough...the colonel, remember?''

''Who can forget colonels?'' Bolan said. ''Thanks, Shawnee.''

''Thank you, big soldier.''

Shawnee rose to her tiptoes, planted a kiss on his grimy face—not a lover's kiss, no, but packing too much emotion to ever be called chaste, yeah—a loving friend from the bottom of her heart. Then Shawnee turned without a backward glance and hurried back to the ER.

Bolan continued on to the command bunker and Colonel Winters's office.

He knocked at the doorframe.

Winters looked up from his desk.

''Oh, come in, Sergeant. Uh, welcome back.''

Bolan entered and saluted.

"Thank you, sir. And thanks for sending those reinforcements in to pull us out."

He realized upon stepping into the office that he and Winters were not alone.

Winters's guest was not the CIA man, Tuttle, as Bolan had half expected.

He was a bit surpised to see that the man, who stood with the colonel when Bolan entered, was in fact Father Eckenrode, the base chaplain. Bolan abruptly realized that the mood in this small, makeshift office was heavy with discomfort.

The chaplain looked profoundly pained, and Howlin' Harlan's normal outgoing demeanor was totally absent, his eyes grim and sad.

"You'd, uh, better sit down, Sergeant," Winters told Executioner Bolan. "I hate to hit you with this just after what you've been through, son, but I'm afraid the chaplain here has some terrible news for you...."

Epilogue
Southern California _____

Bolan dodged back to flatten himself against the front wall of Kenny the Kid Ensalvo's palatial home.

The pitched grenade boomed inside the foyer, blowing the twin oak front doors outward off their hinges.

The power of the blast also spit out in gory pieces one Mafia hood.

A blacksuited Executioner left the night, entering through the front entranceway that now billowed out smoke.

Bolan triggered his Ingram, the MAC suppressor reducing the nasty autofire to indiscreet burping, which sizzled through the scene of shambled foyer littered with torn human bodies.

Amid the wreckage of a chandelier wrenched loose by the grenade blast, upended furniture and Mob hardmen, one peripheral glance told him these punks had already gotten theirs.

Three mobsters were picking themselves up groggily, nicked but healthy enough to look dazedly around for weapons. They saw the deadly apparition in the doorway, then Bolan put them back down again with the Ingram's continued burping.

He tracked on hood number five just as that punk gave up trying to find his rifle in all the mess and decided to grab for hardware harnessed beneath his jacket instead. Bolan triggered the Ingram.

Nothing!

His SMG gun had jammed.

The hood almost got his concealed weapon out, eyes flaring at his good luck and at the same time searching wildly for a place to hide.

Bolan dropped the chattergun and unholstered the 93-R from shoulder leather. He quickly switched the Beretta to his left hand while his right fist speed-drew the .44 AutoMag, Big Thunder, from the hogleg's low-riding, tied-down holster on his right hip.

Big Thunder thundered big and the hood's head exploded into a fine red mist as he toppled back onto the first few ruined steps of a winding stairway leading up to the second floor.

The warrior knew it was there that the boss cannibal named Kenny the Kid Ensalvo and his cold-blooded *consigliere*, Bobby "Trick" Compsari, together with a contingent of Southern Cal street hoods, were supposedly holding their peace conference. But the burst of machine-gun fire from inside this house before the Executioner's assault—the reports had sounded to Bolan like an Uzi, Bobby Trick's favorite weapon—indicated that the peace conference was not so peaceful.

Bolan stepped over the final hood's headless remains and hit the winding stairway three steps at a time. Big Thunder was in his right fist, the Beretta in his left, both weapons an extension of the man, ready for anything to come out of the open door at the head of the stairs. And Bolan knew from his previous hit on this Mafia hardsite that the upstairs room was the San Diego's don's conference room.

The preceding dozen years of Mack Bolan's life had been spent paying back an uncollectable blood debt Bolan owed these walking scumbags, who would tear down and corrupt and destroy everything the trained warrior considered worth fighting for.

Sergeant Bolan's military career ended for all intents and purposes the moment Chaplain Eckenrode dropped his bomb on Bolan that lifetime ago, on an August morning at Special Forces Camp 105-A in the highlands of South Vietnam.

Mack's mother and father and sister were dead.

They had paid with their lives for good-hearted Sam Bolan's mistake of again borrowing from Mafia loansharks in Mack's hometown.

Pop had fallen behind in his payments and insisted that Elsa and Cindy not tell Mack. Pop's pride had gotten them killed when the bloodsuckers had put on the screws.

Johnny alone had survived the horrible massacre, gravely wounded.

A grieving soldier had been granted emergency leave to bury his family—a sad, traumatic homecoming made worse when local police officials told Bolan that, yes, they knew who bossed the Mafia loanshark operation that had cost Bolan's family their lives, but the authorities were powerless to do anything—there was no proof, there were civil rights, they were sorry.

Bolan wasn't sorry.

Bolan was *mad*.

And for the first time, a highly trained jungle-combat specialist realized fully what had to be done.

Realized that, yeah, this soldier had been fighting the wrong enemy.

The police were helpless against those responsible for the deaths of his mother, father and sister, God bless their souls.

Bolan's miltiary mind lost no time in analyzing the situation.

The rules of this home-front war between the cops and organized crime were all rigged against the cops.

They knew who the enemy was, right, but they had to prove it, and even then the hoods always managed to walk out of the courts laughing at those they victimized.

Bolan wrote in his War Journal, the day after his parents' and sisters' funeral: "What is needed here is a bit of direct action, strategically planned, and to hell with the rules. Over in Nam we called it a war of attrition. Seek out and destroy. Exterminate the enemy. I guess it's time a war was declared on the home front. The same kind of war we've been fighting at Nam. The very same kind."

Bolan's existence had been War Everlasting since that day, first against the Mob, then broadening into a widening circle of operational fire, financed by funds appropriated from Mob targets, to be turned against them.

In a continuing one-man war, Bolan came to re-alize that he fought not against isolated enemies, but rather against the whole dark strain of human ills they—and perhaps he, he sometimes thought in his darker moments—represented.

He was the fire that fought fire, sometimes with the help of others—Shawnee, Doc Brantzen, a pilot named Grimaldi, all would cross Bolan's subsequent miles through Hell—righting wrongs where he could, because Mack Bolan saw no other course open to a man of his distinctive capabilities and spiritual and philosophical makeup, certainly not in light of remembered advice from Sam Bolan on Mack's last visit to a loving family.

Bolan's family—ma, pop, Cindy—were no more, not in this world.

The weak needed heavy fire on their behalf if they ever wanted to inherit a savage earth, and these multitudes had become Bolan's "family."

Yeah, pop, this Executioner had learned his lessons well.

Bolan knew *family* to be well worth fighting for and, sure, dying for, if it came to that.

More often than not, this Executioner blitzed alone after that terrible lesson learned when he had assaulted this Mafia site so many lives ago. And it was on this same killground at the beginning of his home-front war, that he had lost the buddies from Nam who had offered to fight with their sniper-team leader again.

Bolan double-timed up the winding stairs, reaching the top, heading straight for the doorway to

Kenny the Kid's conference room, Beretta and AutoMag aching in his fists to deliver more.

The roll call of those good guys who had died here twelve years ago, after getting themselves out of a hell called Nam in one piece, scorched through his mind.

Boom-Boom.

Bloodbrother.

Chopper.

Gunsmoke.

Deadeye.

Dead and gone, all of them.

The way Bolan would be, someday, right.

But not *this* day.

Not *this* night.

Not if he could help it.

There remained miles of Blood River to wade through, too many cannibals who would escape any kind of justice at all if not for The Man from Blood.

The Man from Ice.

The Executioner.

I am not their judge, Bolan had once written. *I am their judgment.*

Gadgets and Pol were still around, helping Bolan from time to time.

After that mission into Cambodia, which had been Bolan's last in the Southeast Asian conflict, Loudelk and Bach Yen had started living together. Bloodbrother had planned to marry the woman who had done so much for them, who had lost so much, to bring her and the child back to the States after his tour and raise the infant Bach Yen had birthed, thanks to Bolan.

Bolan had later learned Bach Yen and the child were killed during a VC attack while Loudelk was gone on patrol.

Everthing had turned to shit for America and South Vietnam and Cambodia.

Bolan's feelings that his country had made a grave mistake getting involved in a land war in Southeast Asia, no matter how honorable its intentions, had proved true with an awful vengeance.

American fighting men had fought their guts out for democracy and freedom in that beleaguered corner of Hell, but it had not been enough. America was still binding, trying to heal, the wounds from that era, wounds of the body, spiritual wounds that ached, haunted, a generation later.

He power-housed into the conference room.

Two corpses lay sprawled across each other near the conference table, bodies riddled with holes that accounted for the Uzi fire Bolan had heard less than a minute ago: two Hispancis in the flashy street garb of barrio hustlers. Their presence here made them the boss and bodyguard of the Hispanic street gangs, and their being dead made it Bobby Trick's handiwork, the smell of burnt gunpowder still acrid in the air.

Two black guys across the room, clothed similarly to the dead, whipped around together.

The warrior pedigreed the duo instantly as being of the same mold as the Hispanics. The soldier almost laughed as he watched the pair tugging at a door, frantically trying to open it, to escape Death. But the door must have been locked on them by Kenny and his *consigliere*, who probably hoofed out that way only eyeblinks before.

The two black street toughs tried to press themselves backward through the wall when a cold-eyed Executioner stalked into the room.

Bolan felt a strange calm descend upon him. He watched both of these degraders of women, these sellers of smack to schoolchildren, these crude lower than sewer filth, the two pimps shrieking, "We're not armed!"

"Tough luck," Death whispered.

The Beretta pilled the guy on Bolan's left through an eyeball. Big Thunder shook the walls of the room, raining plaster from the ceiling, loosing the other hood's head into a daub of blood-and-brains gore across the wall behind him, two hunks of dead meat pretzeling to the floor.

Bolan triggered the AutoMag again without slowing, blowing away the door's lock and part of the door with it. He barreled on through, straight and fast, hurtling down the narrow stairway he found there, faster than he came up, knowing from the long ago hit of this estate that these stairs led to the house garage.

The warrior hit the bottom step just as he heard a car engine gun to life from beyond the closed door separating the stairs from the garage.

Bolan was certain that a boss-of-bosses hairbag named Ensalvo, and his second-in-command, Bobby Trick, would be backed up by Mafia sentries from the front gate, who would have had time by now to run to the garage.

And if he survived taking them out, there would be nothing ahead but more of the same for as long as this warrior's life continued.

For as long as Blood River wended its way through a troubled world that needed all the help it could get.

War everlasting, yeah.

Dirty war. The dirtiest.

A soldier named Mack Bolan would, could, have it no other damn way.

This Executioner intended to storm Hell on until Death itself robbed the good fight for him.

Until the bloody end.

The Executioner sent the door to that garage off its hinges with one powerful kick of rage and fury and blitzed on through with both guns blazing.

What readers are saying about Gold Eagle books and Mack Bolan.

"There are no books about any person, nonfiction or fiction, that I like better than the Executioner series. Mack brings to life the longing of every law-abiding citizen."

S.W., Christiansburg, VA

"I'm a woman sergeant in Army Intelligence and I thoroughly enjoy all your books. Mack is a fascinating, believable character representing so much in our world. Please don't change him!"

L.H., APO, NY

"These works are exactly what the world needs; they demonstrate in good old-fashioned terms, the triumph of good over evil and sometimes at very good cost to the innocent. Mack's intrepid people are just what the doctor ordered."

Y.P., Plattsview, Nova Scotia

"I really must tell you you have created the most interesting series I've ever read. Bolan is the most exciting hero of our times."

H.R., Watertown, NY

"I hope you keep Mack going against the bad people of the world. I believe your books are the best."

J.K., FPO, Miami, FL

"I have read all the books and wouldn't trade them for anything. I love every page. Mack is the meaning of the word American and everything it should stand for."

W.S., APO, CA

"Gold Eagle books are all of the most superior reading—there is a hell of a lot of food for thought in each and every one. Gold Eagle is to be congratulated and commended for the type of books they publish."

M.C., Painted Post, NY

"All the Executioner books are super. Thanks."

M.D., Loveland, OH

"I have been a devoted reader of your books and I've enjoyed all of them. I thank you for writing the type of books that put forward the way things should be handled in this country."

C.S., Canplejeune, NC

"In my own mind, I cannot think of any books I've enjoyed more than yours."

E.D., Round Lake, IL

"We really think your writing is so realistic that it is hard to believe that your books are not based on real-life events."

C.J., NRM, Tempe, AZ

"I hope your books never stop."

D.L., Alliance, OH

"I'm in the Air Force, stationed overseas and if it wasn't for your books, it would be very hard for me here. I only have 9½ months left here and I can't wait to get back to the States to read all the ones I've missed."

N.W., APO, NY

*Names available on request.

DON PENDLETON'S EXECUTIONER
MACK BOLAN

Sergeant Mercy in Nam…The Executioner in the Mafia
Wars…Colonel John Phoenix in the Terrorist Wars…Now
Mack Bolan fights his loneliest war! You've never read
writing like this before. By fire and maneuver, Bolan will
rack up hell in a world shock-tilted by terror. He wages
unsanctioned war—everywhere!

Available wherever paperbacks are sold.

GOLD
EAGLE

Mack Bolan's

ABLE TEAM

by Dick Stivers

Action writhes in the reader's own street as Able Team's Carl "Mr. Ironman" Lyons, Pol Blancanales and Gadgets Schwarz make triple trouble in blazing war. To these superspecialists, justice is as sharp as a knife. Join the guys who began it all—Dick Stivers's Able Team!

"This guy has a fertile mind and a great eye for detail. Dick Stivers is brilliant!"

—*Don Pendleton*

GOLD EAGLE

Able Team titles are available wherever paperbacks are sold.

GOLD
EAGLE